NAUGHTY GIRLS

Also by Alisha Yvonne

I Don't Wanna be Right
Lovin' You is Wrong

Anthology:
Around the Way Girls 3/Double Trouble

NAUGHTY GIRLS

Alisha Yvonne

URBAN BOOKS

Urban Books
10 Brennan Place
Deer Park, NY 11729

ISBN 13: 978-0-7394-8202-5

Printed in the United States of America

Acknowledgments

Special thanks to everyone who support my literary endeavors:

Mom and Dad: Rhonda and Charles Brown

My very supportive siblings: **Donna L. Smith (Boo Boo), Gregory Savage (Rock Jr.), and Ronald Byrd (Mr. B.)**

To my beautiful daughters: Ebony and Imani, I love you.

To supportive friends and family: Benjamin Tutwiler, Paul Tutwiler, Martin Tutwiler, Kendal and Eric Hubbard, Deborah Tuggle, Lillie Garrison (Grandma), Stephanie Wilkerson-Hester, Tonya Samateh, Pam Small, Shamanda Griggs, Sherita Nunn, James Davis, Michelle Coates and Stephanie Perry—thanks for your input.

To some very special online and local book clubs: The Imani Book Club-Montgomery, AL, R.A.W. SISTAZ, Memphis-R.A.W., R.A.W.4ALL, Urban Knowledge-Memphis, Allekaye, Fundamentals, JustUs-Atlanta, ReadInColor, Sophisticated Souls of Learning, Women In Sisterhood, Women Seeking Knowledge, Uchefuna, GFI-Mphs, Black Women Empowered Through Reading, The Literary Ladies, and Unique Women Social Club

Urban Books's staff and my fellow supportive authors: Carl Weber, Roy Glenn, Arvita Glenn, and the entire Urban Books family, LaJill Hunt, Dwayne Joseph, Stephanie Johnson, Angel Hunter, Thomas Long, Pat Tucker, Mary B. Morrison, Cherlyn Michaels, Eric Pete, Cydney Rax, Keith Lee Johnson, Shelia E. Lipsey, Felecia R. Ellis, Regina Neequaye—I'll always remember your graciousness.

To anyone I might have forgotten: Please charge it to my head and not my heart. I appreciate everyone who has been a part of my success.

Special Dedications

Corry L. Richmond
29 June 1974—10 September 2003

Julia Cummings
29 November 1944—6 February 2005

Barry A. Clark
16 October 1965—26 January 2006

Albert Finch
12 April 1972—5 February 2006

Each of you impacted my life in different ways—invaluable experiences. I'll never let go of the memories.

Love Always,

Alisha Yvonne

NAUGHTY GIRLS

Chapter 1
Lights, Camera . . . No Action

The club was off the chain, but that Gerald Warren had made me mad again. Considering he'd been my boy-friend for two years, I would've thought he'd have more respect for me than to openly flirt with the mud duck sitting at the table behind us. He couldn't seem to stop his neck from turning around. I wanted to slap fire from his mouth, but I knew better. We would've been fighting in the parking lot for sure.

Gerald said he needed me, so I went to be with him. I put on my MAC foundation, which matched my caramel tone perfectly, and then squirted a dab of Liz signature perfume on my neck and each wrist. Gerald loved when I glossed my lips, so I made sure they looked kissable. Then I put on the tightest dress I could find, stepped into my stilettos, and bounced. I felt if I wasn't the woman he needed, he'd just find someone else. At twenty-six, I knew I wasn't getting any younger and that I needed to keep my man at all costs. I had no regrets for leaving the house at midnight to be with him—until I saw the flashing red-and-blue lights in front of my apartment.

I was disoriented, and I don't remember placing my car into park before jumping out. Before I could reach the sidewalk, I was hit with a heavy arm in the chest by a policeman, who knocked me to the ground. A bit stunned, I questioned what was happening.

"What's going on? Where are my children?" I asked, rising to confront the man.

"Are you Ivy Lee Jones?" the officer asked.

"Yeah. Where are my children?" I asked, struggling to get around him as he held my arms.

I looked at my apartment, which was on the second level, and noticed a thin, smoky film flowing from the roof. The kitchen door had been kicked in, and the windows were dark and ashy-looking. As I continued to fight to get past the officer, a fireman to my right blasted a hose over my doors and windows. Tragic thoughts flooded my mind.

I wanted to go back to the serenity I felt on the way home when "Trouble Man" by Marvin Gaye crooned across my radio. It was 5:00 in the morning, and I was sleepy, but I woke up when I heard the song's introduction. I never figured that only ten minutes later, I'd get the shock of my life.

I screamed until I had very little energy left. "Let me go! Where are my children? I wanna see my children," I yelled, wrestling with the policeman.

My tight, black Donna Karan dress inched above my waist during the struggle. I was in too much of a fury to worry about my panties being bunched into my ass, exposing my cheeks. I fought until I was tired. I could hear a news reporter talking nearby, and when I looked over my shoulder, my suspicion was confirmed. The whole policeman-versus-civilian scene was being captured on film.

The officer didn't seem to care about me being a woman. He tussled on the ground with me until a female officer came to assist him. She grabbed my arms and tugged them behind my back while he held my feet. I was handcuffed then carried over to a patrol car. While elevated in the air, I spotted an ambulance. I wondered if my children were in there. I began to twist and fight to get away, almost causing the officers to drop me. I was frantic as I thought of the kids.

"Nooooo. Robin . . . Zachary . . . Dillon! Where are you? Please answer me," I cried, looking at the ambulance.

The officers threw me in the back of the patrol car then slammed the door. I kicked the windows on each side, hoping to break them so I could get out. After pounding the glass several times with my signature stiletto Gucci sandals, the female officer opened the door, grabbed my ankles, then strapped them together with a plastic tie. I was exhausted, and I was done fighting. She closed the door then mean-mugged me through the window.

I couldn't believe no one would tell me about the well-being of my children. I tried to dismiss all negative thoughts. I took comfort in the fact that I didn't see body bags lying around. *My kids must be in that ambulance,* I thought. *If they were severely hurt, someone would've told me by now.*

It seemed as if I sat in the back of that car for an eternity. My hair was all over my head, and I felt embarrassed as my neighbors stood gawking and shaking their heads at me. The news cameras were getting an eyeful from all angles, something I later learned after seeing the replays of the eyewitness report.

I used my one phone call to contact my mother. She wasn't thrilled to hear from me, and she let me know it.

"Momma, it's me, Ivy," I said just after she approved the prison phone charge.

"I know who this is. I came real close to not accepting this call," she said.

"Momma, I can explain—"

"You can't explain nothing," she yelled. "Don't even try to fix your mouth to rationalize leaving those kids alone."

"Are they okay?" I asked, fearing her answer.

"Why are you asking? You don't care."

"Momma, if I didn't care, I wouldn't be asking."

"Save it, Ivy. The only thing you care about is yourself and the no-good-ass men you fool around with. Why are you calling me? You should be talking to the man you left your kids at home alone for. Get him to help you. I ain't spending a dime of my money on trying to get you out of jail."

I began to cry. "Fine, Momma. Don't bail me out, but please, please just tell me where my children are and how they're doing. No one's talking to me. The police are saying they don't know how the children are . . . just tell me."

There was a long pause as I continued to sob. She finally spoke up. "They're here with me."

I felt so relieved to hear her response. I took a deep breath. "Are they okay?"

"They're fine. They were out of the apartment before the blaze got too large. A neighbor heard them coughing and crying outside her window, so she peeped through her blinds to see what was going on. She was able to get everyone up and out of the building before the firemen came."

"Thank God—"

"Shut up, Ivy," my mother yelled. "I've told you over and over about leaving those children alone. Robin is only eight years old. She's your baby, not your babysitter. Zachary and Dillon are just stair steps below Robin. Where all your sense is, I don't know. An eight-year-old girl can't be responsible for taking care of a six- and four-year-old. That girl was in the kitchen, trying to fix Dillon a grilled cheese sandwich because he said he was hungry.

She turned on a gas stove by herself then accidentally left the bread bag too close to the fire. Why was she trying to cook, Ivy? You didn't feed them that evening?"

"I fed them well," I yelled back. "I fed them before I put them to bed. Dillon has never awakened hungry in the middle of the night. I thought they'd stay asleep."

"This is what I've tried to tell you before, Ivy. Anything can happen. Do you understand now? Anything, Ivy."

I cried even more. "Robin knew not to be messin' with that stove when I wasn't around."

"Un-un . . . don't you go blaming that baby. Robin is a child, Ivy. What part of that do you not understand? You can't expect children to assume things or automatically know how to take defense when the time comes. You have to be there to guide your children."

"But I can't always pay a babysitter."

"Then you should've listened to my advice and stayed at home with your kids. Nobody else opened their legs and had unprotected sex to get pregnant with them except you. Nobody else labored in the delivery room to have them but you. But, you know what? You might just not have to worry about a babysitter now. You're in a lot of trouble, and any judge in his right mind wouldn't let you have these kids now."

Her words hurt me terribly. "Those kids are my kids, Momma. Let me speak to them."

"Girl, let these kids alone. I'ma raise 'em and give 'em a good home. When you get out of jail, go do what you do best: lay up with men."

She hung the phone up on me. I was devastated. I wanted to talk to my children. I didn't get a chance to let them know how sorry I was and that I loved them. As I slid to the floor, bawling, I heard a female correction officer yell for me to get up 'cause my phone time was over.

She lifted me off the floor then walked me back to my cell. I couldn't eat. I couldn't sleep. All I could do was think of my children and the mess I'd gotten myself into.

Four days went by before I was released. My brother, Kerry, paid 10 percent of a hundred and fifty thousand-dollar bail in order to get me out. Even though he was two years younger than me, Kerry had a good head on his shoulders, and I admired him for it. My mom only had two kids, but people often asked me if Kerry was my older brother because his love for me always seemed strong. From childhood, Kerry had always been my protector.

Kerry came to pick me up from jail. I threw myself into his arms and cried. When he drew back from me, he turned his head slightly because he didn't want me to notice the tears in his eyes. It was too late because I had already seen them. He began to talk as he walked away.

"C'mon, Ivy. I parked over there," he said, pointing toward the car.

"Well, you don't have to walk so fast, do you? I know I might be embarrassing you with this tight-ass dress on, but even if my stuff hadn't burned in that fire, I don't think the police would've given me time to change," I said, huffing as I tried to catch up.

Kerry never turned around, so I had to talk to the back of his tall, lean frame as he hurried to the car.

"Naw. I'm not embarrassed. I'm just trying to get some things accomplished before I have to be at work this evening," he said, opening the car door for me.

"Accomplish what?"

"Let me get in the car. I'll explain." He shut the door then walked around to the driver side to get in. "First, we need to get you some clothes and a temporary place to live."

"Why can't I stay at your place?"

"'Cause Rita just moved in, and I know my woman ain't having it."

I felt Kerry's forehead. I couldn't believe what I was hearing. "What made you decide to move her in? I know you, Mr. I-Ain't-Living-with-No-Woman-Until-I-Get-Married, didn't move your girlfriend in."

"Well, she happens to be more than a girlfriend now," he said, unable to look at me.

"What? You can't even look at me, can you?"

"I'm driving. I'm supposed to keep my eyes on the road."

"Kerry LeNard Reynolds. I know you didn't marry that woman without involving me and Momma, did you?"

Once we stopped at a red light, Kerry decided to look at me. "We went to the courthouse."

"Kerry!"

"Well, I know how you and Momma feel about Rita being Hispanic, so I felt I'd tell you later."

"Kerry, her being Hispanic isn't the problem as much as it is that she's not black."

"Do you hear yourself? What's the difference? Her being Hispanic and not being black is the same thing. And since we're on the subject, Rita's six weeks pregnant, and we didn't want our child to be born out of wedlock."

"Oh, so bump what Momma and I feel? We aren't the ones you love. Or are you even in love at all? Sounds like the two of you figured there's no sense in having a bastard child, right?"

"Rita and I *are* in love, and you need to watch your damn mouth. You oughta be more careful about what you say to the hand that'll help you. I just spent fifteen thousand dollars out of Rita's and my bank account to bail you out of jail. If I didn't love you or care about your feelings, I would've left you to rot."

I had struck his nerve so I remained silent for a while.

He was extremely irritated because I could see his right temple moving as he gritted his teeth. After he pulled into Wal-Mart's parking lot, quiet time was up.

"What are we pulling in here for?" I asked, raising my eyebrows.

He laughed until he started to shake. "Girl, you making my side hurt. I haven't laughed this hard in a while. Why do you think we're here?"

"I know you ain't buying my clothes from here." I could feel my milk-caramel skin turning beet-red as I got angry.

Kerry laughed some more. "C'mon. I don't have all day. Beggars can't afford to be choosey. Didn't Momma teach you that?"

"Kerry, unless something has changed, last I remember, you and Rita are flight managers at FedEx. I know y'all can afford to buy me something from Macy's at least. I've got a reputation to get back intact."

"What reputation? Oh, you mean the fact that you wear brand-new Gucci and Prada, but your kids wear hand-me-downs or whatever Momma and I buy them? Or, do you mean the fact that you can wear designer clothes, live in the projects, and drive a beat-up '87 Toyota Tercel? Huh? Which reputation are you trying to uphold?"

My feelings were hurt, so I kept my mouth closed. I knew Kerry didn't mean any harm, but his frustrations came out the wrong way, causing me as much pain as I felt when Momma hung up the phone on me. Kerry began to bandage my wound by selecting his words more carefully.

"Ivy, you know I love you. I'll do just about anything for you, but I can't take money from my savings to buy what you want. My wife and I want to buy a house. After your bail money, it's gonna take us a minute to build to where we were." Kerry grabbed my hand as he continued. "I wish there was a way I could just snap my fingers and you'd be back on your feet. Unfortunately, life is not a fairy tale. We can't make troubles magically disappear."

"I know. I guess I just need to learn to think before I speak. I've made a lot of bad decisions in my time. I see that you're willing to help me, so I'm going to be grateful for whatever you're willing to do."

We got out of the car then started toward Wal-Mart's entrance. Kerry looked at me from head to toe for the first time since he'd picked me up.

"What the—"

"I know what you're thinking, Kerry, but this is club material. And it's Donna Karan."

"I don't care if it's Donna Summer. Your head and that dress ain't quite matching too well right now."

"Well, I didn't have a comb or curlers in jail," I said, mashing my hair down.

Kerry grabbed me then cupped my mouth. "Shh. Not so loud. You don't have to let everyone know where you've been."

"They're probably wondering where I've been and who I've been doing it with anyway. Better yet, they're probably thinking you're my pimp." I laughed.

Kerry shook his head. "And you think that's funny, huh?"

My brother bought me three hundred dollar's worth of clothes and other necessities from Wal-Mart. He took me to pick up my car then to a motel where he could pay a low weekly fee for my stay. He fussed at me before he left.

"Ivy, you've got two months to get yourself together. After that, you're on your own. I'll always love you, but I've got my own family to think of," he said.

"I know. I'm going to find me another job because I don't wanna go back to my old one. I'm too embarrassed, but I promise I won't let you down."

"Good. Now I've got to get some sleep before I head to work tonight," he said, leaning to kiss me on the cheek.

I lay in bed thinking about my kids and all of the material things I lost. I also became angry with my mother for fighting against me. I knew she had my children's best interest at heart, but it was unfair for her to fault me for what she didn't teach me. Sure, she told me not to leave my kids home alone, but she made me feel more like she was trying to run my life than help me. She didn't volunteer to babysit one time.

I had to straighten up around my little brother. All he wanted was for me to live a better life. Unlike my mother, he'd been in my corner through thick and thin. If anyone said something bad about me, he would be ready to fight. I think we developed a close relationship because he felt sorry for me over the years. Kerry witnessed how cruel and hard on me Momma would be on the account of my father leaving her before I was born. She denies it, but I still feel she named me Ivy in reference to poison, and my middle and last name is my father's. I've asked her before why didn't she just name me Poison Lee Jones since that's the way she feels, but she didn't answer me.

After withholding my kids, I could no longer call her Momma. She became Bessie Mae Reynolds to me. I didn't give a damn if she and I got along or not. I wanted my kids, and my mind was made up to show Bessie Mae how poisonous I could be if she kept standing in my way.

Chapter 2
To Backtrack is Whack

I had only been in the motel three days before Gerald spotted me. He caught me when I went to check the mailbox at the old apartment. All of the boxes were connected together near the office. When I pulled up, he was sitting on the sidewalk, looking like he'd lost his best friend.

"What's up, Ivy? Why you ain't called me?" he asked just as I stepped out of the car.

"Gerald, I've got a lot of shit on my mind, okay?" I responded sarcastically.

"So, I just didn't cross your mind at all in the last few days?"

"Yeah. I just said I've got a lot of shit on my mind. You're part of the shit I was talking about," I said, rolling my eyes. I continued opening my mailbox.

Gerald stood and walked toward me. His shirt was open and his jeans hung slightly off his waist, exposing the band to his Joe Boxers. He'd been sitting in the sun. Sweat ran down his chocolate face and abdomen like a steady flowing stream. His wet six-pack was sexy as hell. I looked away and continued scanning through my mail.

"That's cold, Ivy. You know that's not right."

"Whatever, Gerald," I said, throwing up the talk-to-the-hand signal.

"Hey, why're you so mad at me?"

"I've just had some time to think, and I realize I don't need you to do bad. Why don't you go sit around somebody else's mailbox? Leave me the fuck alone."

"Baby—" he said, stepping closer.

"Don't come near me, Gerald. You're sweaty." I frowned.

Gerald's tall, masculine frame towered over my five-foot-six body, causing a calming shade over my face as his back blocked the sun.

"Baby, I don't understand why you're taking things out on me. I saw you on the news. I felt so sorry for you. I wanted to help you . . . do something for you, but I didn't know where to find you."

Before I knew it, we had stood and talked for half an hour. Somehow Gerald was able to smooth talk me into letting him ride back to the motel. The fact that I was lonely and needed his affection certainly didn't help, but I also wondered what his company could hurt.

When Gerald bent me over the bed then stuck his tongue into my ass, I quickly got past the feeling that he shouldn't be there. In fact, I began to beg him for more sexual favors. I wanted my lips licked, my clit sucked, and the walls inside my canal needed to be tapped. He did just as I'd asked him, when I asked him. I knew this man was no good, but all that mattered to me was he was good to me at the moment.

Gerald caused my shoulders to be sore because as he lay on top of my back, he gripped under my arms and repeatedly rammed himself into me. I moaned and screamed for more. He liked it when I made all sorts of inviting sounds.

Many of them were fake, but I did what I had to do to make him come.

Gerald sexed me up then asked if he could borrow my car. I was very apprehensive.

"Borrow my car for what, Gerald? If you need me to take you somewhere, I will."

"I need to go holla at my partner about this money he owes me. He doesn't live in the best of neighborhoods, and I can't take you over there. He said he'd pay me today. I didn't want to let the day go by without at least talking with 'im."

"Well, there's a phone over there. I'm sure the charges won't be too high. You can't possibly have that much to talk about anyway."

"Really, I just prefer to go see him. He might try to tell me he doesn't have it if he's not in my face. Besides, I see you could use some things around here. You got that kitchen over there, but no groceries. What's up with that?"

"Gerald, you know I don't have a job anymore. I can't go back to the Southern Bell Phone Company. I've been a no-call, no-show since I went to jail. They wouldn't let me back to work even if I wanted to."

"That's what I'm talking about. Do you want me to go get this money or not?"

Gerald kept talking and finally convinced me. Sex with him had made me lazy and sleepy anyway. After he left, I went to take a shower. I put on the nightgown I bought at Wal-Mart then got into bed.

I rolled over and looked at the clock. I couldn't believe I'd slept all night. It was 7:00 the next morning, and I felt like I'd been whipped with a plank. I lay there for a minute, contemplating my next move. It suddenly dawned on me that I'd been with Gerald the night before, and he still had my car.

I jumped out of bed and ran outside to the parking lot in my gown. My car wasn't out there. I ran back inside to make some phone calls to see if I could locate Gerald. I had no luck finding him. I sat and waited till evening then I called my brother.

"Kerry, what's up?" I asked just after he picked up the phone.

"What's up, sis?" he said, grunting.

"Look. I know you were probably trying to catch a nap before going in to FedEx tonight, but I have a slight problem."

"Uh-oh. What kind of a problem, Ivy?"

"Gerald came over last night and asked to borrow my car."

"I know you didn't," he yelled as if he was suddenly awake.

"I did. And he hasn't returned with it. And I'm hungry, have no money, and need to get out of this room before I lose my mind."

"Ivy, I could wring your damn neck. When you do stupid stuff like this, you make me ready to wash my hands of you."

"I know, Kerry, but I really thought he was going out to get some money from his friend and would be back."

"Since when has Gerald started doing right by you?"

I couldn't answer him right away. "Kerry, I just need you to come take me to see if you can help me find my car. I have an idea where it might be."

"I ain't going nowhere to get my ass blown off. I'll come bring you something to eat then I'm coming back home to finish my nap."

"Kerry—"

"Enough said. I'll see you in a minute," he said just before hanging up the phone.

Kerry made it over to my motel with a chop steak dinner from Picadilly's and some tea. He gave me forty dollars and offered to help find my car the next day if Gerald still hadn't brought it back. I kissed him on the cheek then walked him to his car. After eating my food, I couldn't sit still.

I picked up the phone to call an old girlfriend to come get me. I dialed six of her seven digits then changed my mind. I realized I wasn't ready to face old friends after the fire. I remembered that Kerry had given me forty dollars, so I decided to call a taxi.

The first place I decided to look was over to Sherita's house, a woman I'd known Gerald to cheat on me with. As we pulled up, I saw my car in the driveway, beat up worse than it already was before I let Gerald drive it. The windshield was bashed on the passenger side, the doors had huge kick marks in them, and the entire body looked like it had been beaten with a bat. Dents were everywhere. I asked the taxi to wait, but he sensed I was up to something fishy, so he sped away.

The lights were on in the house, but when I knocked on the door, no one answered. The curtain was cracked, so I decided to look through the window. I could see Gerald sitting on the couch, apparently drunk. There were several beer bottles on the coffee table as well as on the floor. The television blared while Gerald sat in front of it dazed.

I decided I should try to open the door. Just as I had suspected, it was unlocked. I walked right on in. Gerald was so out of it, he didn't hear or see me. He sat unblinkingly in the same spot. I checked the entire house for Sherita. Although her car wasn't outside, I wanted to be sure she wasn't there. I was satisfied to know she wasn't there because it was about to be on with Gerald.

I headed back into the living room to confront him about my car. I went through the kitchen on the way and spotted a broom and decided to take it with me. Once back in the living room, I stood in front of Gerald. He had drifted off to sleep. I used the pointed end of the broom to wake his ass up.

"Get up, muthafucker. Wake yo' ass up," I yelled, poking him repeatedly.

He didn't like the nudging of the broomstick too well. He woke up cussing. "What the fu—" he started.

"It's me, nigga, now get up!"

Gerald tried to sit up, but in his drunken state, the best he could do was sit lopsided. He looked really stupid with his knees together and his hands between his lap. He kept bucking his eyes at me, trying to keep them open. I reached back and slapped the shit out of him.

"Heeeeyyy, got-dama," he yelled as he jumped off the couch then fell back down.

"What the fuck happened to my car, Gerald? Did yo' bitch fuck up my car?"

"I dunno. Whaddaya mean?" he slurred.

"Why my shit sitting out there all bashed up like that?"

"Uh . . . 'cuz it wuz already raggaly," he said, falling over on the couch.

"My car didn't look like that. You done brought it over here to yo' bitch's house, ain't thought about my feelings, and you drunk."

Before I realized what I was doing, I began pounding the broomstick over his body. I couldn't count the blows if I wanted to because I delivered them fast, hard, and furious. He lifted his leg in the air, trying to block the next blow, and the stick finally broke in half. I picked up the piece without the sweeper and continued to batter his body until I got tired.

I looked around the living room for my keys. They were lying on the floor next to the coffee table. I picked them up then headed to beat Gerald's drunk ass some more. Once I got tired again, I left the house.

It took several tries to get my car to crank. As I backed out, I spotted Sherita's Ford Taurus slowing down, blinking to pull into the driveway. Immediately, I got angrier. I placed the car into park then jumped out. Sherita's car was still sitting in the middle of the street. She saw me coming then rolled up her window.

"Naw. Don't get scared now, bitch," I yelled. "You were a bold ass when I wasn't around, so don't get scared now."

Sherita cracked her window. "Yeah . . . and . . . so what? He had no business bringing that piece of shit over to my house," she yelled in a shrilled voice. "Get the hell out of my driveway."

"Gladly," I screamed, storming back to my car.

I mashed the gas pedal to the floor, aiming for her car, severely wrecking the front end. I pulled forward to back up and crash into her again, totaling my back end in the process. I didn't care though. I just wanted Sherita to feel some of the anger I was feeling.

I sped away to my motel. After I arrived, I jumped out to look at my car. Steam elevated from the hood, and the trunk was completely destroyed. I ran into my motel room and cried like a baby. Things just didn't seem to be going right. My car was already a piece of junk before Gerald and his woman got ahold of it. Wrecking it myself certainly didn't solve anything.

I slept peacefully, but the next day around noon, Gerald was back over to my motel, ranting and raving about me showing up over to Sherita's.

"Open the damn door, Ivy. I know you're in there," he yelled as he beat on the door.

"Go away before I call the MPD," I screamed back.

"I don't give a fuck who you call. Once I get in there, it's gonna take SWAT to get me off your ass, so you might as well call 'em now."

I dialed 911 and asked for the police. The operator wanted me to hold the line with her, but I told her I needed to get off the phone and find something to protect myself. I hung up, but it rang back immediately.

"Hello," I answered.

"This is the motel management. Are you okay up there?" a man asked.

"Yes, I'm okay right now. The police are on their way. I just called for them."

"Oh, I called several minutes ago, too. I was just checking with you. Don't open the door."

"Don't worry," I responded.

After hanging up, I yelled to Gerald to let him know the police were on their way. He continued his rage as if he didn't hear me.

"I'm going to fuck you up, Ivy," he yelled.

When I pulled back the curtain, I could see Gerald standing on the balcony with no shirt on, sweating like a hog. There was no sign of shade, so the hot sun must've been driving him even more insane as he continued his fit. I wasn't going to open the door, so I yelled at him through the window.

"Not if I blow your ass off first, Gerald. I'm asking you nicely to go away. If you give me a reason, I'm going to send you to an early grave."

Gerald stepped toward the window and leaned in to lock eyes with me. His eyebrows meshed together just above his nose as he frowned. He was close enough to the window for me to see the beads of sweat as they produced, one at a time, on his forehead. I stood still, pretending to be brave, anticipating his next move.

Gerald reached behind his back and pulled a gun. I gasped, but I became paralyzed and couldn't run from the window. He turned the butt of the gun around then bashed the glass with it. The whole pane shattered. I stood screaming with my eyes closed and hands to my ears. I kept waiting for Gerald to either shoot me or grab me, but he never did. I paused, wondering what was going on. Although my ears were muffled, I could hear voices. I opened my eyes to find Gerald outside the window, lying on his stomach with his hands behind his back. I opened the door and saw a policeman with his gun drawn, instructing Gerald on what to do. Another policeman ran up the stairs then cuffed him.

To say I was relieved was an understatement. I began to shake worse after everything was over because I realized how close I'd come to losing my life. It was a good thing the motel management beat me to calling the police because those minutes saved me. But, not only did management call the police, they also called my brother since the room was registered in his name. Kerry pulled up just as the police drove away with Gerald. I stood on the porch watching him speak to the manager. They both headed up the stairs.

"Ivy, get your stuff. Let's go find you somewhere else to stay," Kerry said.

"Why? Gerald's locked up now. He won't be back," I said.

"Yeah, but you can't stay here. You're being evicted," Kerry said.

I looked at the manager. "Evicted? You think him coming over to harass me was my fault?"

"I don't know, ma'am, but I can't take any chances. I'm trying to run a quiet and safe environment. Any tenant who violates the peace has to go."

I was angry and stunned. Kerry was mad, too. Not just because I had to leave, but because he was also being charged for the motel window. I apologized all the way to the next motel.

Kerry had to have my car pulled from the old motel to

a junkyard because it was dead. It had suffered its final abuse the day I decided to ram it into Sherita's car, leaving me with the Memphis City Transit Bus System as my main source of transportation.

I went to court two days after moving into the new motel. Although a judge had awarded me visitation rights with my children, Bessie Mae was determined not to let me see them. No matter how I tried to convince her I'd changed and that I didn't hear or see from Gerald anymore, she stayed firm with keeping my children from me.

Two weeks later, I still had no job. I became depressed because each day Kerry came to see me, he counted down the time I had left to find a job and get out of the motel. I didn't know what I was going to do. I began to mope around, feeling sorry for myself. I became more and more bitter about the way my life was going. I still loved my kids and my brother, but when it came to Bessie Mae, I didn't give a fuck.

Chapter 3
Lean on Momma—Not

Kerry took me over to Bessie Mae's house, hoping to persuade her to let me in. She loved Kerry and would do just about everything he asked.

"Hi, Mom. I brought Ivy over to see the kids," Kerry said to her through the closed wooden door.

She opened the door and looked over Kerry's shoulder at me with an evil eye. "I done told her already she ain't welcomed here, and you know it, too. Why'd you bring her?"

Kerry reached back for my hand then pulled me around him. "Mom, you know those children love their mother. Don't do this to them. They want to see her. Robin told me so the other day. Mom, please let us in."

She gave me another evil eye, glancing up and down at me and the giant gift bag I had in my hand. "Hmph. I guess she can see 'em, but only for a minute," she said, stepping back to let us in.

When I first stepped inside, I didn't see my children. Bessie Mae's house was spotless as usual, but it smelled like cooked greens and fatback. I could also smell corn bread in the oven. As I stood waiting for my children to come around the corner, Bessie Mae hugged Kerry and acted like I was a stranger. Although it had been a couple of weeks since she'd last seen me, she hardly looked at me, and she never even offered me a seat. I finally sat down at my own leisure. Bessie Mae didn't like that too much.

She snarled at me. "Don't get too comfortable. When I bring these kids out to the living room, you've only got five minutes with 'em, then you gotta go," she said, heading toward the bedrooms.

Kerry and I looked at each other. He seemed at a loss for words. I shook my head, rolled my eyes, then pointed my finger down my throat as if I was about to gag. We both burst into laughter. Soon Bessie Mae was back with my kids lined up behind her. Once they saw me, they ran and gave me a group hug. I looked over their shoulders and noticed Bessie Mae standing with her eyes bucked, her wig crooked, and one hand on her hip while flashing an open palm at me as she mouthed, "Five minutes." I closed my eyes and relished the hugs and kisses coming from my children.

"We miss you, Mommy. Can we go home now?" Zachary, my middle child, asked.

"No, son. Not yet. I'm working on getting you home with me though. Mommy misses you, too. And I love you all so much," I said, trying to prevent my voice from trembling.

"Mommy, I'm sorry. I didn't mean to leave the bread bag too close to the fire. I was only trying to be a big girl like you always ask me to be," Robin said, holding her head down.

I stroked her chin. "Shh. I know, sweetheart. Don't apologize. You are a big girl. You're my big girl, and I'm the one who should be apologizing. I'm sorry I left you all home alone. I should've been there with you, and when you come back to live with me, things are going to be much different."

"Nanna said you don't care about us. She said all you do is look for no-good men to be around."

Kerry and I looked at each other then turned our attention to Bessie Mae. When I looked back at Kerry, he had dropped his head, seemingly sorry to hear Robin's words. I tried to respond without signs of bitterness. "Well, sweetie, things might've seemed that way to Nanna, but she just doesn't understand."

"Really? So, you don't look for no-good men?"

I cleared my throat. It was tough thinking of the right words to say to my child. "No, actually I don't. I'm hoping for a knight in shining armor."

"What's a knight in shining armor?" she asked.

Boy, she's asking a lot of questions, I thought. "A man who'll treat us good and love us all forever and ever. Now stop asking so many questions," I said, stroking her face.

Apparently Bessie Mae had heard enough. "All right, children. You've seen your mother. Now go get washed up for dinner," she said, pulling them from my arms.

"Wait," I said, looking up at Bessie Mae. "Please. Just two more minutes. I want to show them the gifts I brought."

The children began jumping up and down as I pulled out each of their favorite toys they once owned. Thanks to Kerry's financial support, I had gone to Wal-Mart before visiting the children and picked out an African American Fever Fashion Barbie for Robin, a blue Big Rides Hot Wheels truck for Zachary, and a Fun 2 Learn Laughtop for Dillon. The children were ecstatic, bouncing up and down as they all smothered me with kisses.

"Mommy, how did you find my laptop?" Dillon asked just after calming down. "I thought it burned in the fire."

"Uncle Kerry and I went shopping for you all. Make sure to thank your uncle, too."

They all turned their attention to Kerry and applied the same kisses on him as they did to me. Bessie Mae was just plain fed up. She clapped her hands twice. "C'mon now, children. It's time for dinner."

Robin and Zachary got down off Kerry and headed to wash up. Dillon began to cry. My heart was broken.

"C'mon, boy," she fussed.

"Wait. Please just let me talk to Dillon a bit," I pleaded with Bessie Mae.

She let his arm go. "Hurry up, Dillon," she said, walking toward the kitchen.

I wiped Dillon's tears as he cried. "Hey, little man. What's wrong?"

"I wanna go witchu," he mumbled.

"I want you to go with me, too, son, but you can't go today. What's wrong? Isn't Nanna being nice to you?"

Dillon shook his head. I panicked because I didn't know what to think. Four-year-olds can exaggerate the truth at times, but the look on Dillon's face seemed sincere. I looked over at Kerry who seemed confused then I questioned Dillon more.

"What do you mean, little man? What's going on?"

Dillon looked at the kitchen opening as if he was trying to see if Bessie Mae was coming. Seemingly satisfied he didn't see her, he leaned in, grabbed my face, and whispered, "Nanna gon' make me eat dem nasty greens."

I sighed to release the deep breath I'd been holding. Kerry and I chuckled softly. Although I knew in my mind that Bessie Mae wouldn't hurt my children, I was still relieved to hear that Dillon was only afraid of eating healthy foods.

"Sweetheart, you not wanting those greens is mainly my

fault. Momma never cooked many vegetables before, but trust me, you'll like them. Tell Nanna to put some vinegar on them for you. Okay?" I said, rubbing his head.

"Okay," Dillon said sadly.

Bessie Mae came out of the kitchen. "C'mon here, Dillon. Go wash your hands," she said, reaching for him.

I was sad to see him go. I watched him walk down the hall to the bathroom. Bessie Mae gave me a stern look and then reminded me that my time was up.

"Five minutes left long ago," she said.

I stood. "I'm leaving, Bessie Mae," I snapped. She looked shocked to hear me call her name. "By the way, please put some vinegar on Dillon's greens. He's not use to that kind of food."

"Yeah? Well, that food is good for him, and I done told those kids that I'm gon' make sure they eat healthy from now on. Dillon will get use to it."

"I'm sure he will, Bessie Mae. At least put a little sugar on the greens if not vinegar to help him out. Please, and thank you," I said, walking to the door.

Kerry followed me. Bessie Mae began to act like her feelings were hurt. "Kerry, you leaving, too?" she asked.

"Yes, ma'am. I have to. I drove Ivy over here," he responded.

"Well, why didn't she drive her own car?"

"That's a long story, Momma," he said.

"You gonna come back? I cooked enough so you could eat, too."

"Umm. I might come back later on, Momma. I need to go check on Rita first. The bigger she gets, the crankier she gets."

"I can imagine. Well, take her on," she said, pointing at me. "Check on your wife, then come on back over and get you some greens. I made some corn bread, too. Ask Rita if she wants some," Bessie Mae said, stepping outside as we walked off the porch.

"Thanks. I'll call you after I get to the house," Kerry said.

I turned around and looked at Bessie Mae. "I guess I'm not your child anymore. You ain't gon' offer me dinner?"

She snarled at me once more. "I didn't make enough for you. I didn't know you would be here. I'm feeding your children. Isn't that enough?"

I walked toward her. "If my children are really that much of a burden to you, then all you have to do when we go back to court is let the judge know you feel I'm a fit parent, and perhaps *my* children can come home with me."

Bessie Mae shook her head. "You don't deserve to be a mother. You're trash, and that's all you'll ever be. Get off my porch, slut."

Tears welled in my eyes. I was so hurt that I charged at Bessie Mae. Kerry caught me around the waist before I could reach her. I pulled and tugged on Kerry's arms, trying to break free. He lifted me and carried me to his car. Once at his car, he put me down and began to curse me.

"What the hell is wrong with you, Ivy? That is your mother standing over there on the porch."

"She ain't acting like my mother," I yelled.

"No . . . fuck what you think. Whether she acts like it or not, she's still your mother. You don't have a choice except to respect her."

"I do have a choice. She needs to respect me, too," I said as tears streamed down my cheeks.

Kerry was silent as I stood sobbing. I looked at Bessie Mae. She shook her head then turned to walk into the house. She slammed the door shut. Kerry opened the car door for me.

"Get in," he said softly.

"Kerry, I just want another chance. I want my kids back," I cried.

He hugged me. "I know, Ivy. Give her some time. Work on getting yourself together, then regardless of what Momma says to the judge, you'll get your children."

"I love my kids, Kerry."

"I know, Ivy. And Robin, Zach, and Dillon know it, too," he said, rocking me in his arms.

I got into the car. Kerry took me back to the motel. After walking me to my room, he sat to chat with me for a few minutes.

"Ivy, what are you planning to do with your life? I mean, would going back to the phone company really be that bad?"

"You don't understand the people I use to work for, Kerry. And besides, if I wasn't fired the day my story hit the news, then I'm sure fired now. I've been a no-call, no-show for close to a month now."

"Could it really hurt to try? All they can do is say no, Ivy. Just explain your situation with being embarrassed. You never know. Perhaps your boss would understand."

"I hear ya, li'l bro, but I don't know if I can stomach my coworkers looking down on me."

"Ivy, you were on the news, on every channel, for nearly a week. The fire at your apartment complex and you tussling with the police, trying to resist arrest was the biggest thing to happen in Memphis in a while. The news reporters made a big hoopla for so long because there wasn't much else going on in the city at the time. So, any job you get, you'll more than likely be recognized. You could either take the snarling looks from the people at the phone company or from another job."

"I think I'd rather take the looks from another job," I said frankly.

"A'ight. Just remember the time frame we're working on here. I'm not paying for your motel room after next month. You hear me?"

"Fine. I hear you, Kerry. Stop drilling that into my head. I'll have a job by next week. You'll see."

I didn't know where or what kind of work I would find, but the pressure was on.

Chapter 4

First Impressions are Lasting Ones

K erry had left me with a hundred and fifty dollars to get some food and toiletries. I desperately needed to shake the depression I was slipping in, so I caught the bus downtown to get out of the house. I had also seen a job posting in the *Commercial Appeal* for the local health department. The job was clerical, and I felt I had enough experience, so I went there to fill out an application.

There were several people lined up inside the building, but I seemed to be the only one inquiring about a job. After asking the security guard for directions, I was instructed to apply online and fax a resume over. I was frustrated because I knew I wasn't going to get online any time soon. I turned to leave and noticed the line of people had grown. *Damn, is anybody free from sexually transmitted diseases in Memphis anymore?* I thought. Many of them seemed to be looking down, but there was one woman who held her head high. She even smiled and winked at me as I headed out the door. I didn't know anything else to do except smile back.

The weather was nice and breezy, so I walked farther

into downtown. I spent most of my day walking and sightseeing. I went inside a corner store to buy everything I
needed then headed down Second Street to the bus station. Second is a one-way street, and I was walking on the
opposite side so I could see the cars coming toward me. I
spotted the 10 Cottonwood bus as it slowed to stop at the
shell where everyone was waiting. It was the one I needed.
Confident no cars were coming, I hurried out into the
street.

Just as I was halfway across the street, a huge SUV sped
toward me then slammed on the brakes, stopping just
inches from hitting me. The crowd on the sidewalk all
screamed in unison. My heart damned near fell out of my
chest as it beat fast and irregular. I took a deep breath
then looked up at the truck. It was a black Hummer. That
thing seemed like a huge army tank as I stood motionless
in front of it. I looked up past the headlights to the windshield in order to make eye contact with the male driver.
Although I couldn't see his eyes through his dark sun-
glasses, he seemed perturbed that I was in his way. His
nose was wrinkled and his lips were twisted.

I couldn't move no matter how much my mind told me
to get out of the way. The man slid his shades down his
nose then leered at me with piercing eyes. His eyes looked
red like fire, and he squinted as he continued to frown. I
was frozen solid—that is until he opened his door. Afraid,
I ran as fast as I could, dropping my bags in the middle of
the street. I jumped on the bus and begged the driver to
drive away. He did as I'd asked.

As I went to have a seat, I could see the man in the
Hummer bending down to retrieve my things. I was
pissed. I didn't have money to buy more groceries, and I
didn't want to have to tell Kerry what happened. I didn't
want him to think I was careless. I stood, holding on to the
top rail of the bus, watching to see what the man would do

with my bags. After the bus turned the corner, I could no longer see him.

I took a seat, trying to catch my breath. I went into a daze about almost getting run down in the street, and then I was startled by the yelling bus driver.

"Ma'am, you forgot to pay your fare," he screamed as he continued to drive.

The bus came to a stop at a red light, so I got up to put one dollar and forty cents in the change acceptor. I wondered how I managed to hold onto my purse, considering how scared I was of the stranger. I went back to have a seat.

The lady in front of me turned around to make conversation. "Wow. I saw what happened. Are you okay?" she asked.

"Yeah. At least I think so," I said. "I'm still a little shaken."

"I can imagine so. I'm glad you're all right."

"Yeah. Me, too." I laughed.

"Why'd you run away and onto the bus so fast?"

I huffed, exhausted from the rush of adrenaline. "That driver was scary looking. I didn't know what was on that fool's mind. He looked like he wanted to beat my ass for being in his way."

She gasped. "Really? Damn. He might've been crazy then. Good thing you can run."

We sort of chuckled a bit. I had a sudden flash. She was the same woman who smiled at me earlier at the health department. I began to wonder why she had been there, but then I dismissed all negative thoughts. Some people go to the health department to get condoms or just for information. Besides, I didn't feel it was fair of me to judge her. She continued to make conversation.

"Did you see the truck before you heard the screeching brakes?"

"No. I don't know where he came from. Do you?" I

asked. The woman shook her head. "Me either. I could've sworn there were no cars coming when I stepped out there."

"Well, the important thing is that you're all right. I guess it could've happened to either one of us. We just have to be more on the lookout. People are crazy. That man was speeding, you know?"

"That's what I kind of figured," I responded. "Anyway, I hate riding these buses. I wish my car was fixed."

"I know what you mean. My car is in the shop, and I don't have a job, so it'll be there for a while."

I shook my head. "Mmph . . . maybe something will change for us soon."

The woman smiled at me again. I took a good look and noticed her beauty. Her complexion seemed smooth and caramel like mine, and she wore the sharpest cornrows I'd ever seen. I got a glimpse of her on the way back from paying my fare, and I noticed that her braids were waist-length. They were neatly zigzagged at a slant over her head. She sat turned around in her seat, staring at me. Under any other circumstance, I might've felt uncomfortable, but something about the woman's eyes was soothing. I calmly returned the stare. When she smiled at me, I wondered what she was thinking.

"Why are you staring at me like that?" I asked.

"I don't know. I guess I just want to make sure you're okay."

"Well that's awfully sweet of you," I said.

"You're pretty. How old are you anyway?"

"I'm twenty-six. Why? Don't I look it?"

"No. You actually look a lot younger. I would've guessed about twenty-one."

"Thanks. I guess some of us women just keep that girl-ish quality about us," I said, rubbing my hair.

She smiled. "You know that's a good thing. I'd rather

someone think I was younger based on my looks. How old do you think I am?"

"Oh, I don't know. And, I don't like guessing games."

"G'on. My feelings won't be hurt. I promise."

I shook my head. "Nope. I don't do guessing games at all. I stay out of trouble that way."

"I heard that," the woman said.

I attempted to interrupt her train of thought. "My name is Ivy Lee Jones by the way. What's yours?"

"I'm Candy," she responded, stretching her hand to shake mine. "Candy Cane."

"Are you serious?"

"Very. My name is Candy Cane."

"Yeah, right. And I suppose if I ask you again, you'll tell me the same." I laughed.

"I have no choice 'cause that's my name," she said, laughing.

I shook my head in disbelief then told her she had a stripper-type name. She gasped, and covered her mouth.

"What?" I asked.

"Nothing. What's up with you?" she asking, shrugging.

"Why did you gasp and cover your mouth as if I said the wrong thing?"

"I think I remember you."

"Oh? I remember you, too, but I wasn't going to say anything." I leaned in and whispered. "You're the woman who spoke to me while you were in line at the health department, right?"

She raised her eyebrows. "Yeah. That was me, but that's not where I first remember you from. I remember you from the news. You left your children at home while you went out to party with your boyfriend."

I became angry and almost blew a fuse. "And? So what? My children are fine."

"You mean to tell me you didn't get jail time behind

that? I'm surprised to see you sitting here rather than locked up," she said.

"Well, don't be surprised. And what's it to you anyway? I did a bad thing, but that's behind me now."

"Hmph. I hope so. That's why I don't have kids. I'm twenty-eight years old, and I know I'm not through chasing men and being a ho yet, so ain't no need in me birthing nobody's baby."

I was extremely offended. "Bitch, you don't know me," I yelled. "I ain't no ho, and I love my kids. I made a bad choice in leaving them home alone because I'm human, and I made a mistake. I know better now, and I'm not gon' let you and nobody else tell me I'm a bad mother. My kids love me."

"Hey, I didn't say they didn't—"

"Yeah, but you said enough. Like I said, you don't know me, so you can just turn yo' smiling ass around and leave me the fuck alone."

The bus driver put his two cents in. "And you ladies don't know me. I don't tolerate loud talking, profanity, and violence on this bus. I will put you off whether we've arrived at your destination or not. Respect the other riders, please."

"Well, tell this female to turn around and get out of my business. She sitting here tryna judge me like she ain't got issues. This ho just left the VD clinic. I know because I was there applying for a job, but her ass was in the shot line. She better get up off me," I said, all but spitting fire.

"Ma'am," the bus driver yelled, "you gon' have to calm down or else I'm gon' stop to put you off. I'm not going to keep driving around, listening to you huff and puff. Now make up your mind. Are you gon' sit quietly, or do I need to stop the bus?"

I closed my mouth. I had no more money, and I was too

far from the motel to get put off the bus. Ms. Candy Cane finally turned around and stopped aggravating me. I stared at the back of her head. Her cornrows were zigzagging all the way to the nape of her neck. If looks could kill, Candy would be dead or else bleeding because I traced every braid with my eyes, trying to pass time.

Chapter 5
Who Do You Turn To?

As bad as I didn't want to, my growling stomach forced me to call Kerry for some more money. When I got back to the motel, I tried to drink water on top of water to fill me up, but all it made me do was pee back to back, and I became hungrier by the second. Kerry was livid, and his wife was in the background raising hell, too.

"Every time I put some trust in you, Ivy, something else happens to make me think I'm wasting my energy on you," Kerry said after I finished telling him how I lost my bags.

"So, what . . . you think I'm lying?"

I could hear his wife, Rita, in the background fussing. "Something just doesn't sound right, Kerry," she said. "You need to quit believing everything that girl tells you."

"Tell your wife 'that girl' happens to be your sister. And I ain't lying to you. I was afraid of that man. He looked like he was about to get out of that truck and beat my ass. I don't even recall dropping the bags. I just remember running for my life."

"But, damn, Ivy. A hundred and fifty dollars don't come

easy for me. I hear what you saying about being hungry and all, but I don't have any more money to just let you have."

"A'ight. Well, just bring me something to eat out of your refrigerator then. I don't want no more of you and your wife's money. I just need something to eat," I pleaded. My voice cracked as I began to cry. "Please, Kerry. I know it all sounds untrue, but I would never lie to you. You're all I have."

He sighed. "Ivy, if I find out you're just trying to get over on me, I'm washing my hands of you. You hear me?"

"Cool. 'Cause I know I'm not lying."

"You better not be. I'm on my way, Ivy. I don't have much money, but I'll give you something."

"No problem. Thanks, li'l bro. I appreciate you being there for me as much as you have."

Kerry didn't respond to my last comment. He just hung up the phone on me. I stopped crying then went to take a shower. It was late in the evening, and I knew it wouldn't be long before Kerry came over since he had to be at work at 8:00. After getting out of the shower, I took advantage of gathering my laundry so I could go wash the next morning.

I shook out all the clothes and found two dollars in loose change. My stomach was giving me the blues, so I went downstairs to the snack machines and bought some chips, a candy bar, and a Coke. I had gobbled half the candy bar and drank most of the Coke before I returned to my room. Once I got to the door, several plastic bags were sitting on the ground, blocking the entrance. I bent down to look in one of them and discovered many of the products I lost earlier when I was downtown. I searched a couple of more bags and discovered they all belonged to me.

I looked around to see if someone was near or watching me, but I didn't see anyone. It was dark, and the silence began to spook me, so I ran into my room. I quickly locked the door then went to peep outside the window again. I still didn't see anyone. I became extremely nervous because I didn't know who would've set those bags in front of my door other than the mean-looking man in the Hummer. I remembered seeing him pick up my bags when the bus was driving away. *He must've followed the bus,* I thought.

I tried to remain calm, but the thought of that scary man knowing where I lived terrified me. I had my mind made up to ask Kerry if he didn't mind moving me to a new location for the next couple of weeks. I grabbed my chips and soda off the table then sat on the bed. Before I could get comfortable, there was a knock on the door. I was afraid to peep out the window again, so I yelled to the visitor.

"Who is it?" I asked.

"It's me. Kerry."

My heart was beating so fast, I could hardly catch my breath. "Okay. I'm coming."

When I opened the door for Kerry, I wrapped my arms around his neck, potato chips and soda in hand. "Boy, am I glad to see you," I said.

Kerry pushed me away from him. "What the hell is all that on the table, Ivy?"

He came in then closed the door behind him. I looked over at the bags then attempted to explain.

"That's why I'm glad to see you. See, I went downstairs to the snack machines, and when I returned, my bags were waiting for me at the door, but—"

"Ivy, you obviously think I'm a fool. I knew I should've listened to Rita."

"Say what?" I frowned.

"You had me losing sleep to come over here because you said you were hungry and didn't have any money. But when I get over here, not only are you snacking, but the bags you supposedly lost are sitting right in my face," Kerry argued. "I told you if I found out you were bullshitting me, I was gon' be done with you. You thought I was playing or something?"

"Naw. I'm trying to explain what happened, but you won't let me. What's wrong with you? You never come around me acting funny like this before."

"You know . . . I'm starting to think Momma and Rita are right. I really need to start practicing some tough love with you, 'cause if I don't, you're gonna run me ragged and into the poorhouse."

"I can't believe you'd say that. I told you the truth. Some man terrified me today. I didn't mean to drop those bags. You think I like throwing away your money?"

"You didn't throw it away apparently. You just thought I'd give you some more on top of what you already have. I must be out of my mind to keep listening to you."

"Oh, so if that's the case, then I guess that makes me a damn fool because any idiot running game would've at least hid the bags before you got over here."

"Whatever, Ivy. I'm tired, and I ain't falling for your mess anymore. I'm putting my money back into my pocket. I'm through feeling sorry for you. You're a grown woman, and it's time you start acting like it."

Kerry turned to walk out on me. "So, you just gon' leave?" I asked, tearing up. "I'm standing here trying to explain for nothing. It seems as if your mind was made up before you ever came over here."

He placed the bag he brought with him on the couch by the door. "Rita cooked this tonight. Enjoy because this will be the last time I go all out for you like this," he said, sounding tearful.

"I can't believe you won't listen to me. I told you the man from downtown must've been over here. Why would

I lie to you about that? You know I don't have anybody else I can depend on," I yelled. "Why are you doing this to me?"

"You did this to yourself. From losing your kids, your job, your apartment, car, Momma and me . . . you did it all to yourself. I have my own household to look out for. My unborn deserves the best at birth, but I see now if I keep bailing you out of trouble, my own family will suffer. I love you, but I can't let that happen."

Just like that, Kerry turned and walked out on me. I broke down and cried. Everything happened so fast, I had to replay the whole argument back in my mind to comprehend what transpired. I sat on the floor near the bed and bawled my eyes out. I looked up at the door and realized it wasn't locked, so I jumped up to fasten it. I ran to the phone to call Kerry back. *Maybe he'll listen now,* I thought as I dialed his cell. *He was just tired.* Kerry never answered. I got his voice mail instead.

"Kerry," I cried after the beep, "I don't know what happened between us tonight. I just know you didn't give me a chance to tell you how everything came to be. I know if you just listen, you'll understand. I never meant to make you angry, and you have to believe that I'm not lying to you. Please call me back. We need to talk. Thanks. I love you, li'l bro."

I was sure Kerry would be returning my call during one of his breaks. I tried to stay awake for as long as I could, awaiting his call. I dozed a few times, but as soon as my head would nod, I jumped up. I even put water on my face a few times because the later it got, keeping my eyes open became a severe struggle.

I was excited to see the 5:00 A.M. hour because I knew it wouldn't be long before Kerry made it to his car and got my message. I literally watched the time pass on the clock radio. By the time it was 5:45, I knew he should've gotten my message. I tried calling him, but his phone went straight to voice mail. I became nervous something might've happened to him, so I called his house.

"Hello," Rita answered groggily after the third ring.

"Hi, Rita. I've been trying to reach Kerry on his cell, but he hasn't answered," I said.

"Mm-hmm," she groaned.

"So, I'm worried. Is he okay? Has he made it home yet?"

"He's fine. He's in the bed, Ivy. You wanna leave a message for him?"

"No. I wanna speak to him. Tell him to get up. Didn't he get my message?"

"Yes, Ivy. He got your message," she said just before pausing. "He doesn't want to speak to you. And if I were you, I'd find me a job quick, because time is running out on your stay at that motel under Kerry's credit card."

"Bitch, you don't tell me what to do. You put my brother on this phone, dammit, and I mean now."

"I've already told you he doesn't want to speak to you," she said, elevating her voice on the last two words.

"I'm his blood. You can't come between us like this," I said, huffing. "He told me you always feeding him bullshit about me, telling him I'm running game on him. For your information, I don't need to lie to my brother. He loves me, and I love him."

"Ivy, what are you talking about? I'm not trying to come between you two. I know you love him, but I love him, too. And anyway, I'm his wife."

"Bitch, that ain't blood."

"Well, it may as well be, because in a court of law, *wife* counts as blood."

I was fuming. "Wake Kerry's ass up now," I yelled. "I'm sick of talking to you. Put my brother on the phone."

"Ivy, don't make me change my phone number because I will. I'm tired of you stressing Kerry. Don't call here anymore. Lose his cell phone number, too."

"Rita, you've really got me fucked up, you know that?"

"No, Ivy, you've got yourself fucked up. You can get next to Kerry, but you can't get next to me. That's why as his wife, I'm going to protect him. I need him sane and in his right mind, not crazy because of you."

I slammed the phone down in her face. I felt like my world was tumbling down. My brother was my rock. I didn't know if I could survive without him. I felt sick that he'd turn his back on me when he knew I needed him. I cried my eyes out some more then got in the bed.

I thought of how my kids were with Bessie Mae and how Kerry seemed to be choosing Rita over me. I cried until my eyes were dry and couldn't produce more tears, then I became angry. I figured that if my only brother and so-called mother weren't going to have my back then to hell with them.

Chapter 6
A Close Call

Igot up at 5:00 in the morning to do my laundry. The sign on the washer room door said it opened at 6:00, so I wanted to be ready. From previous experience, I knew I should go early or else chance missing all the good machines. Last time, I was fire mad about wasting my money on three loads of half-cleaned clothes, and it took four extra dollars just to get them dry.

Being that it was April, the sun was up before I left my room. Just as I had suspected, the washer room was empty. I separated my belongings into three machines then started them. I grabbed my two hampers then turned to leave. I was startled by a man standing in the door. It was the man who almost ran over me downtown. He stood silently staring at me.

He was blocking the door, and I didn't know what to do. He seemed to be about six-four and at least two hundred and fifty pounds. Considering I only weighed one hundred and twenty pounds, I knew I couldn't wrestle with him if I wanted to. I looked around for an escape, but the room seemed to only have one exit. I scrambled my mind for something to say.

"Excuse me, sir," I said, starting toward him. "You're blocking the door."

"I know," he said matter-of-factly.

His voice struck me as deep and sexy, but this was no time for admiration. There was no telling what he planned to do with me, and I was afraid. I put on my acting shoes, pretending not to be scared as I moved closer.

"Then do you mind moving out of my way? I've got things to do."

"Yeah. I mind. I mind it very much."

"Why?" I asked, looking up at him. "Do I know you?"

He laughed. "Yeah. You do."

I stood waiting for more response, but it never came. I was sick of his short responses, so I kept the conversation going, hoping he wouldn't turn mean. "Do you care to elaborate? Or, do you want me to just stand here and let you keep looking in my face?"

He leaned his tall frame down to speak just inches from my nose. "Let's get one thing straight: you can't *let* me do anything. I'm Stormy Daniels, and I do what I want to do."

I wondered if he could hear my heart beating because I was scared silly. I refused to let him know it though. I frowned and set one of my hampers down.

"Okay, Stormy Daniels. If your name is supposed to mean something to me, then I'm sorry because I still don't know who you are. Now, if you don't mind, I need to get around you. I've already told you I have things to do, and I hate repeating myself."

"Cute," he said.

"Excuse me?"

"I think it's cute how you're standing here pretending like you don't remember me."

"Oh . . . I thought you were trying to say I was cute. I was just about to say you're a little desperate if you think I'm pretty in this beat-up T-shirt and sweatpants," I responded, trying to throw in a little humor. "I mean, I didn't even comb my hair. I'm standing here looking like a jacked-up chicken by the head." I laughed.

Stormy must not have seen the humor in what I said because he didn't laugh. Instead, he had a ruthless expression on his face that signaled me to get moving. I scrambled for more to say. I drew a blank for about a minute.

The longer it took for me to say something, the more Stormy frowned, putting the fear of God in me. I wondered if I'd seen my last episode of *Good Times* when I got up at 5:00 in the morning. But, despite how frightened I was, I was certain Stormy couldn't see it. We stood silent, having a staring contest. Surprisingly, after a few minutes, he moved out of my way. I wanted desperately to take off running, but instead, I picked up my hampers and walked calmly back to my room.

I locked the door then peeked out the window. When I saw Stormy getting back into his truck, I felt I could breathe again. I wanted to pack up and move right then. I called Kerry and left him several voice messages, letting him know the man I was telling him about had found me and that I was scared. Obviously Kerry didn't believe me because he didn't bother to call back.

I went to put my clothes in the dryers and two one-dollar bills fell out of a pair of pants. I smiled then walked to a nearby newspaper stand for the daily paper. I wanted to search for a job. After circling several possibilities, I went down to the motel office to see if someone could help me. There was a woman there I'd never seen before.

"Excuse me, ma'am. My name is Ivy Lee Jones, and I'm one of your tenants," I said, reaching to shake the woman's hand.

"Okay, Ms. Jones, nice to meet you. I'm Jennie Brooks, the manager here," she said.

"It's a pleasure to meet you, too, Ms. Brooks. I'm here to ask for a favor." I paused when she looked at me funny, but then I put my newspaper on her desk and continued. "See . . . I need to go look for a job, but I don't have bus fare. I was wondering if I could borrow a few dollars . . . just enough to get me back and forth, and I'll repay you."

"Ms. Jones, I don—" she started.

"Please," I said, shushing her, "call me Ivy."

"Hmph." She grunted, sitting up in her chair. "Okay, Ivy. What I was trying to tell you is that I don't believe I should be loaning money to tenants. You seem like a nice girl and all, but I don't want to do anything that would put my job in jeopardy."

"Put your job in jeopardy? What do you mean?"

She sucked her gold tooth before replying. "Well, you borrowing money could become a *ha-bitch-ual* thang," she said, stressing the part about *bitch*. "And, at some point, I'm gon' be looking for my cash back. And uh see, I know me betta than anybody know me. I'ma act a fool about mine. My money is too hard to come by."

At that point, I realized how ghetto she was. I didn't know it walking in the door, but once we kept talking, she began to let it all hang out. I started having regrets that I'd approached her, but I continued to plead because I didn't have anywhere else to turn. I was about to have a nervous breakdown, thinking about Stormy and what he might be thinking of doing to me.

"Ms. Brooks—" I began.

"Un-un . . . you can call me Jennie," she said as she continued to lick her gold tooth. "You wanna be on a first-name basis, we can do that."

I was about to say something, but she bent down and I could no longer see her face. When she came from under the desk, she had a tube of lip gloss in her hand. Before she bothered to look back at me, she stroked the gloss over each lip several times. I wanted to tell her she was overdoing it, but I didn't want to offend her. She put the tube up then looked at me, raising her eyebrow as if she was waiting for a response.

"Well, Jennie, I promise if you loan me money this one time, I won't bother you for any more. All I need is a few dollars. I just want to be able to catch the bus to one of these places and back," I said, pointing at the circled job openings in the newspaper.

Jennie sat back in her chair and twisted her frosted lips. Her skin was so black and shiny, I swear I could almost see my reflection on her forehead. I use to want to be her complexion because I'm color struck, favoring dark-skinned people, but as I got older, I came to accept my caramel tone. I actually thought Jennie was pretty until she started talking. Her attitude took away from her beauty as she continued to be ugly toward me.

"You from Memphis?" she asked.

"Yes."

"What area you grow up in?"

"Why? What does where I'm from have to do with whether you're going to loan me money?"

She stared at me before speaking. "I betchu one of them rich kids, ain't it?"

"Huh? I'm standing here looking tore up from the floor up. How do you figure I come from a wealthy family?"

"'Cause I done seen yo' kind before, sweetie."

"And what the hell does that supposed to mean?"

"You ain't all fixed up today, but I know you're a prissy one."

"Look . . . I don't know you, and you don't know me. You can't assume something about me that isn't true."

"Mm-hmm . . . I can tell you from a rich background,

and now that you done slipped on yo' ass, yo' family don't want nothing to do witcha . . . messin' up they good name and all. I saw you on the news."

My feelings were hurt, and I didn't know what to say. Jennie was right about seeing me on the news, but she was far wrong about my upbringing. Tears filled my eyes, but I held my head back and looked up at the ceiling so they wouldn't fall. Jennie kept talking, but her words began to sound like *blah, blah, blah,* as I drowned her out with positive thoughts of my kids.

I wondered how many new friends Robin had made at her new school. She could always make friends very easily because of her nice spirit. I imagined my boys were accustomed to their new environment because they were tough. Dillon loved child care, but I couldn't call it that around him. He said he attended Head Start. I guess that sounded more grown-up to him than child care. I thought of my children for several minutes as Jennie rambled. I didn't even hear her when she called my name.

"What's wrong witchu? Don't you hear me calling you?"

"Uhm . . . yeah," I lied.

"Well then answer me. If I didn't know any betta, I would think you were tuning me out," she said, reaching into her bra.

I wondered what she was doing, and I even wondered if I should look away. She dug like she was digging for gold, damn near popping one of her breasts out—a sight I didn't care to see. I figured I better say good-bye and be on my way.

"Well, Jennie, I would love to be able to stand here and talk more with you, but I've got to roll. I really need to get going if I'm going to find somebody to loan me some money."

She called for me as I was walking out. "Hold up, li'l

momma. I thought you wanted my help," she said, pulling money from her bra.

"I do, but I don't want a beat down if I can't pay you back when you're ready for me to."

"I done got it out now. Here . . . take this," she said, handing me a five-dollar bill. "You don't owe me nothing. I just wanna know the results when you get back. I might seem mean at times, but I got a sister about your age. If she needed help, I'd want someone to help her. Now take it."

I smiled. "Thanks, Jennie," I said, placing the money in my pocket. "And I'll still pay you back."

"I told ya. I ain't lookin' for that. I just wanna know you tryna do something positive with yourself. Good luck," she said.

I was glad to have left there on a positive note. It was 8:00 in the morning, and I still hadn't eaten anything. I retrieved my clothes from the dryer then went up to my room, got dressed then went to the Burger King down the street. Time was running out on me. My bus was scheduled to run in less than fifteen minutes once I got there. The sausage croissants were on special for ninety-nine cents, so I ordered one and a cup of water to go.

I made it to the bus stop in the nick of time. Just as I paid my fare, I spotted Stormy's truck passing by. He slowed to make sure I saw him then sped off. I plopped down in my seat thinking, *Lawd, let me hurry up and find a job, so I can get out of here.*

Chapter 7

Rescue Me

I got off the bus in front of the Burger King after a long day of constant disappointments. I filled out application after application, but I got rejection after rejection. The disheartening thing that made me give up and decide to go home was after a manager at a dry-cleaning store had to turn me down. She seemed excited about hiring me, but then she asked for two forms of identification. My Social Security card was destroyed in the apartment fire, so the only ID I had on me was my driver's license. She told me to come back when I had a more permanent address and a second ID.

As I walked back to my motel, I spotted Jennie sitting at the front desk. I didn't feel like a long conversation, but I went in anyway. I had my mind ready for the lashing she'd give me, telling me how I didn't try hard enough, and so on and so on. She filed her nails nonstop with an emery board, even after looking up to notice me walking toward her.

"What's up? How'd it go?" she asked.

I shook my head. "Terrible," I said just before breaking down in tears.

"Hey, hey, hey. Don't be doing that up in here. Not in front of me. You go do that up in yo' room. I ain't good with consoling people when they crying," she said. "Now, I know you must've had a bad day . . . hell, I bet you even hungry. I didn't give you much money to do anything with. G'on up to yo' room, and I'll send the pizza man up in a bit."

I stood up straight then began wiping my face and eyes. "Thanks, Jennie," I said. "I'm sorry."

"You welcome, but no need to apologize. You gon' be a'ight, you hear me?"

"Okay," I whispered, tears filling my eyes again.

"Now g'on upstairs," she said, picking up the phone. "Hello, Pizza Hut? I'm gon' need a deliv'ry."

I headed to my room. I didn't know what Jennie was ordering, but considering how my stomach was growling, it didn't make a difference. I rushed to the shower because I figured it wouldn't be long before there was a knock on my door with my food.

Once I got out of the shower, I caressed my body with lotion then put on some lounging clothes. The long-awaited knock finally came. I went to answer it.

"Who is it?" I asked, standing behind the door.

"Pizza Hut," a man said.

I opened the door to let him in. "Hi. You can just sit the box down on the table over there."

"Okay," he said. "How are you doing this evening?"

When he turned to look at me, I noticed how fine he was. I stared at him intently. He had a flawless smile that made me weak at the knees. His skin looked like smooth, creamy peanut butter—a delicacy I hadn't devoured since I was a kid, but he certainly made me ready to sop him up with the quickness. I wanted to ask if he had a girlfriend, but I felt uncomfortable and unattractive in my lounging clothes. I opted to remain quiet—that is, until he broke my trance.

"Hello, Miss. Are you okay?" he asked.

"Oh, yes," I responded, snapping back into reality. "I'm fine. Thanks for asking."

The pizza smelled so good, I had to go over to the table to see what it looked like. I opened the box and discovered much of it missing. "What happened? Where's the rest of it?" I asked.

He looked confused. "The lady who paid for it took a few pieces then told me to come up here to bring you the rest," he said.

"Oh . . . well, I hope she took care of you because I'm broke."

"She took care of me a'ight. She let me have the dollar and twenty-seven cents change from her twenty-dollar bill."

I felt bad and didn't know what to say. "Sorry."

"Don't worry about it," he said, backing out the door. "I'll be all right."

I shut and locked the door behind him. I ran over to grab a slice of pizza. Just as I bit into it, another knock came. I wondered what the pizza man needed, so I opened the door.

"Hey, what did you—" I started before noticing it wasn't the pizza man standing there.

"Hey, yourself," Stormy said, stepping in, closing the door behind him.

"What are you doing? You aren't invited to come in. I'm calling the police," I said, backing to the phone.

Stormy grabbed my arm. "I wouldn't do that if I were you."

I forgot all about how to pretend to be tough. I swallowed hard then cried. "What are you planning to do to me?"

He looked lost. "Girl, what are you talking about?"

"You've come to do me harm, right?"

He laughed then let my arm go. "No. I just wanna talk to you."

I wanted to make a run for it, but I figured I better use my head and listen to him for a minute. "Okay. What's up?"

"Wipe your tears, and go eat your food first. I don't know about you, but I don't like cold pizza."

"I'd rather hear what you got to say then I'll eat."

"And I'd rather you eat first," he said, taking a seat on the sofa. "I'll be here. I ain't going anywhere."

Stormy crossed his legs as he sat on the sofa and stared at me as I ate. I was so nervous I could hardly swallow. I questioned him after I'd had enough.

"Now . . . why are you here?" I asked, standing in front of him.

"Do you make it a habit of running out in the street in front of speeding trucks?"

I couldn't answer for a minute because I was baffled. *Surely this man didn't come here to chastise me about being a grown woman who doesn't know how to cross the street,* I thought. "When I stepped out into the street, nothing was coming. What? Do you think I'm crazy?"

"No. I don't think you're crazy, but I do think you're beautiful."

I was really confused. "You what? Each time I've seen you, you've frowned and made me feel threatened."

Stormy found what I said funny. He laughed heartily. "People tell me I have an unapproachable look. I guess I should start believing 'em, huh?" He laughed some more. "I'm not a mean guy, but at times I can be serious."

I started to relax a little bit, so I sat down next to him. "About what?"

"About my business, about people I love, and about how attracted I am to you," he said, leaning in closer. "You know I've been watching you, right?"

"I've seen you lurking. You've been scaring the hell out of me, too."

"I didn't mean to. I just wanted to see if I could find out who your man was."

"Well, you could've just walked up and asked me. That's what the average man would do."

"Something you have to learn about me: I don't operate like the average man."

"I know . . . you're Stormy Daniels. You get what you want and do what you want, right?"

He laughed. "You better believe it."

I don't know why, but I began to feel comfortable with Stormy. It could've been the fact that I missed having company since my brother would no longer visit me. I don't know what was going on with me, but it felt nice to have someone to chat with. No one could have told me that I would soon begin to admire the same man I once ran from.

I loved listening to his sexy, profound voice as he spoke. I even began to realize how good-looking he was. He had thick, coal-black hair that deep-waved to the back of his head into a long ponytail. His skin tone was a medium brown, making him borderline milk chocolate. I could tell he worked out because his arms were chiseled, and his shirt and pants fit him well. I relaxed and continued a conversation with him.

"So, you don't do things like the average man, huh? Well, maybe you should try being normal for a change. I had labeled you a stalker," I said.

"Stalker? I'm thirty-four years old, and I've done a lot of things in my life, but stalking has never been on my agenda."

"I can't tell," I said, surprised by his statement. "Following my bus to find out where I live is stalking." We both laughed. "Standing in the door of the laundry room just after six A.M. is stalking. Driving past the bus stop—"

"A'ight . . . a'ight . . . I hear you," he said, doubling over with laughter. "But, you've gotta believe me. I'm not crazy. Just trying to get with you."

"All I'm saying is you had a sista worried. I was scared to death of you."

Stormy looked shocked. "I might've looked mean, but I never attacked you. C'mon now. Don't put me on the Memphis most wanted list for being an admirer."

"Well, like I was saying, snooping around where someone lives is stalking in my book."

"Really?"

"Yes, really."

"Well, I guess I've learned something new tonight. My momma says I can never get too old to learn." He smiled.

We sat silent for a moment. I finally got a chance to see a pleasant look on his face. I began to feel a bit shy as he stared into my eyes. I wondered when he would say something else, but since he didn't, I tried to spark the next conversation.

"So, what's on your mind? You think we should just begin a relationship at the drop of a dime?" I asked.

"Yeah, and before you reply, just know that I'm going to have you. I told you: I'm Stormy Daniels. I get what I want."

I wanted to tell him he could have me since no one else seemed to want me, but I continued to play hard instead. "I don't know you. You don't know me. What makes you think I'm even available?"

"C'mon now. You're living in an extended-stay motel. I've been watching you for a while. You should know I've figured out you don't have a man. And it's a good thing you don't. The poor guy would've gotten his heart broken the day you had to tell him you were leaving him for me."

"Hmph. I'm glad you're so confident, but you can't make someone want you, Stormy. Did your momma teach you that?"

He got up and went over to the table. He opened the pizza box and grabbed a slice then headed back to sit with me. I didn't think I'd actually see him take a bite since it was cold, but he bit a large chunk then offered it to me. I declined.

"How many times do I have to tell you I don't take no for an answer," he said, just before shoving most of the pizza into my mouth.

I chewed then swallowed as fast as I could. "Why did you force your germs on me? I don't know where your mouth has been," I said.

"Yeah, but you didn't spit it out either."

"Stormy, I'm not gonna lie. You intimidate me. Do you make it a practice of telling people what to do?"

"And I'm not gonna lie—just my woman, and the people who work for me," he said nonchalantly.

I felt frustrated about his attitude and inconsideration for my feelings, but I tried to turn the negative energy around instead of cussing him out. "Speaking of not lying . . . you said you don't like cold pizza, but you just ate some. What's up with that?"

"I didn't lie. I said I don't like it. I never said I wouldn't eat it. I'm sure when you're hungry, you find a lot of things to be tasty that you wouldn't normally eat."

"Well, excuse my manners. I guess I should've offered you some while it was warm. But, anyway . . . are you avoiding my original question?"

"No . . . just refresh my memory."

"Did your momma ever say to you that you can't make somebody want you?"

"No. She never told me that. You tryna say you don't find me desirable?"

"No. I'm just saying we should find out more about each other before jumping into something we both might regret."

"Okay. So let's spend a couple of hours talking then you can get your bags and come move in with me."

I was dumbfounded. The look on Stormy's face was very serious. "What? Why me?" I asked.

"Because I like you, li'l sexy. I don't have anyone, and I'd love to have a beautiful woman like you on my arm."

"You don't know me. You don't know if I'm healthy, got a pea for a brain, or what. Why would you move me in so quickly?"

"We can get our HIV/AIDS results back in less than two weeks. As for whether you're smart . . . I'm willing to teach you what you don't know," he said then smiled.

He left me speechless. I thought about the nice truck he drove then wondered what his home looked like. "Where do you live?" I asked, giving him an attitude.

"Harbor Town."

"Downtown?" I asked excitedly. "You mean one of those nice, big houses overlooking the river?"

"Yeah. As a matter of fact, I have six bedrooms, three-and-a-half baths, a four-car garage, and a swimming pool damn near large enough to cover a tennis court," he said proudly.

"Damn. That's a mansion. I wouldn't know how to act living large like that."

"Trust me. You'll get use to it."

"Why do you need such a big house? Do you have children?"

"I have a ten-year-old son, but he doesn't live with me. I get to see him about every other weekend though."

"What do you do for a living?"

"I own several businesses in town and across the bridge in West Memphis and Little Rock, Arkansas."

"Your businesses must be successful for you to have a home like that. What line of work are they?"

"I have two car washes and a small restaurant in Memphis. I also own a dry-cleaning store in West Memphis, Arkansas, and a night club in Little Rock that's doing quite well."

"And how old did you say you are?"

"Thirty-four. Why?"

"I'm just impressed at your accomplishments. How'd you get the money to fund your businesses?"

"Well, let's just say I was born with a silver spoon in my mouth." He laughed. "My father was a bright man before he died a few years ago. He taught me all the business sense I need to keep things going."

"Really? I wish my folks were rich. Hell, I don't even know where my father is."

"You don't need him."

"I don't?"

"I'm here now, and I'm all the daddy you need," he said then locked his lips with mine.

It felt so right to kiss Stormy that I just let myself go. I tongued him like I owned him. We both seemed to have forgotten we had pizza on our breaths—or else Stormy didn't care. Our tongues enjoyed having playtime together.

Stormy let his lips glide down my neck—my spot. I went wild, curling my fingers through his ponytail, pushing his face into mine. I couldn't believe how quick I was giving in to him. He began talking to me between breaths.

"You ready to pack, li'l sexy?" he said, sucking on my bottom lip.

"Un-un," I moaned.

Stormy shoved his tongue deeper into my mouth and pushed me down on the sofa as he climbed on top of me. He was strong and could easily crush me, but he was careful not to put too much weight on me. "What do you mean?" he asked, kissing my neck.

I let out a loud moan. "Aaaahhh . . . Stormy, wait. Let me up. I need to explain something."

Stormy was a gentleman to get up as I'd requested. I had made a mess of his hair while twirling my fingers in it, so he took down his ponytail holder and shook his head. His hair flowed in deep waves down his back. I teased him about having so much hair. "Pretty boy Ricky," I said, laughing.

He laughed, too. "Hey . . . hey . . . now. Watch your damn mouth. I don't play that. You don't wanna know what happened to the last man who called me that."

"I'm just kidding, Stormy."

"You better be," he said while smoothing his hair, putting his ponytail back together. "Now why is it that you're not ready to pack?"

"It's a long story, but you might—"

"Try me," he said, cutting me off. "Give me the short version."

I paused then took a deep breath. "I got into a little trouble because of a man, and I lost custody of my kids. I'm due to be back in court in six months, and I've got to have a job, a car, and my own place if I want to get my children back. Your place sounds lovely and all, but it would probably hurt me to tell the judge I'm staying with another man."

"Kids, huh?" he said, sounding dismayed. "How many?"

"Three. And I'm not ashamed. I had them, and they're mine."

Stormy nodded then stared at the floor for a few minutes in silence. I waited for the moment he'd get up and walk out on me, but he didn't. Instead, he looked up quickly as if a lightbulb had gone off in his head. "Hmm . . . a job, a car, and a place to stay, right?"

"Yes," I said in more of a question tone than a statement.

"Then I guess you need to decide if you want to work in the restaurant or the cleaners because you're not working in my nightclub. And I hope you don't have a problem staying downtown because I want you near me. Last, but not least, if you can't drive a stick, get someone to teach you quick because the three hundred ZX I'm going to transfer in your name tomorrow doesn't come in an automatic."

Damn! This nigga is playing for keeps. I like him already.

Chapter 8
If You Can't Beat 'im, Join 'im

Three weeks later, Stormy created a title for me at his restaurant called Exquisites. I was named the events coordinator, and I had paperwork to prove a hundred and thirty thousand dollars a year salary. I didn't know whether Stormy really intended on paying me that much money, but I was too scared to ask. He'd been nice to me since we'd started kickin' it, and I didn't want to risk pissing him off. Besides, he had just bought me a two-bedroom condo overlooking the mighty Mississippi River.

I could truly say the place felt like it was all mine because Stormy rarely spent the night. He said he didn't want to get me into trouble in case the Department of Human Services tried to snoop and ask my neighbors if I had someone living with me. I was cool with his decision. Besides, I didn't care to share my beautiful home with him or anyone else. It was where I found peace.

When I stepped out onto the patio, I could see the beautiful arches of the Hernando de Soto Bridge, which resembled an *M*—a just cause since it's located between Memphis, Tennessee and West Memphis, Arkansas. I could also see the Pyramid—thirty-two stories of stainless steel off the bank of the Mississippi River, which serves as an entertainment facility for concerts and more. My condo couldn't have been located in a better spot.

Every room looked like something Stormy had peeled straight out of an interior decorating magazine. He said he'd hired a designer to create and furnish the place. There was no need for curtains or blinds because the condo sat on a hill, high above a bluff.

I absolutely loved my new home, especially the quiet nights because the bridge and the Pyramid were lit. I even loved the rainy days and nights because I could watch God work as lightning crackled, illuminating the sky. On clear nights, the atmosphere was calm and surreal, like nothing I'd ever experienced before. I loved Stormy for giving me the opportunity to be happy and serene. I began to feel he was indeed my knight in shining armor.

It was after I'd been living there for two months when I realized Stormy never intended for me to work. He gave me a thousand-dollar weekly allowance, which I pretty much junked up on shopping, but I started to feel less than adequate. I wanted to get up every day and prepare to work. My new job title sounded exciting, and I wanted to try my hand at it.

One evening, I sat in the living room on the *U*-shaped, cream-colored sectional to think about how I'd approach Stormy with my concern. When he walked through the door, he stepped in front of me with a puzzled look on his face. I stared back, too intimidated to speak.

"What's up, li'l sexy? What's wrong?" he asked.

"What makes you think something is wrong with me?"

"First of all, you're sitting here on the sofa, looking dazed, with a drink in your hand and no music or the big screen playing. It's too damned quiet in here. What's up?"

He continued to stand over me, but I had an urge to speak anyway. "Storm, have a seat, baby," I said, patting the sofa.

He sat down. "I hope like hell you're not about to give me some bad news."

"Naw, Storm. Relax, baby," I said, rubbing his shoulder. "I just need to ask you a few things . . . that's all."

"A'ight. Well, g'on hit me with it before my nerves shoot through the roof." He laughed.

"Okay. It's about that position you gave me at your restaurant." I paused because Stormy's smile faded.

"I'm listening," he said.

"Well, I'd really like to try my hand at it. I think I could do well as an event coordinator." Stormy sighed, but I kept speaking. "Hear me out, Storm. What'll happen when the judge asks me to describe what I do? I need experience to answer that."

"No, you don't. You can just tell his ass you arrange party engagements, live entertainment, business meetings, and other shit like that. It doesn't take a rocket scientist to figure out what an event coordinator does."

I could tell my request agitated him, so I continued the conversation with caution. I looked toward the patio window and spoke softly. "What if he asks me to give examples?"

"You're thinking too much into this now, Ivy. I'll have the answers for you before that time comes. Right now, all I want you to do is continue to be my li'l sexy. You hear me?"

I thought about it, but I couldn't accept his demand to just stay at home and look cute. "Storm, I wanna work," I said sternly.

He jumped up, snatched my glass of red wine out of my hand then threw it. He seemed untouched by the huge splatter of deep red that began to spread as it ran down the vanilla-colored wall in multiple streams. I got up quickly, ready to defend myself if I had to.

"What's wrong with you?" I asked. "Damn! Did it even occur to you that I was still drinking that?" I yelled.

"Yeah, but it obviously didn't occur to you that I don't give a fuck. That wine's gone to your damn head. I keep you fed and lookin' good. I spend more money on you a week than I do myself. I don't give a fuck about you feeling like you need to do something self-fulfilling."

Although he towered over me, I became angry and bold enough to step closer. I pointed up to his face as I spoke. "Well, you need to give a fuck," I said. "Just don't bother then 'cause I'm only your freak, the woman who'll let you screw her anytime you want, in every hole imaginable. But I guess that doesn't matter, huh?"

He laughed with an evil tone then tried to grab a fistful of hair but couldn't because of my super-low haircut. I jumped back, but he grabbed my arm then picked me up by my shoulders. I struggled to get free, but his grip was firm. My first mind told me to kick him where it would hurt, but I refrained.

Storm began to speak to me through clenched teeth. "You must be out of your rabbit-ass mind," he stated. "Don't think you can threaten me with the pussy because you're not the only bitch with a hole between her legs."

He put me down. I was so angry, tears fell rapidly down my face. "I didn't ask to come here, Storm, and all I want is some identity rather than just being your play toy."

"If you're unhappy, then leave! I'm not forcing you to be here. I think I treat you pretty damn good, but go if that's what you wanna do, I'll find somebody else who'll appreciate the man I am."

"Yeah . . . the man you are, hmph . . . it takes a punk to put his hands on a woman—not a man," I boldly stated.

"Well let me show you how much of a punk I am then," he said pushing me down on the couch.

He started slapping me nonstop. I tried to throw him off me, but he was too heavy. With every blow and every sting, I could feel my face swelling. I covered my face with my hands. Stormy became even angrier.

"Move your fucking hands," he yelled, trying to pry them apart. "Move your goddamn hands."

When I didn't take my hands down from my face, he began punching the back of my hands as if he was boxing Mike Tyson. My palms added very little cushion to my face as he continued to pound me. I wondered when his brutality would be over, or if it would be over. After several more harsh blows, he got off me. I jumped up and ran to the middle of the room.

We stared at each other in silence. Stormy's eyes pretty much dared me to say another word, so I kept quiet. When he began to walk toward me, I begged for mercy.

"No," I screamed. "Stormy, please. No more, please."

He stopped in front of me then brushed against me hard, nearly knocking me to the floor. Before he turned the corner toward the bedroom, he stopped and looked at me. "Clean that shit up," he said, pointing to the mess he'd made on the wall.

I was fuming. I thought about leaving, but I didn't know where I'd go. I had spent all the money he'd been giving me on clothes and other material things, so I knew I had better chill. I learned that I wasn't going to always be happy with Storm, so I began a game plan to save any money he gave me.

When I finished cleaning up, I went to take a look at my face in the hall bathroom. The mirror was unkind. I looked like the Playskool toy, Mrs. Potato Head. My entire face was swollen. My chin felt heavy, my cheeks burned, and my lips felt like there were rocks in them. My eyes felt like they were protruding out of my head, but they weren't.

I went to the freezer to retrieve some ice. My hands ached so bad, I could hardly move them. I filled two large plastic freezer bags then went back to the bathroom. I closed the door then sat on top of the toilet. I took the huge bath towel off the rack behind me then stretched it across my lap to keep my thighs from getting cold as I soothed the back of my swelling hands. I bent over, placing the other pack between my palms and my face. I kept my face buried.

I felt ashamed for letting Stormy disrespect me. I cried, but the more I cried, the more my face hurt. My hands felt frostbitten as the coldness stung the back sides and my palms. I only took breaks to catch a good breath. I wanted to give up because my fingers were numb.

I heard Stormy enter the bathroom. I kept my head molded into the ice pack and continued to cry as though I didn't know he was there. I silently wished he would go away. I could feel his presence, so even after lifting my head to breathe, I didn't look his way. He didn't resist the opportunity to talk to me.

"Hey," he said.

I looked over at him. He blinked several times, seemingly surprised by the sight of my battered face. I attempted to suck up my tears, but despite my efforts, they kept falling. Stormy just stood and watched. I believe he was taken aback by how much damage he'd done. He kept blinking without uttering a word. He soon turned and walked out.

I decided to leave the bathroom after the ice melted. It was so quiet in the condo, I wondered if Stormy had left. I checked the bedroom and found him in there asleep. Considering this was our first altercation and the severity of what happened between us, I thought he'd have trouble sleeping. He looked as if he had no problem at all. I seized the chance to leave the condo without him knowing it.

It was after 7:00 in the evening and turning dark. I drove toward Kerry's apartment, looking for comfort. I couldn't remember what nights he had off from work, but I risked driving over there anyway. His car wasn't there, but I still knocked on the door. Rita answered.

"Ivy? What the hell happened to you?" she asked, peeping through the cracked door.

"Rita, may I come in?"

She seemed teary-eyed and concerned, but she refused. "Ivy, I'm sorry. I was told that under no circumstance am I to let you in here when Kerry's not here."

I was hurt and shocked. "What? Why? Who would tell you that? Kerry wouldn't turn me away when I'm hurt like this, would he?"

"I'm sorry, Ivy. I can't let you in. Go see if your mother will help you. On second thought . . . don't go to your mother's house. Your kids probably shouldn't see you all beat up like that," she said just before closing the door.

"Rita," I yelled, "tell Kerry I have a cell phone now. My number is five-nine-one—"

Rita opened the door. "Start over. Tell me the number slower. I'm going to write it down."

I repeated the number then Rita shut the door in my face again. I drove around a few more hours, trying to clear my head. I thought of my children. I decided that my condo and fake job position was the best option for getting my kids back in the house with me. I made up my mind to stay with Stormy, but I needed to figure out a way to keep him from being around so much. That way, I wouldn't piss him off and he wouldn't make me angry.

When I entered the condo, everything was dark. I could hear soft music coming from my bedroom, and there was a flickering light dancing through the cracked door. As I walked closer, I determined the sexy male vocalist was Will Downing. I slowly pushed the door open. Stormy was sitting on the bed in navy silk pajamas. The shirt draped him, but left his muscular torso exposed.

White candles aligned the dresser and headboard. The aroma was heavenly, but it did nothing to alter my feelings of hatred toward Stormy. He looked up quickly after sensing me walking through the door.

"What's up, li'l sexy?" he said in a low, gloomy tone.

He got up and came toward me with his arms opened. I stood, awaiting his embrace, but I didn't have the mind to return the hug. I stood with my arms at my sides as he gripped me lovingly. He took a step back to look into my eyes. "Baby, I'm sorry," he whispered. "I don't know why I got so angry. I shouldn't have bruised my angel. You were right about what you do for me. Any woman who can be here for me the way you have is definitely my angel. I hope you can forgive me."

He stared, looking as if he was awaiting my response. "I forgive you," I lied.

Stormy smiled then squeezed me tightly. "C'mere," he said, leading me into the bathroom. Sweet-smelling candles aligned the Jacuzzi bathtub. A bottle of champagne chilled in an ice bucket near the faucet with two glasses beside it. Stormy stripped me then held my hand as I stepped in the water.

The warm water felt wonderful. I sat back, closed my eyes and imagined Stormy wasn't there. For a brief moment, I really felt alone and happy again, but then he ruined my peace by speaking. "Here's some champagne for you, baby," he said.

I flashed a fake smile then got the glass from him. I took a sip then looked at him. He sat on the edge of the Jacuzzi and stared at me as if I meant the world to him. If

I didn't know any better, I would've thought he was in love with me. This was the first time since I'd known him that his eyes seemed gentle and kind. I began to feel confused, as if perhaps I should consider forgiving him.

I couldn't find words to say to Stormy, and he soon began to question my silence. "Li'l sexy, I thought you said you forgive me," he stated.

"I do, Storm."

"Then why can't you talk to me? If you're still angry with me, just say so. I can't blame you if you are," he said, stroking my chin.

"I'm cool, Storm. I'm still in a little shock, but I'll be okay."

"I hope so, li'l sexy. I truly hope so. I'm going to make it up to you, too. G'on finish your bath. Drink as much champagne as you like. I'll be in the bedroom. I'm gon' turn the covers back on the bed, and get you a bite to eat."

"No, Storm. I'm not hungry."

"Huh? Have you eaten? You really should try to eat something. You know it's not good to go without eating, especially since you're drinking," he rambled, hindering a quick response from me.

"I know. I'm not going to drink much more. I just wanted to taste it. Go ahead and get the bed ready. Are you spending the night?" I asked.

"Yes, of course. You really thought I would leave here tonight without taking care of you? I feel terrible about what I did, and I intend to make it up to you."

I smiled then nodded. "I'll be out shortly."

After Stormy left me, I soaked a few minutes then washed myself. I blew out all the candles then dried off and put on my robe. When I entered the bedroom, Stormy was stretched out across the king-size bed eating strawberries and whipped cream.

"C'mere, baby," he said, motioning me with his finger.

I sat beside him. He tried to put a strawberry in my mouth. "Storm, please. I'm not hungry."

"I know, baby, but this is different. It's light and you'll have something in your stomach if you eat enough of them."

"Just give me one. That's about all I can swallow right now," I said, opening my mouth.

Stormy shoved the strawberry in my mouth then tongued me just as I began chewing. I wanted to throw up, but I managed to get through the ordeal without getting sick.

He got up then pulled me up. "I don't say it often, but I think you should know I love you," he said, untying my robe.

He pushed the robe off my shoulders then let it drop to the floor. He massaged my breasts then sucked on each nipple gently. I wanted to be tough and not let him faze me, but slowly and surely I fell weak. My nipples were extremely sensitive and hardened with every flick of his tongue. I panted and watched as he licked and sucked my breasts with tender loving care.

Stormy stroked me between my thighs and discovered a heap of moisture. Apparently it turned him on because he moaned, groped me more then sucked my breasts even harder. I let out a series of loud moans. I wanted him to have me right then, but he kept taking his time with me, teasing my belly button with his tongue then blowing in it between every circular motion. "I love you, Ivy," he said.

I hadn't heard him call me Ivy since I'd moved into the condo. I had begun to wonder if he'd forgotten my name. I was proud to know that I was "li'l sexy" because of what he felt for me rather than because he didn't remember my name.

Stormy drew a wet line down my stomach until he reached my hot spot. He lifted my leg then eased it down on the bed. I could hardly stand when he spread my lips apart to better have his way with sopping my juices. I held his head and did a slow grind on his face until I climaxed. I trembled uncontrollably then collapsed on the bed.

He wasn't through with me yet. While I lay breathless, Stormy put both of my legs over his right shoulder then entered me with long, deep strokes, hitting my right wall. I dug my fingernails into the covers, damn near gripping the pillow-top mattress. He spoke sweetly as I moaned.

"Ahh, yeah. You like this, baby?" he asked. "You like this, don't you?"

I couldn't speak. I was in ecstasy, and all I could do was let out cries of pleasure. Just when I thought I was going to come again, Stormy started talking and then switched things up on me.

"Whatchu know about algebra, baby?" he asked.

I was confused. I was extremely close to climaxing and he brought up some shit about algebra. "What?" I asked as he continued to lay the pipe to me.

"You know much about algebra?" he asked again, panting and stroking me nonstop.

"Yeah," I said, moaning, totally pissed that he'd broken my concentration toward my next orgasm.

"Good. 'Cause complete lovemaking equates like algebra," he said, stopping to switch my legs over to his left shoulder. "And if you know anything about algebra, you know that what you do to one side, you must do to the other."

Stormy then began to give me the same long strokes on my left side as he'd pleasured me with on my right side. At that moment, Stormy sent me into a level of ecstasy I'd never known. My mind was gone, and I wanted him to be mine forever. I let him know it.

"Storm, baby, thank you," I panted each word, "for choosing me. I want to be with you always, baby."

"Oh yeah? What about the man attached to the dick? Tell me you love me, Ivy."

I was silent and contemplated answering. Then Stormy began to go deeper. I could hold back no longer. I was pretty sure my neighbors heard me as I exploded, and then Stormy came with me. As we lay exhausted, trying to catch our breaths, I told him what he wanted to hear.

"I love you, Storm. Just be good to me. That's all I ask."

He rolled over on my shoulder. "I will, li'l sexy. I will."

Only time would tell whether he meant what he said, but his words helped me feel content again. We made love several more times through the night. I rubbed Stormy's head and watched him as he slept. I declared in my mind that he was mine and knew that any female who tried to trespass would have hell to pay.

Chapter 9
Haven't We Met?

One month later, Stormy came home with a surprise conversation, ending with a statement that he'd decided I could work in the restaurant. I was ecstatic. I began researching details of my job on the Internet because I wanted to put forth my best and make Storm proud. He came to me shortly after I began my position, telling me about the great job I'd been doing.

By late September, I'd been instrumental in organizing events like poetry slams on Wednesdays, jazz concerts by various local artists on Thursdays, family nights on Fridays, and a few Memphis Idol shows on some Saturdays. Stormy paid me two thousand two hundred dollars a week—not quite the one-hundred-and-thirty-thousand-dollar a year salary he'd stated several months before, but it was well above what I was use to earning. I gladly accepted my check with no complaints.

One afternoon, before it was time to get off work, I called my mother to see if she would allow me to see my children. More than five months had past since I'd spoken to them. I had made several attempts to see and talk with them over time, but Bessie Mae would slam the door or hang up in my face. I thought perhaps she'd accept money and gifts for them via mail, but all of my packages were returned unopened and marked: PLEASE RETURN TO SENDER. My failed attempts to reach my children hurt me, but I never stopped trying. I felt at some point, Bessie Mae would give in if she saw that I wouldn't quit.

I had awesome news to share with Bessie Mae about my success at the restaurant, and I had hoped she'd be happy for me. She picked up on the first ring.

"Hi. It's Ivy," I said then paused.

"What do you want, Ivy?" she asked in a harsh tone.

I was disappointed with her continuous lack of enthusiasm to hear from me, but I was polite anyway. "I just wanted to speak and see how you and the kids are doing."

"We're fine, and what is this Exquisites place on my caller ID? What type of establishment are you calling me from? A club?"

I had to bite my tongue because she was working on my nerves. "No, ma'am. Exquisites is a restaurant with good food and tasteful entertainment. I'm employed here as the event coordinator. I make a healthy salary, and I live in a condo downtown near the river. I've got two bedrooms, and I was wondering if you'd let the kids come spend the night with me."

She yelled at me. "Have you bumped your head? I don't care what kind of life you say you're living. I'm not entrusting these kids into your care for a second. Kerry told me how messed up you are. You tricked him out of his money and got men beating you up, running you over to his place. Stay away from his home. Kerry has a seven-months' pregnant wife to take care of. He don't need your stress."

"Kerry told you I'd been over? Why hasn't he called

me? I gave my cell number to Rita. He could've at least checked to see how I was doing."

"Like I said . . . leave your brother alone and stay away from his place. Can't you see we're all sick of your trifling ways? Even these children are tired of your mess."

"Say what? Don't put words into my kids' mouths. And, you know I hate it when you say these or those kids. Call them who they are. They're my kids. Does it kill you to say they belong to me?"

"Yes, to be honest it does. Because you're no kind of mother to them. Never have been and never will be. Oh, why don't you just leave us all alone?"

Tears fell from my eyes. "You talk like you were the best mother known to mankind," I said, sniffling. "I guess you can't understand that I got most of my ways from you, huh? You were starving for attention from my dad and neglected Kerry and me all the time. Have you forgotten that Aunt Luanne took care of *your* kids for five years while you ran up whoring behind my daddy?"

"Shut the hell up. You don't know what you're talking about. Whatever Luanne told you was all lies," she said, huffing.

"No, Bessie Mae. She didn't lie. I was old enough to remember. My daddy never really wanted you. He left you before I was born—until you kept throwing yourself at him. You put yourself off on him, and he used you . . . even after you messed around and had a baby by Kerry's married father."

"Married or not, Kerry's father took care of him. He even came back to marry me after his wife died. Your no-good-ass pappy never shelled out a crumb for you."

"And . . . was that my fault? I didn't deserve your cruelty then, and I sure don't appreciate it now. I messed up. I've told you I understand that now. Can't you just allow me to have a little time with my children? They're mine. I birthed them."

"A dog can lay down and have children, too, Ivy. So what?"

"You know sometimes I think I can't stand you."

"And I can't stand you either. You've got no respect for me as your mother—back talking, loudmouthing me, and calling me by my name. And not just that . . . you don't even know how to respect yourself. No! Seeing the kids is out of the question. Go bark up somebody else's tree, bitch," she said just before hanging up on me.

I threw the cordless phone against the wall of my office. It made quite a bit of noise as it slammed against the surface then crashed on the floor. I went over to pick it up, but was startled by the head chef as he opened the door. He saw that I was crying.

"Ms. Jones? Are you okay?" he asked.

I wiped my face, but I couldn't stop sniffling. "Yes. I'm okay. Thanks for asking um . . . um . . ."

"Jaabir," he interrupted.

"Yeah . . . Jaabir. Thanks for asking. I've just got some issues I'm trying to deal with right now, but I'll be fine."

I leaned over to pick up the phone and forgot about the short skirt suit I was wearing. Once I rose, I noticed Jaabir admiring me from the waist down. I was a little embarrassed because I wasn't sure how much of my behind he might have seen. I walked back around the desk and quickly sat down. He gave me a tissue from the box near the window.

"Let it all out if you need to. I know sometimes crying makes me feel better," he said, extending more Kleenex to me.

I dried my face and nose then looked up at him. Jaabir was a thick, muscular guy with a strong resemblance to Stanley "Tookie" Williams.

"Hey, has anyone ever—"

"Told me how much I look like the younger version of Tookie Williams? Yes. All the time . . . but, I'm taller and a little less stocky, right?"

"I guess. I never had the pleasure of meeting him, but judging from the pictures, you look just like him. I mean, the body and the facial structure are what give you the likeness. I like your dreads, too."

"So, should I say thank you, sister? Or is looking like Tookie a bad thing?"

"Definitely not a bad thing. Tookie was a beau in my opinion," I said, flirting.

"Cool. I'll accept that because I see it puts a smile on your face—a beautiful one at that."

I tried not to blush, but I failed miserably. I glanced at the clock on the desk and realized I should be leaving. "Jaabir, I hate to cut our visit short, considering I hardly ever see you here, but I need to get going," I said, standing.

I grabbed my black leather quarter-length swing coat. We'd had a lot of rain over the past week, bringing about cool weather. Jaabir helped me put on my coat then handed me my purse and keys from the desk.

"Usually you're gone before I get here. I'm sure I'll see you around sometime soon though. In the meantime, just try to remember to never let anyone rob you of your joy."

I was speechless. Jaabir gave me butterflies. He had a captivating smile, framed by a neatly trimmed goatee. I wanted to spend more time talking with him, but I kept reminding myself that I had to answer to Storm. Although I walked out to my car alone, I had the butterflies to keep me company. Jaabir's voice kept replaying in my mind, ". . . *never let anyone rob you of your joy.*"

I turned the key in the ignition, but my car wouldn't start. I tried several times to crank it, but it only made a clicking noise. I called Storm to pick me up. I felt it would be better to stand outside the restaurant rather than to be inside. I knew if Storm caught Jaabir flirting with me, not only would I be in hot water, but Jaabir's ass would be grass, too. Storm had shown me the bad side of him, and I never wanted to see it again.

Forty-five minutes went by before I saw Storm's Hummer speeding into the parking lot. *It's about damn time,* I thought. After he came to a stop, I reached to open the passenger's side door, but he hadn't unlocked it. I stood on my toes to knock on the glass then he let down the back window to talk to me.

"Get into the back, Ivy," he said.

I was shocked to say the least. I could see someone sitting in the front seat, and I couldn't figure out why Storm would make me, his woman, get into the backseat rather than tell his friend to get out. I stood with my hand on my hip, huffing. That is, until he yelled for me to get in.

"C'mon, Ivy. I don't have all day," he screamed.

I was angry, but considering how the cool wind kept blowing up my skirt, I went ahead and got into the backseat. I slammed the door behind me, attempting to make a statement of how upset I was at his lack of respect, but he ignored me by turning up the radio then speeding off.

I looked at the back of the passenger's head and realized it was a woman. I was fuming. *Calm down, girl,* I thought. *You don't know if this is his sister or what. Just cool off before you say something you'll regret.*

She never turned around. She and Storm just nodded to the beat of the music during our ride. I continued to stare at the back of her head then had a flashback. This woman had long, cornrowed braids that zigzagged like the woman I'd argued with on the bus several months before. I kept trying to catch a glimpse of her face in the side mirror, but the heavy tint made viewing her difficult.

I could feel myself about to lose it, so I fought harder to

remain calm. I rocked my knee until Storm pulled up to my condo. He got out then told the woman she could go inside, too. Once I got out of the truck, I came face to face with the woman, and indeed she was who I'd suspected. I could no longer hold my silence.

"Stormy," I yelled, "who is she to you?" I asked, pointing at the woman.

"This is Candy. She said the two of you knew each other," he responded, looking back and forth at each of us.

"You met me on the bus, remember?" she said.

"And? Why are you here? How do you know Storm?" I questioned, demanding answers.

She laughed then looked at Stormy. He laughed, too, then jerked my arm and pulled me into the condo. He pushed me farther inside then beckoned Candy in. I stood shocked as he helped her get more comfortable. He took off her coat then hung it up. After he returned from the closet, I pitched a fit.

"What the fuck is going on here? Storm, you need to tell me what's up, right now," I yelled.

He looked at Candy. "You can have a seat on the couch," he told her. Then he looked at me. "You might as well have a seat, too, Ivy."

"Why?" I asked, giving him a major attitude.

He stepped in my face and spoke through clenched teeth. "Because I said so," he said.

He reached for my hair, but his fingers slipped through just like the first time he'd tried to violently grab me. I ran to the other side of the room. Thankfully, he didn't follow me.

I was hurt, and I wanted to cry, but I refused to let Candy know how much she had gotten to me. She sat silently as if Storm and I were a picture show. He stood, staring at me as if he knew I had more to say that would piss him off.

"Storm baby, what's going on? Just tell me straight out, baby. What's up?" I asked, standing with my hands on my hips.

He walked over to me then grabbed the sides of my face. He kissed my lips before explaining. "Ivy, you know I love you, right?"

What the fuck ever, I thought. "Yeah, baby. I know that, and I love you, too. But, please stop beating around the bush."

"Okay. Candy is a personal friend of mine. I met her when she was getting off the bus the day I almost ran you over." He smirked.

"I met her on that damn bus, too. And I had seen her before that at the damn health department."

"I know. She told me about all that and said she knew you."

"She don't fucking know me. We spent two minutes conversing then I spent another three minutes cussing her ass out," I stated, looking at Candy. "Did you ever get your VD results, or were you getting tested for AIDS?"

Storm and Candy snickered. "She's clean," he stated calmly.

I huffed. "And how would you know?"

He turned to look back at Candy then at me. "She's a personal friend of mine. We talked about why she was on the bus that day as I did with you, and I've seen the paperwork."

I wanted to smack the taste out of his mouth, but I refrained. "A personal friend, huh? How personal, Storm?"

My breathing got heavier as I tried to keep my cool. He couldn't look at me. He kept turning around to look at Candy as if she could offer assistance with explaining. She sat with her legs crossed and hand under her chin. When she smiled and winked at me, I damn near lost my mind. I grabbed Storm's face and turned it so he'd face me.

"Are you fucking her?" I asked angrily.

He smiled. "Yeah. Something like that."

Before I knew it, I had landed a hard blow across his face then reached back to throw another one. He caught my hand before I could hit him again. He twisted my arm behind my back, and I screamed so loud, I scared myself.

Storm began treating me like a bitch on the streets. "Who the fuck do you think I am? You don't raise your muthafucking hand to me . . . let alone actually hit me," he yelled. He twisted my arm harder, causing me to scream some more. "Shut the fuck up. I'll break this muthafucker. Shut the fuck up." I panted, trying to suck up the pain. "Now grin and bear it," he continued. "You obviously want me to beat your ass or else you wouldn't have jumped bad."

I was in so much pain, I prayed to pass out. My knees gave out, and I ended up on the floor with my arm twisted backward in the air. I pleaded for him to let me go.

"Storm, please, baby. I'll do anything you say. Let me go," I whimpered.

"You gonna do anything I say whether I let you go or not. If I want you to bark like a dog, you will or else get your head stomped."

I thought my arm was gonna snap any second. I tried to remain calm because he'd told me to shut up, so I took deep breaths as tears rolled down my face. He finished cussing me out about five minutes later then let me go. I couldn't move my arm. Although I didn't hear it pop, it might as well have been broken because it hurt to lift it. I sat on my knees with my arm limp at my side.

After a couple of minutes of me kneeling with my back to him, Storm picked me up by the choker necklace I was wearing, nearly slicing my neck. He turned me to face him.

"I don't give a fuck if you down with me being with

Candy or not. I'm gonna have her. You hear me? But if you got issues with it, I suggest you bounce. So what's it gonna be?"

I wondered where I could go. *Nowhere,* I thought. "I'll stay," I answered regretfully.

I looked at Candy. She gave me sympathetic eyes as she sat motionless. Storm let me go then walked over to her. He leaned over and kissed her on the lips.

"I knew she'd be down. You think you can do her?" he asked just after kissing her.

She seemed nervous. Although she tried to appear calm, I could see her chest heaving. "Sure, Stormy," she answered, nodding.

"Good," he said then kissed her again.

I wondered what they were talking about. *Do me,* I thought. *What the hell?* I figured Stormy couldn't have wanted me dead or else he wouldn't have told me to accept Candy or bounce. The only other thing he could've meant was for Candy and me to have sex. *Sex? Oh, hell no!*

Chapter 10
Do I or Don't I?

Candy and Storm left the condo shortly after his intimidation scene with me. I wondered when and if they'd return. I got my answer when they popped up, drunk and singing as they came through the door about midnight. I couldn't sleep, so I sat on the couch, watching *Diary of a Mad Black Woman* on DVD. When Storm noticed what was playing on the projector screen, he cussed me out.

"Turn that shit off," he demanded.

I did as said then prayed he didn't want to start another fight. To my surprise he walked over, kneeled, and then kissed me. Candy came over and sat down next to me. "How you doing, Ivy?" she asked.

I suddenly felt angry enough to spit in her face, but I didn't. "I'm okay," I answered.

Storm smiled. "That's my baby," he said, sticking his hand up my nightgown to rub my thigh.

He gave Candy a wink then she reached for my shoulder strap. I was extremely uncomfortable.

"Wait," I said, pulling my strap back up. "I still don't know your bill of health."

She smiled. "I thought you'd say that." She conveniently pulled out her HIV results and Pap smear from her purse. The date was current and everything was negative. I tried to think of another excuse to get out of the ménage à trois fantasy Storm obviously wanted, but I was at a loss for words. Apparently the two of them had been planning to get me into bed with them for months.

Storm reached up my gown again then pulled off my panties. I was nervous, as if it was my first time having sex again. Candy smiled a lot. I guess she did so in an effort to make me feel comfortable with her, but what she didn't understand was there was nothing that could put me at ease.

I'd never been intimate with a woman before, but of course Candy and Storm were willing to show me the ropes. Storm spread my legs then licked me lovingly as he'd always done. I still had a tough time trying to get into the moment though. I closed my eyes to concentrate, but Candy began rubbing my breasts and kissing my neck, causing me to become more distracted. She pulled each of my straps down then sucked one of my nipples. When I closed my eyes again, I imagined she was T.I. and Storm was Usher. Then my moisture flowed.

Storm decided to invite Candy to share my nectar. I didn't know what to expect, but I soon found out. Her tongue was a welcomed instrument inside my tunnel. The more she lapped, the more heated I got. I looked at Storm. He was excited to see Candy pleasing me. He stroked himself then entered her from the back. She moaned as he gave her the long, hard strokes I was use to.

After several minutes, I began to feel ill. I lost my concentration as I watched Storm screw her. His facial expressions let me know he definitely enjoyed what he was doing. Soon he asked us to switch. I wanted to cry. Candy got on the couch then laid spread-eagle. Storm grinned then looked at me.

"Go ahead, baby," he said. "Don't you wanna taste it?"

Hell no, I thought. "You want me to?" I asked.

"Yeah. Why not?"

"Storm, I ain't ever done anything like this. I wouldn't know what to do."

"That's okay, baby. It's not hard. Here . . . let me help you." Storm opened Candy's lips then pointed at her clit. "This is the thing you wanna concentrate on. She likes it to be sucked and then blown on. Stick your fingers in her when you blow and wiggle them. Repeat that several times and she'll come before you know it."

I looked at the pinkness of Candy's hole and almost vomited. It dripped and made noises as she played with herself. Tears formed in my eyes, but I didn't dare let Storm see them. Candy began grinding then placed her hand on the back of my head. I closed my eyes and held my breath. I waited for Storm to enter me like he did Candy, but he didn't. I wasn't sure what he was doing, so I opened my eyes briefly to look up. He stood over Candy, smiling and massaging her breasts while she gave him head. When he looked over at me, he nodded then winked. I closed my eyes and cussed him out in my mind.

Storm banged me then banged Candy some more. Candy got off more times than I ever knew a woman could—that is unless she was faking like me. I pretended to come, trying to get Storm off me, but he must've taken some Viagra or energy pills before we got started because his shit was on forever hard. Several hours passed before the whole scene was over. We had started in the living room, but ended in the bedroom. To say I was disgusted and tired would be an understatement.

The three of us lay in the bed with Storm in the middle. I got up to use the bathroom. I noticed Candy sprawled across Storm like he was the best thing going and she didn't want to give him up. At one point, I thought I would kill any woman who looked at Storm the wrong way. But as I looked at him and Candy in bed, I didn't care if she took him away from me for good. I also knew that wouldn't happen without him taking away my fancy living conditions.

When I came back from the bathroom, I got back into bed with my back to Storm. He sensed me in bed then turned and placed his arm over me. He kissed the back of my neck and shoulders.

"You know I love you, don't you, Ivy?" he asked softly.

"Yeah," I murmured.

"Huh, baby? I didn't hear what you said."

"Yeah, Storm," I said, speaking up.

He kissed me some more. I silently prayed he wasn't getting geared up for more sex. "Good," he said. "I just want you to know how I feel. I don't want you to leave me. You've made me so happy since coming into my life, but I'm happy with Candy, too. I think the two of you will get along fine. I promise I'll always take care of you, okay?"

I couldn't believe what I was hearing. I found out early into the relationship that Storm had an evil streak, but I had no clue he was the monster he had turned out to be. He rubbed my side as he awaited an answer. "Okay, baby?" he asked again.

"Okay," I whispered.

He turned me to face him then tongued me. Knowing his face had been between Candy's legs made me sick, but I dared not kiss him back. I must've kissed him a little too good because he spread my legs then got on top of me. Candy opened her eyes and noticed what was going on. She reached to stroke my breasts, but Storm stopped her.

"Un-un," he said, pushing her hand away. "I just want some time with my baby. You can lay there and watch."

And watch she did. Storm made passionate love to me like he would when no one else was there. I even forgot Candy was watching. That is, until she started moaning as she played with herself, which also broke Storm's focus on me. He had been hitting me from the back, but suddenly stopped.

"Oh, I'm sorry. You want some, too, don't you?" he said, pulling Candy to him.

He got off me then asked me to lie on my back. Candy's face went between my legs as he fucked her from the back. Pleasuring a woman was something she obviously liked doing because she was damn good at it. I figured since there was no safe way out of my situation, I may as well relax and enjoy Candy's trade. Unlike the last round, I was more into her doing me, and it wasn't long before I came.

The next morning, I woke up solo in bed. I smelled breakfast, so I figured Storm and Candy were in the kitchen. I ignored the heavenly scents and went straight to the shower then turned the water on as hot as I could stand it. I felt dirty and worthless. I hoped to scrub some of what happened the night before off me, but my mind was still tainted.

I dressed for work then went into the kitchen. Candy was sitting at the table, eating half-naked. She looked comfortable with her bra and panties on like it was a traditional thing to do in the morning. Storm was in a business suit, which let me know he was probably going to the restaurant. He looked me up and down like I had lost my mind.

"You going somewhere?" he asked.

I placed my purse on the table. "Yeah. At least, I kinda thought I was," I responded.

"Really?" he asked, scratching his head. "Now let me see
. . . last thing I remember was that I had to pick you up
from work . . . which means you don't have a car."

"So, what're you saying? You're not going to take me?"

"That's exactly what I'm saying," he said matter-of-factly.

I was pissed. "Why not? I don't understand. Aren't you
going to the restaurant?"

"I might. And?"

"And . . . I don't see what's wrong with you dropping
me off if you're going that way anyway."

"I see a lot wrong with it. You might not understand,
and perhaps it isn't meant for you to understand, but what
matters the most is, I say you're not going to work today.
Besides, you've got company," he said, pointing at Candy.

Candy never looked up from her plate. Storm went
over to kiss her on the forehead then he walked over to
me and kissed me on the lips. "Don't do anything I wouldn't
do while I'm gone," he said sarcastically then laughed.

When I heard the door shut, I cussed. "Fuck! I don't believe this shit," I screamed, throwing my purse across the
room.

Candy took a bite into her Hungry Jack biscuit then
shook her head at me. I sat at the table, using all the ob-
scenities I could think of. The more I cussed, the more
Candy shook her head. "Mmph, mmph, mmph," she said.

"What the fuck are you shaking your head for?" I asked.

"Girl, you can't let a man get next to you like that. Just
chill. Hell, he's taking care of you, ain't he? You living a
fabulous lifestyle—better than where you came from, I'd
say. What more do you want?"

I hit the table with my fist. "I want a faithful man who
loves me and me only. I don't wanna have to share him
with some stank-ass woman, let alone be a part of his sexual fantasies with her."

She laughed. "What you tryna say? You mean you didn't

like it when I coated your lips with my cream?" She laughed some more.

I was ready to lunge across the table. "Don't make me fuck you up right here and now. I ain't in the mood for jokes."

She rolled her eyes. "Girl, life is not a fairy tale," she said, taking another bite of her biscuit. "You better ask Fantasia. She wrote a book about it," she said, barely audible between chewing.

"Life is not fairy tale . . . if one more person tells me that shit, I'm gonna scream."

Candy shrugged. "So, scream, but it's true. Besides, men come and go. If Storm won't be what you think he ought to be to you, then move on. I'd say you're a fool if you do. He'll just have somebody else up in here living large the day after you leave."

"I really wish I could say I don't care, but the truth is I do. I want Storm, but I want him to myself."

Candy sipped her juice then shook her head. I wanted to scream at her to stop it, but she intervened. "Look, Ivy. Stormy's got you blinded. There are some things you obviously don't know about him, but I fault you because you've never tried to know more about him."

"Say what?"

"I'm just saying, if you never knew Stormy ain't the type to be with one woman then I can imagine you're blinded by some of the other shit he does."

"What other shit?"

Candy didn't answer right away. She got up to put her plate in the sink. "If you don't know, I ain't the one to tell you. My reasons for being with Stormy differ from yours. I don't give a shit about having a one-woman man. What I want from Stormy, he provides—a good fuck and money in my pocket. You need to open your eyes to some things."

"I've asked you what kind of things, Candy. I don't wanna

hear mess about me being blind if you're not going to tell me what I need to know."

She sat back down at the table. "I've seen Stormy damn near tear your arm out of its socket. I'm not going to get my ass beat over telling you shit. But, let me ask you this: have you met any of his friends?"

I had to think a minute. After being with Stormy for more than five months, I still hadn't been introduced to his clique. I'd heard about them, but I never met them. "No," I answered. "I've never met his friends."

"Well, all I'm gon' say is you should meet them. And pay close attention to details. If you do, you'll learn some things you never knew about Stormy."

I gasped then jumped up from the table. "That mutha-fucker ain't gay, is he?" I asked, raising my tone. "Huh? Is he bisexual?"

Candy's eyes grew wide. "Naw." She laughed. "Hell, naw. I didn't mean anything like that."

Whew, I thought. "Then what is it? Oh, never mind. I'll just ask him if I could meet his friends."

"No," Candy shouted. "Don't do that. I don't want him to think I told you anything."

"Okay. I won't ask him. But, since you won't tell me, I've got to figure out a way to get him to introduce me," I said, walking away.

"Where're you going?"

"To work," I answered nonchalantly.

Candy shook her head. "You're a crazy bitch. I've never seen anyone like you. Last night it was your arm, but by the time Stormy finds out you went to work after he told you not to, it's gon' be your ass."

"Yeah, and my momma use to beat my ass every time she felt I disobeyed her, but she'll tell you her beatings never stopped me. When my mind is made up to do some-thing, I'm going to do it. I know Storm will probably draw blood from me later on. It wouldn't be the first time and damn sure won't be the last time. We'll see," I said just before closing the door.

Candy opened the door then yelled at me. "I take that back. You're not just a crazy bitch, you're a stupid one, too. When Storm gets ahold of you tonight, I'm leaving. I'm not going to sit here and listen to you whine while he beats your ass. Stupid bitch!"

I flicked her the bird and kept walking.

Chapter 11
Actions, Consequences, Reactions

I was determined to see Jaabir. My work at the restaurant wasn't nearly as important as being near him again. I longed to see his smile and to hear him say something soothing. I realized I wasn't thinking so bright, especially considering how insane Storm could be. But for some strange reason, I felt like taking my chances.

I walked about a mile then called a cab. As we pulled up to the restaurant, I prayed I wouldn't see Storm's truck in his reserved parking space, and to my relief, it wasn't there. I paid the cabdriver then went inside. I became nervous once I realized Storm could show up any minute, so I racked my brain for a good excuse. I kept drawing a blank, especially when I looked in the kitchen and saw Chef Jaabir.

I stood and watched as he walked about the kitchen giving orders. He was wearing a white wrap over his dreads that twisted into a bun in the back, a white chef coat, and black pants. I began to fantasize about how good his lips would feel against mine, how magical his hands would feel as they caressed my inner thighs, and how hard his dick would be as I rode him. I was snapped out of my trance once Jaabir spotted me and began waving. I waved back then walked toward my office.

I could hear voices coming from the other side of the door, so I stepped closer to listen. The speech was muffled, but I could make out much of what was being said. Storm's voice was the most distinctive.

"Ivy ain't no fool. I've had to put my mark on her a few times, but by now, she knows I ain't shit to be played with," I heard Storm say.

"Yeah, and you can't let up on the bitches or else they'll be trying to run game on you before you know it," a male voice said.

"Not my bitches," Storm responded. "Ivy Lee and Candy Cane are gon' be my best moneymakers yet. You'll see."

"Yeah . . . yeah . . . yeah," another male voice said. "You say that about all the girls." They all laughed.

"Okay, but listen," Storm said. "All kidding aside. What's up with this nigga Snowball? I've warned his ass about invading my territory, but he still hasn't moved his business. Ain't enough room for both of us running cane on the same track. I thought one of y'all told me that muthafucker is dealing heroin, too."

"Yeah, he is. He got pushers all over the Mound working for 'im," one of them said.

"Then that's where he needs to stay. I run East Memphis. Ain't no damn two ways about it . . . just me," Storm replied.

"I told that nigga, man. He won't listen," a voice said.

"Yo', I ain't no hater, and I'm all down for niggas wanting to make that paper. But when it begins to dip into my pocket, that's when I got a problem with it."

"I feel ya, Storm."

"So, since he can't understand what I mean in plain

English, pop a Beretta in his face—a French one. See if he understands that. If he still plays dumb, send him to meet his maker," Storm said.

"Dig that," one of them said.

"Wait a minute," Storm said.

There was silence for several minutes. My first mind told me I needed to tiptoe away. Just as I was about to turn around, the door suddenly opened. I jumped, unsuccessfully masking my guilt. Storm stood, staring me in the face.

"He-hey, b-babe," I said, stuttering. "I was—"

He grabbed my arm then jerked me inside. "Get your ass in here," he said, closing the door behind me.

I looked around the room. There were two rather large men inside. Storm went to sit on the desk. He reached for my hand then pulled me near him. I shook like a leaf on a tree.

"Fellas, this is Ivy," he said, stroking the back of my hand with his thumb.

"Oh, yeah," the high-yellow, bearded one said, rubbing his hands together and licking his lips.

The dark, big-bellied one echoed the other. "Oh yeah?"

Storm laughed. "Ivy, that's Drake," he said, pointing at the red bone. "And that's Bling over there," he said, pointing at the fat black one.

"Whuzzup, shawty?" Drake said.

"Yeah, what's up, li'l bit?" Bling seconded, smiling, exposing a mouth full of gold and diamonds.

Storm laughed again. "Calm down, fellas. Chill out. Ivy got some explaining to do." Storm gently stroked my arm. "How long were you standing out there, Ivy?"

"Not long," I lied, trembling uncontrollably.

Storm stopped rubbing me then placed my palm on top of his. No matter how I tried, I couldn't stop my hand from shaking. "Really?" he asked. "Then what's wrong, baby? Why are you so nervous?"

I looked around at the other guys, buying time as I thought of how to tell a convincing lie to Storm. I knew if I had told him the truth about everything I'd heard, he'd kill me. Then it hit me. "Well, Storm, I guess I'm nervous because you told me not to come here . . . and well, here I am. You've caught me."

"Oh, that's right," he said, cupping my hand. "You're supposed to be at home keeping Candy company, aren't you?" Storm's calmness was awkward and frightened me even more.

"Yes," I said in an innocent tone.

"Then your reason for being here must be good. Surely you wouldn't risk me blowing a fuse for something trivial, would you?"

"No, baby. C'mon. You know I wouldn't go against your demands without a good reason."

"Okay. So tell me. Why are you here, Ivy?"

I looked at the other guys. They stood, listening attentively. I swallowed hard. "Storm, I can't tell you in front of these guys. It's kind of embarrassing," I said, acting timid.

"Yes, you can. Don't mind them. They're family."

"No. Trust me. I really need to tell you in private, Storm."

Storm let my hand go then rubbed his forehead. His voice elevated. "Ivy, I'm really losing my patience with you, baby. I don't want to click on you, so just tell me now. Why are you here?" he asked, rising from the desk.

I took a step back. "I wanted to try something spontaneous with you. I miss my dick, and I thought you could stand to let me give you a good blow job in the office," I said, using my best Eartha Kitt voice impression.

"Dayum," Drake exclaimed.

I rolled my eyes at him then looked back at Storm. "But

I can see you're busy, so I'll just give you a rain check, baby."

I turned to walk away, but Storm pulled me back. "Hold on. We don't need a rain check. If my baby wants to taste her candy stick then what kind of man would I be to starve her?" he asked, looking back and forth between the men.

"You got a point there, boss," Bling said.

Drake and Bling started out of the office. Storm stopped them. "Hey, hey . . . where y'all going?"

"I thought you and your girl needed some privacy," Drake answered.

"Man, this meeting isn't over. Close that door," Storm said, unzipping his pants. "My baby, Ivy, came to do a job, and we're not going to stop her . . . just like she's not going to interrupt our work. Besides, ain't no shame in her game. Is it, Ivy?"

I didn't respond. I stood shocked. I felt humiliated before ever dropping to my knees. I paused, thinking, *This isn't happening!* I just wanted to wake up and be grateful that the entire day had been a dream. Storm pulled himself out of his pants then sat on the edge of the desk. Drake and Bling stared at me, seemingly awaiting my performance.

"C'mon, baby," Storm said, pulling me to him. "I love you, girl. No meeting or anything else could make me let you go hungry." He kissed me then pushed me down on my knees.

I wanted to cry, but I sucked up my tears. When he helped me put ten inches into my mouth, I gagged. A twangy taste stained my tongue, and immediately I knew what it was when I smelled urine reeking from his drawers. I'd seen him on numerous occasions piss then stick his dick back in his pants without shaking or wiping it. I had suspected his underwear would have a stench, and unfortunately my suspicion was confirmed.

Storm hissed and moaned. "Ssssss, oooh, yeah, baby . . . mm-hmm . . . that shit is good," he said, rubbing my head. "So, fellas, what about that Snowflake . . . oooh yeah, Ivy . . . I mean, Snowball nigga?"

"Don't fret it. That's gon' be taken care of, boss," Bling said.

The meeting went on as intended. I bobbed my head around Storm's stick forty minutes before attempting to stop. I sat on the floor, massaging my jaws. Storm wasn't having it.

"Yo', what the fuck are you doing?" he asked.

"My face hurts, Storm."

"Your ass is gon' be hurting in a minute if you don't get back here and finish sucking my dick. It was your bright idea to come here, remember? My shit is hard, and you gotsta get me off."

"Storm, I can't," I said with tight jaws. "I can barely open my mouth to speak."

"Okay then. Get up."

I didn't move because I didn't know if he meant what he said. "Are you mad?" I asked.

"Naw. I'm not mad. Get up," he responded, motioning for me to stand up. "Excuse me, fellas."

As soon as the men both nodded, Storm turned me around then bent me over the desk. I screamed and wrestled to keep my pants up. "Storm, stop. No. Please, no," I begged.

Storm huffed and puffed as he struggled to speak and get my pants down at the same time. "You should've known I meant it literally when I said your ass would be hurting in a minute. I know it's been a while, and I hope you got enough anal opening because I certainly don't have any grease."

I wouldn't give up the fight. He was not going to tear

my ass apart in front of his boys. "Wait," I screamed. "I'll suck it. Wait. I'll suck it."

Storm let me go. I fastened my pants then got down on my knees. He made me put my hands behind my back then repeatedly and intentionally gagged me with all ten inches. I thought I was going to die when he sent his come gushing down my throat. His boys were completely entertained. They laughed and high-fived when Storm took himself out of my mouth then slapped it across my face several times, making sure all traces of his come was wiped around my lips.

"Thanks, baby. I hope you feel like being spontaneous more often," he mocked. "G'on in the bathroom and clean yourself up."

The office had a bathroom, so I was spared the disgrace of having to go out into the restaurant with Storm's secretions coating my face. When I came out of the bathroom, Storm was the only one in the office. I was scared and contemplated running away.

"C'mere, baby," he said, motioning for me. When I got close, he pulled me down on his lap. "How're you doing?" He kissed my cheek.

I felt I would break down and cry if I spoke, so I nodded instead. Storm rubbed my side then pointed at a small monitor under my desk. I could see the entire hallway leading up to the office. *So that's how I got caught,* I thought. Storm picked up a remote and began switching the screen to various parts of the restaurant. I couldn't believe my eyes. I had noticed what seemed like a small box under my desk weeks before, but Storm told me it was private materials and not to touch it. *Damn, how naive can I be?* I thought.

I took a deep breath then tried to explain my actions. "Storm, I don't know what you're thinking, but I really only came here to be with you," I said.

"No, you didn't, Ivy. But, that's okay. You don't have to tell me what's up. I'll figure it out sooner or later."

I sat quietly, looking into his eyes. He stroked my chin as if he loved me then kissed my lips before asking me to stand. He walked out of the office without saying anything more or looking back. I sat at the desk feeling sick. I wondered what I had become and why. *I use to be pretty tough . . . not taking shit from any nigga,* I thought. *Yet, I let Storm treat me worse than any man. Why?* I had no real answers.

I paced the floor, brainstorming on how to get rid of Storm and still gain custody of my children, but not being with Storm also meant losing my condo and my job—a serious problem. The east and west walls of my office became very familiar with me as I paced for nearly thirty minutes. I was forced to take a break when Jaabir stepped in.

"Excuse me," he said. "The door was open, and I couldn't help noticing you look worried about something. Are you okay?"

The butterflies returned, and I was excited to have them. "Yes, Jaabir. I'm fine. I was just thinking about something."

"May I come in?"

"Well, I was just about to get online to work on an event, but I guess I have a few minutes," I lied. "Would you like to have a seat?"

"No, thanks. I just have one question for you. Do you mind?"

I prayed he wasn't going to ask anything personal, especially about Storm and me. "Okay. Shoot," I said.

"I'm sure you must know I find you attractive," he said, clearing his throat. "You seem to be a bright young woman. I think you're extremely beautiful, and here's my question to you: Will you let me take you out? I'd love to get to know you better."

I blushed so hard I thought my skin tone would remain beet red for the rest of my life. "Wow. You're awfully kind to say such nice things, Jaabir. I . . . I just . . . I um—" I stuttered.

Jaabir walked closer then grabbed my hand. "Before you say no, just give it some thought."

I smiled. "Sure. I'll think about it."

We stood like two shy schoolkids, grinning and holding hands. Jaabir didn't seem to want to let go. Truth is, I didn't want him to. His hands felt strong and safe. He gazed into my eyes and gripped tighter, giving me comfort and reassurance of my worth—definitely what I needed at the moment. His eyes spoke to me, saying he could be into me and not just my body. I never felt so good in my life. Our moment was abruptly interrupted when Drake walked in on us. We quickly dropped our hands to our sides.

"Ahem," he said, stomping toward the desk. "I think I left my hat in here."

Jaabir winked at me then headed out the door. "I'll rap to you about that later, sister. I'm sure I'm needed in the kitchen."

"No problem. Talk to you later," I responded.

Drake had been rambling around the desk until Jaabir walked out. "What's up with that nigga?" he asked.

"What do you mean?" I folded my arms, giving him much 'tude.

"What did he want?"

"Excuse me?" I asked. Drake kept rambling instead of responding, so I continued. "You ain't my man. Who do you think you are to question me? And what the fuck are you looking for around my desk? Your hat is obviously somewhere else, so get out."

Drake frowned, pressing his tongue against his top row of teeth. He began to back out of my office one small step at a time. I was glad to see him going, but then he stopped just as he got outside the door.

I put my hands on my hips. "What are you looking at?" I asked, frowning.

"Um . . . let me see . . . a *trick*."

Chapter 12

Saved by the Candy Licker

I had only been working about fifteen minutes when I got a call from Storm. "Get your ass home," he yelled.

"Okay, but I—"

"Now," he roared then hung up.

Go and take your whipping like a woman, Ivy. You can't say Candy didn't try to warn you, I thought. I wondered if I could tell Jaabir everything and he'd save me, but then I remembered he worked for Storm. I knew better than to expect him to jeopardize his career by running interference. I made sure to let him know I was leaving then I called a cab.

All sort of crazy thoughts ran through my head on the ride home. I wondered if Storm was going to meet me at the door with a fist to the face. I imagined him kicking me nonstop. With Candy being gone, I wondered how I could get him to stop beating me. *I'm just going to have to fight back,* I thought. *It's time for the old me to rejuvenate. Enough is enough.*

I put the key into the door then slowly pushed it open. The lights in the living room were dim, and there was no

sign of Storm. I remembered his truck was parked outside, so the silence in the condo was confusing. I closed
the door then tiptoed toward the bedroom. That's when I
heard him.

"Oh, shit, Candy baby! You fucking the shit out of me.
Oh, shit, good-googalie–moogalie," he screamed.

I could hear Candy laughing in between his jabbering.
"Be still, Stormy," she said, giggling. "I'm trying to ride
you until I hit that spot, baby. I can't get a good rhythm
with you wiggling like that." She laughed some more.

I tipped away from the door then sat in the living room.
For some reason, Storm was being awfully loud. They were
back there, keeping up noise for more than an hour. I
even knew when Storm busted his nut because he screamed
like a bitch. Candy laughed like she had just heard the
funniest joke ever. Any other woman might've raised sand
about her man screwing another woman in her bed, but
as far as I was concerned Candy needed to take him off my
hands. I was well past sick of Storm. After the way he
treated me in front of his boys, I didn't care if he ever
touched me again.

I sat up when I heard the bedroom door open. Storm
came down the hall naked, staggering and mumbling.

His speech was slurred. "I can't believe this bitch ain't
made it home yet," he said, pressing numbers on his
phone. "She must think I'm play—" he said, cutting himself off after spotting me on the couch.

His cell phone hurled at me so fast I barely had time to
react. *Plack!* My arm felt like he'd stung me with an open
palm. I jumped up off the couch before he darted toward
me. Candy was soon behind him, wearing one of my
robes. She threw her arms around his waist, hindering his
roll.

"Stormy baby, I thought we agreed you'd keep your
cool tonight," she said.

"It ain't dark outside yet," he said, trying to pry her hands from his waist. "It's still daytime."

He was limp and swung loosely as he struggled to get away. Thank goodness he was drunk or else he probably would've sent Candy flying into one of the walls. I don't know what came over her, but I could've kissed her for sticking around and taking up for me although she'd said she wouldn't.

"Sit down, baby," Candy said, leading Storm to the couch.

"Naw. I gotta teach that bitch a lesson," he said.

"Okay, but let me fix you a drink first. You like the last one I made for you, didn't you?" Candy asked.

"Yeah, but that bitch owe me some teeth. I'm ready to leave my fist print in her jaw," he said, falling onto the couch.

"Hold on," Candy said, slumping over with him. "She can't suck your dick with swollen gums, baby. You just told me how good she was at the restaurant. How you think she gonna be able to do that again if you fix her mouth so it won't close? Huh?"

Storm didn't respond. He just kept trying to get off the couch but couldn't. I began to feel a little at ease knowing he couldn't stand straight. How bad could he hurt me while in such an inebriated state? From the looks of things, he wasn't going to be able to do much. Candy easily held him down on the couch.

"Wait right here," she said. "I'm going to fix you a Cape Cod."

"Naw," Storm said, fussing. "Let me up."

Candy huffed, seemingly frustrated. "Ivy, go get my purse off the dresser," she said.

I was confused as to why she wanted her purse, but I hurriedly did what she said. Once I returned, I noticed she was sitting on top of Stormy with her back to him. His eyes were partially opened, and he wasn't putting up much of a fight. She reached for her purse then pulled out a bag of pills. Stormy was so out of it, he didn't notice anything. Candy took out two round white pills then handed them to me.

"Go fix him a Cape Cod, but be light on the cranberry juice. Those will dissolve pretty fast," she whispered.

I looked around her at Storm. He seemed to be fighting off sleep. He opened and closed his eyes several times in the few seconds I looked at him. "What are these? Are you trying to kill him?" I asked.

"No. They're just sleeping pills. Now go," she said with urgency.

I did as Candy instructed. She was right. The pills dissolved extremely fast. By the time I made it back to the living room, Storm was on his feet, trying to push Candy out of his way.

"G'on, Candy. Get outta my way. I'm gonna talk to Ivy. I need to know why this bitch can't mind me. I'm the daddy around this mutha—" he said just before falling onto the couch.

Candy beckoned me. "C'mere with that," she said, taking the drink from my hand. "Here, Stormy. Take a sip. It's made just the way you like it."

I was surprised to see Storm drink the concoction. I wondered why he couldn't taste the medicine in it, but at the same time, I was glad he couldn't. Soon, Candy no longer had to wrestle with him. He sat on the couch, drinking from the glass and singing to himself. He seemed to be unaware of his surroundings. Candy and I called his name several times, but he continued to sing the theme song from the old *Beretta* sitcom.

I was so glad to finally see him slumped over, sleeping. I sat on the floor in front of the couch to watch him. I wanted to make sure he kept breathing. Candy looked at me like I had lost my mind.

"What are you doing?" she asked.

"Trying to make sure he ain't dead. I'm in enough hot water as it is," I replied.

She shook her head then went to the linen closet and brought back a pillow and blanket for him. She covered him then sat on the floor next to me. "You see his stomach and chest moving?" she asked, pointing at Storm.

"Yeah."

"That means he's still alive."

"Shh . . . don't be so loud," I said, letting my nerves get the best of me.

"Calm down. He can't hear us. And he's definitely down until morning."

"You've done this with him before?"

"No, but I've done it enough times with other men to know what I'm talking about. Stormy won't be a threat when he wakes up either."

"Really? Why do you say that?"

"'Cause he's gonna have trouble piecing together what went down tonight. He won't remember much. He'll probably think we fucked the shit out of him and left him on the couch."

"Well, that's comforting to hear. I must admit, you saved my ass."

"I like you. I don't know why, because you do some foolish things, but I still like you. I was just about to leave when Stormy came in talking about all that he was going to do to you when you got here. He was on the phone with a member of his posse. I think I heard him say Drake."

"That figures. Drake saw me talking to Jaabir."

"Who's that?"

"A long story," I said, looking at the floor. "Anyway, I kinda knew he was gonna instigate my ass whipping. I'm just glad you were here." There was a long silence between us. "I'm thinking I should just bounce. I heard you say he told you about what he did to me at the restaurant. There's no telling what this nigga is gonna do to me next."

"Ivy, don't go. Stormy's trying to move me in. He says I live too far away from him. If you leave, I'll have to deal with him by myself."

"Sounds like a personal problem to me, Candy. Thank you for saving my ass, but I can't hang around and be abused because you don't want him to yourself. You like his money more than I do. That's your bad. You'll be fine. And anyway, he doesn't abuse you like he does me."

"Yeah, but I don't know that he won't. Besides, we can control him. Look at 'im," she said, nodding in his direction.

We both looked at him, snoring and slobbering as he slept with his mouth opened. He looked like a big punk. At first we snickered, but then we ended up having a hearty laugh. It felt good, too. Storm never woke up. Candy was halfway to making her case clear.

"Every time he abuses one of us, we'll just make his ass pay for it," she said.

"What? You think dropping a sleeping pill in his drink every now and then is payback?"

"No, but hitting him in his wallet will more than suffice," she said, looking at me with a sinister smile. "You do know by now what his true profession is, right?"

"Yeah . . . so?"

"So, he's got plenty of money we could juggle, and he wouldn't know the difference because he keeps too many people around. When did you find out about him?"

"I just overheard him today at the restaurant. This muthafucker has a Ph.D. in pharmacy," I said jokingly. "He told me he was born with a silver spoon in his mouth."

She laughed. "He was if you count the fact that his momma was the highest paid whore in Memphis and his daddy was her pimp and drug dealer."

I gasped. "Girl, no. Where'd you hear that?"

"I got him drunk one day, and he spilled the beans."

"He told me his daddy shared a lot of business sense with him before he died, but that's all he said."

"Yep. And his daddy had a shitload of money in the bank and around his house before he was killed by another drug dealer—all Stormy's inheritance. He was grown and in the business by then."

"Why is it that he shared so much more with you than he did with me?"

Candy shrugged. "Maybe because he values what he has with you. It might sound crazy, but I believe deep down he cares about what you think of him."

"Hmph. And he'll beat my ass every chance he gets, too," I said, rolling my eyes.

"He said you wanted a loving relationship. We couldn't tell you about us in the beginning because he knew you wouldn't be game, but I let him know from the start . . . I didn't care about whom he was seeing or what he was doing. All I care about is a piece of the pie. He agreed to share with me, and I agreed to be his every desire—sexually or otherwise."

I looked at Candy, wondering how she could be so nonchalant. I suppose it was because she didn't have children. I began to think about my kids and the upcoming court date. I dropped my head in despair. Candy reached to touch my shoulder. "Hey," she said. By the time I looked up at her, I was in tears. "What's wrong?" she asked.

"Just when I thought I could prove to the world I could be a better person, everything has crashed in my face. In order to get my kids back, I was told I needed to have a job and good living conditions that didn't include a man. Storm gave me that for awhile, but he snatched it back.

"My car isn't working, Storm is here pretty much every

day, and now you're telling me he's even asked you to move in with me. No judge is gonna award me custody of my children hearing all of this. And even if I lied, my mother would find out and report me. She's driven to keep me at my lowest. She's not satisfied unless it seems I need her.

"You should see my babies. My boys are going to be some tough, no-shit-taking young men when they grow up. They like to wrestle, knocking over all of my breakables." I laughed. "It was my fault for thinking I could leave figurines on the coffee table around them anyway.

"My Robin is the sweetest little girl you could ever know," I said, wiping tears. "I named her Robin because her father's name is Robert. I tried to name all my children after their fathers."

"You have three, right?" Candy asked.

"Yeah, and three different baby daddies, too, but that doesn't make me a bad person though," I replied defensively.

"I know. I didn't say you were—"

"I'm sure you were thinking it," I said, cutting her off. "I was young and dumb, not bad. My heart was in the right place with every man I fooled with. Their heart just wasn't with me. But, I love my babies. I wouldn't trade 'em for nothing in the world. It's hard trying to take care of them by myself, but I was blessed to have them, and they're mine." I cried hard, giving myself a headache.

"Look, Ivy, I really don't know what to say. I just know that you're in a no-win situation. If you stay, you won't get custody of your kids, and if you leave, you still won't be deemed suitable to take care of your children. I'm behind you on whatever you decide."

Candy listened to me talk about my children some more. I reminisced on good and hard times. I found myself wishing for any of those days with my children back. Candy's eyes were sincere, and I could appreciate her understanding me at that moment. I sucked up my tears.

"Court is in two days," I said.

"I'll go with you," Candy said, patting me on the back.

"Are you serious?"

"Yeah. You've got a good heart, and I like that about you. I'm in your corner. Let me know how I can help."

"I don't know. I guess I'd just appreciate you being there."

"Cool. Consider me there," Candy said, heading to the bedroom.

When we finished talking, it was 5:00 in the evening. I fixed me something to eat then went to the bedroom to see why Candy hadn't come back. I heard the shower running so I knew she was busy washing off Storm's funk. I got comfortable in a fitted lounging dress then began changing the sheets on the bed.

Candy stepped out of the bathroom, dripping wet. "There're no clean towels in the bathroom. You mind getting me one out of the hall closet?"

"No, I don't mind," I said, heading to get a towel.

I took a peep at Storm lying on the couch. He was still in the same position as he was when we left him, slobbering and snoring. I went back into the bedroom then gave Candy the towel. She dried herself off then sat on the bed to lotion herself. I hadn't finished making it up.

"Do you mind? You're rumpling up the covers, and I need to tighten them," I said, tugging on the sheets.

Candy turned around and grinned. "Okay, but I don't know why you're tightening them when they're just going to get messed up again in a minute."

I stopped and put my hand on my hip. "Excuse me? By who? It's not even six o'clock yet. Stormy is going to stay where he is 'cause I can't carry his big heavy ass, and ain't nobody else getting ready for bed up in here."

Candy walked over to me then stroked my thigh and massaged my breast. I slapped her hand down. "You don't have to do anything. I just wanna taste you," she said.

I walked around to the other side of the bed. "Leave me alone, Candy. I only got down with you because I felt I had no other choice. I'm not a lesbian, and I don't appreciate you coming on to me right now."

She smiled then surrendered her hands in the air. "Okay. I never force anybody to do something they don't wanna do."

Three O'clock in the Morning. . . .

"Aw, fuck! Yeeeeessss," I screamed as I nutted in Candy's mouth.

Chapter 13

Feels Like the Weight of the World

When Candy and I got up to fix breakfast, Storm was still asleep. We didn't dare disturb him either. We danced around the kitchen, listening to the *Hot Wake Up Show* with DJ Nappy and TK on Hot 107.1 FM. I loved to hear Nappy snicker because he'd make me laugh right along with him. I loved to hear TK tell things like they really were, keeping it real.

Candy and I were in the midst of taking the bacon out of the oven when the radio suddenly stopped playing. We turned around and saw Storm dressed in a gray and black suit. He eyed us without saying a word. Candy tried to break the ice.

"Good morning," she sang. "Would you like some coffee until breakfast is ready?"

He didn't say anything. She took a cup out of the cabinet then poured him some coffee. I couldn't tell what was on his mind, so I kept quiet, fearing he remembered everything from the day before and was ready to snap. Candy didn't seem to have a fretful bone in her body.

"So, did you sleep well?" she asked, handing him the coffee.

He took the cup from her then looked inside it. He shook his head. "Give me black," he mumbled.

He looked drained, and I almost felt sorry for him.

"Huh?" she asked.

"Black. I can't drink this. Give me black."

"Oh, you want black coffee? No problem. Coming right up. I'll just drink this one," she said, setting the cup on the table. She poured him another cup. "How's this?"

He took a sip. "Better," he said, barely audible.

"Great. You didn't answer my question. Did you get some good sleep?"

He leaned on the breakfast bar. "I don't know. I sorta feel like I got too much sleep. I can't shake this grogginess."

"Sometimes it be like that," Candy responded, shrugging. "Ain't that right, Ivy?" She winked.

"Mm-hmm," I said, sipping my juice.

Storm set his coffee on the bar then eyed me with an evil eye. After several seconds, I questioned him. "What? Why are you looking at me like that?" I asked.

He continued to stare for a minute. "What'd you do last night?" he finally asked.

I frowned in confusion. "Huh? What do you mean?"

"Don't answer my question with a question."

I became nervous. "I didn't do anything. After you fell asleep, Candy and I watched movies until we fell asleep. Why?"

He ogled me, sucked his teeth, then picked up his coffee to take a sip before answering. "You think you're slick, but I'm watching you." He headed out of the kitchen.

"Storm," I called, "what's that supposed to mean?"

He turned to look at me. "Just be careful," he said.

"Wait," I said, walking toward him. "I go to court tomorrow. What do I say to the judge?"

"What did I tell you to say?"

"Storm, you know I'm supposed to be living alone."

"You do. I don't live here . . . nor do I intend to. I have my own house. Did you forget?" he asked. I shook my head. "Why would you want your kids to live with you anyway?"

His question cut me. "Because they're mine, Storm. They should be with me. I'm their mother."

He stepped to me and cupped the sides of my face. "Have you noticed your surroundings? Do you not realize how much things have improved for you over the last six months? Why would you wanna go mess it up now? Children can really complicate your life, you know?"

"Storm, my children *are* my life. Why do you think I spend so much time calling and going over to my mother's house, trying to see them? Who do you know in their right mind will continue to send gifts somewhere only to get them back untouched? My kids are everything to me," I yelled. "You hear me? Everything."

He picked me up by my head, so I'd look him at eye level. My feet dangled and my brain felt like it was going to pop as he squeezed, trying to keep me extended in the air. I tried to hold on to his arms, but they were no support to me.

Candy ran over. "Stormy baby, chill out. What are you doing? Why are you so uptight this morning?" she asked, rubbing his back. Her eyes were filled with sheer panic.

He dropped me to the floor. I held my head as my ears began to ring. I could barely hear him fussing at me. "Do what the fuck you think you need to do, Ivy, but this is my place," he said. "Your kids aren't welcomed here."

"You told me you'd help me," I yelled. "I've always

wanted my kids with me. That's been no secret. You knew my intentions when you moved me in here."

Candy tried to calm me down. She kneeled on the floor next to me. "Shh . . . don't piss him off any further," she whispered in my ear.

Storm came back toward me. "I know, and I've changed my mind. Am I allowed to do that?"

I pushed Candy away. "No," I screamed at Storm. "Not at the expense of my children. I only moved in here because you said you wanted to help me. You've done nothing but hurt me."

He kneeled next to me. "Are you sure about that? Huh?" he asked. "When I met you, you were close to being evicted from an extended-stay motel. I rescued you from that, and now you're reestablishing your credit by living in a luxury condo, overlooking the river. I ask you again: are you sure all I've done is hurt you?"

Tears came to my eyes. "You use to love me—or at least I thought you did. I also thought you'd fall in love with my children, but I guess that's what I get for thinking, huh? Next time I'll make sure I know what's up before moving in with a man."

Storm stood then walked to the opening of the kitchen. "Move your kids in, Ivy, but from now on, I expect you to work all the hours I pay you for, and you need to pay the lease, get the car fixed, and pay all the other bills around here. Since you wanna act like you're running things, I'm just making sure you won't be committing perjury tomorrow," he said before walking out on me.

The Next Day During the Trial

"Ivy Lee Jones, do you have yourself together?" Judge Melvin Prather asked.

"Yes, sir, Your Honor," I said, looking over at Kerry and Bessie Mae.

"Bailiff, give me her check stubs," the judge said.

I handed a folder to the bailiff then waited anxiously while he looked over my pay stubs, the lease to the condo, and other proof of responsibility. Candy was right by my side. Judge Prather scribbled notes on a piece of paper. I just wished he'd hurry up because I was ready to get away from there. I got sick having to stand there in the presence of my so-called family over on the other side of the courtroom.

"Your Honor, do you mind if I take a seat?" I asked.

"Why, Ms. Jones? What's wrong with your feet?"

"Nothing's wrong with my feet. I'm just suddenly feeling ill."

"All right, but when I finish looking over these documents, you've got to stand."

"Yes, sir. No problem," I responded.

My nerves had clearly gotten the best of me. I thought of Storm and my kids then realized it wouldn't be a perfect mix. Judge Prather asked me to stand.

"Ms. Jones, how did you manage to get such a high-paying job?"

I cleared my throat. "A close friend owns the restaurant, your honor. I applied for a job after hearing he needed an event coordinator. It just sounded like something I'd love to do. He gave me a chance, and it's been working out."

"So what have you done about saving money?"

"I have an account with First Tennessee Bank, your honor."

"Checking or savings?"

"Savings. My statements are all there in the folder."

"Then how do you pay your bills without a checking account? I'm sure you don't pay your landlord with cash, do you?"

"No, sir. I pay by money order—"

"Why?" he asked, cutting me off.

"Because I know I'm not balanced enough to keep a checking account yet."

He looked at Candy. "And who's your friend?"

"Can—" I started.

"I'm Stephanie Perry, Your Honor," she interrupted.

I was shocked. She told me the day I met her on the bus that Candy Cane was her real name. I couldn't wait to check her about that. The judge didn't catch that I was about to call her by a different name.

"Why are you here, Ms. Perry?" he asked.

"Your Honor, I'm a friend. I've known Ivy for the last six months."

"Hmph. Right after she got herself in trouble for child neglect, huh? And you're here to tell me what?"

"I'm mainly here for moral support, Your Honor," she answered.

"Well, if you have anything you'd like to add, you better do so now, because I'm about to make my ruling."

I interjected, "Your Honor, may I say something?"

"Go ahead, Ms. Jones."

"I've gotten myself on the right path, and I intend to stay on it, but at this time, I'd like to withdraw my request for full custody of my children," I said. Loud gasps filled the room. "I . . . I'm not ready, Your Honor. Although I'm improving my lifestyle, I still have a long way to go."

My mother flipped. "Say what? Oh no! You've drilled it to me on more than one occasion that those kids are your kids. What are you trying to pull?"

I began to cry. "I'm not trying to pull anything. I love my children . . . that's why I don't want to take them back until I know I can be all they deserve me to be."

"You just wanna be child-free," my mother yelled. "Now that you've gotten a halfway decent job and a place to stay, you just wanna whore around and not have to worry about a babysitter."

"No," I cried. "Stop trying to tear me down. That's not what I want."

Judge Prather banged his gavel, interrupting us. "Then what do you want, Ms. Jones?" he asked.

I shed more tears before I could reply. "I want what's best for my children, and right now, I know they're better off entrusted in my mother's care."

I saw my mother look at Kerry. "Oh, I don't believe this," she said. "Why are you trying to run away from your kids now? You think it's fair to me that I raise your children while you run free?"

"No, ma'am," I said, wiping my face. "I love my children. I just need you to give me a little more time—six months to a year. I promise I'll take 'em back."

Kerry looked dumbfounded. The judge asked him if he wanted to say something. He shook his head then turned away from me. Candy grabbed my hand then spoke to the judge.

"Your Honor, I'd like to say something," she said.

"Go ahead."

"In the six months I've known Ivy, I've heard her cry and speak of her children on countless occasions. I've also seen her do nearly a one-hundred and eighty degree turnaround. She's on her way to being who she needs to be for her children, and please believe it's killing her to have to withdraw her request for custody at this time."

"Well, I wish one of you would tell me what's hindering her responsibility to her children," Judge Prather said. "Never mind. If Ms. Jones feels she's not ready, then I'm not going to press the issue." He looked at my mother. "Ms. Reynolds, if you are no longer able to uphold responsibility for the children, let me know. I can turn them over to other temporary foster care since Ms. Jones claims she's not ready to care for them."

My mother dropped her head then shook it. Kerry patted her on the back. He didn't bother to look at me. I wanted to tell him I loved him, but I sensed by his reactions that he wouldn't acknowledge me. My mother raised her head then rolled her eyes at me.

"I'll keep the children, Your Honor," she said, "but since she claims she's not ready for them now, then she needs to stay away until she is. She'll look like the picture of health to them . . . we don't need to confuse them any more than they already are. And, I'd like for you to set up an order for child support. Ivy's working now, and I'm sure she can afford it."

"All right. Well, if there's no more that needs to be said, I'll issue my ruling."

Judge Prather slapped me with a three-thousand-dollar a month child support order. I couldn't tell him that Storm had exaggerated my pay on those stubs, so I was left to suffer the consequences. The bottom line was that the money didn't matter. My kids deserved it.

As I headed to leave out of the courtroom, my mother and brother weren't far behind. "I don't know what you're up to, Ivy Lee Jones, but you'll get yours. You ain't right," my mother screamed, walking behind me. "Ain't no good gon' come to you, 'cause you ain't right."

As we exited the courtroom, her voice echoed in the hallway as she continued to fuss. Kerry tried to get her to be quiet, but she wasn't trying to hear him. "Momma, c'mon now. You're making a scene," Kerry told her.

Candy put her arm around me and escorted me toward the door. "Just keep moving, Ivy. We'll be away from her in a minute," she said.

I looked back at Kerry. He seemed to be embarrassed at

all the hooping and hollering. I wanted to stop and make him talk to me, but I didn't.

Just before I stepped out of the building, my mother's voice echoed loudly. "Don't come around, Ivy. You hear me?"

Candy tried desperately to make me keep walking, but I had to answer her. "Loud and clear," I said as she got in my face. She stared at me like I was a piece of shit. "I love you, too," I said before walking away.

Chapter 14
Party Hardy

Candy and I returned to the condo before noon. Court went faster than I'd thought it would. I was feeling pretty somber, and all I wanted to do was sleep the day away. I had hoped I'd awaken from a dream that I had given up my kids to Bessie Mae. I could care less if I saw the rest of the day. I just wanted to see a new day.

As we headed into the condo, I questioned Candy about her name. "So, when were you gonna tell me your name is Stephanie?" I asked with an attitude. "Didn't you hear me almost tell the judge your name was Candy?"

"That's why I stopped you. The last thing we needed up in there was to start a conversation about my name," she responded.

"So is your name Candy or not?"

"Not."

"Now back to my original question. When were you gonna tell me—"

She cut me off. "Look it's a long story. I'll tell you about it one day. Just not today, okay?"

I could hear Storm in the bedroom, slamming dresser

drawers. He came into the living room when he heard
Candy talking to me. He was casually dressed in a navy and
white–striped Polo and blue jeans. I knew he wasn't heading to the restaurant or about to conduct any other business because he looked too relaxed. Candy complimented
his attire.

"Ooooweee, Stormy. This is the way I like to see you
dressed. You look like a real person now," she said.

"Oh, so I guess I look like a fake person when I'm in any
other gear, huh?" he asked, shaking his head at her.

"You know what I'm saying. You look like you can be
about more than just business. This is a different style for
you, I'm just glad to see a change, that's all. Where're you
headed anyway?"

"Out," he snapped. "You know better than to question a
grown man."

"Gosh. I didn't mean any harm. I thought it was okay
for a friend to care about what the other's day is like. Forgive me for caring."

Storm stood looking at her with a smirk. "A'ight 'friend,'"
he said.

I went to sit on the couch. I felt like tucking my tail between my legs. I felt like I was worse than a dog—more
like a cowardly bitch. *How could I sacrifice my children for the
likes of a man who means me no good,* I thought. *This life he's
providing for me is okay, but is it really worth the pain?* I shook
my head, and Storm must've taken notice because he sat
next to me.

"What's up, li'l sexy? How'd it go in court today?" he
asked.

"Okay," I said shortly.

"Okay? Just okay?"

"Mm-hmm."

"What is just okay? You know you have to elaborate if
you want me to understand."

I sighed. "I withdrew my request for parental rights. The kids are going to stay with my mom for a little while longer."

Storm cocked his head to the side then shrugged. "Okay, then why the gloom? You obviously made that decision because you felt it was best, right?"

I shook my head. "I felt backed against the wall, Storm. You gave me an ultimatum: without my children, you'd still take care of me. Otherwise, all living expenses would be on me."

Again he shrugged. "Is taking financial responsibility supposed to be a bad thing?"

"It is when you're willing to do it for me, but not my kids. If you can't love my children, you don't truly love me."

"I disagree, Ivy. I didn't have those kids. They got daddies. I only have one son I'm responsible for—that's it. I don't have to clothe and feed nobody else's children."

Candy and I looked at each other. Her facial expression didn't appear to mean the same as mine. She didn't seem to be shocked at all by Storm's response. I was hurt he'd be so cold. I turned my attention to him. "That's not how you made me feel the day you asked me to move to the condo, Storm. I poured my heart out to you, telling you what my kids meant to me. Now you say you won't take care of somebody else's children."

"Problem?" he asked coldly.

I dropped my head in disgust. "You've got to care, Storm. You're being hard right now, but if you care anything for me, then you've got to be acting. I thought I was beginning to know you. I guess I'll never understand you."

"Don't try to understand me. Just accept things for what they are and as they come," he said nonchalantly.

"Umph, umph, umph. But, you love me, right?"

"Look around you. You think I don't?"

"Hmph," I said, getting up. "Yeah. You love me." I rolled my eyes then headed to the bedroom.

"Wait," Storm yelled. "I'm having a party at my house tonight." He stood then pulled a wad of money out of his pocket. "I need for you and Ivy to be there. Go shopping, buy some new outfits then get your hair done," he said, peeling off hundreds of dollars. "Candy, take Ivy to get some braids."

I rubbed across my head and realized my hair was too short to cornrow. "My hair isn't long enough for cornrows. Besides, I don't like my hair braided to my scalp."

"I didn't ask you what you like," he responded. "You need some damn hair on your head."

"I thought you liked my hair short."

"Hmph. Well, now you know."

"Why don't I just get a wig? You just wanna see some hair, right?" I asked, getting smart.

"You can get micros," Candy said. "I know a place where they can have 'em done in five or six hours."

Storm looked at his Rolex. "That should be good timing. The party isn't going to be popping off until about eleven tonight anyway."

I didn't mind the shopping part, but the braid shit was pissing me off. I kept my cool though. "And how are we supposed to get around? Did you forget Candy's car isn't out of the shop yet and the contraption you gave me is still on the restaurant parking lot, broke down?"

Storm stepped to me, drew his hand back, and then faked a swing at me. "Shut the fuck up, Ivy. You didn't let me finish," he said. "I was about to tell you to drive my Lexus. It's parked outside."

"That burgundy coupe I saw out there?" Candy asked excitedly.

"Yeah, that's it," he responded. "Will that be all right?"

"Hell yeah," she said.

"Enough said. Get going because we're on a time frame here. I need you at my house no later than eleven-thirty."

Candy and I went to Josephine's in East Memphis to shop. Storm broke us off two grand each, so I bought some new Gucci sandals and a dress. Candy decided she wanted her hair re-braided, so just bought some new Louis Vuitton sandals to rock with an outfit and purse she already had at home.

She took me to a braid shop in the Hickory Hill area where the braiders were all Africans. We couldn't understand much coming out of their mouths, but they braided the shit out of our heads in five hours. There were two and three women doing our hair at all times. We both got micros, but Candy went honey blond on me. Her skin complexion complemented it well.

Storm wasn't there once we made it back to the condo to get dressed. He left a note on the bed with the address and direction to his house. I couldn't believe I was actually going to get to see his house. Before the party, I never really even cared whether I ever saw where he lived.

I looked at the clock and noticed it was eleven. "Candy, we need to hurry up. You know what time Storm said he wanted us to get there," I said in a panic.

"Fuck him," she said. "He'll be all right until we get there. Hell, he should know how long it takes for women to get ready for something like this. He just sprung this on us earlier today."

"I know, but I really don't feel like hearing his damn mouth. You know he can get crazy."

"Well, I suppose if we showed up sweaty and funky he'd act crazy about that, too. I don't know about you, but I'm not putting on my clean clothes without bathing first."

"I wasn't suggesting that, Candy, and you know it. I'm just saying we need to hurry up. I'll go to the shower in the hall, and you bathe in the master bath, but don't be all night."

"Yeah . . . yeah . . . yeah. I hear you," she said.

It was eleven-thirty by the time I finished putting on the final touches of my makeup. I ran into the bedroom to get Candy. "Girl, do you see the time?" I asked.

"Yeah. And? He doesn't live far from here. We'll just be a little late," she responded, applying lip gloss.

I rolled my eyes. "Just come on," I said, grabbing the keys off the dresser.

A few minutes after midnight, Candy and I strolled up to Stormy's enormous house and rang the doorbell. The music was so loud, I wondered if anyone would hear us. Just as I was about to ring the bell again, the door swung open. Stormy stared at us with fire in his eyes. I waited for the tongue-lashing he was known for, but it didn't come. He stepped away from the door without saying a word. I pushed Candy inside first then closed the door behind me.

There were men as far as I could see. They were all drunk and loud. The more I scanned the room, the more I could see Candy and I were the only women. I wanted to question Storm, but he wouldn't even look at me or Candy. I tried to play off my worry, but after ten minutes, Candy let me know I wasn't being inconspicuous.

She walked up to me with two drinks. "Do you have to let everyone know you're not enjoying yourself?" she asked, handing me one of the glasses.

"Huh?"

"Standing on the wall, wringing your hands doesn't exactly say you're having a good time."

"Candy, he didn't even speak to us."

"Will you let that go? Stormy's entertaining his guests.

He's not thinking about you, or me for that matter," she said, pointing at a laughing Storm.

I looked at my drink. "What is this?" I asked.

"Cape Cod. I didn't know how you'd like it, so I just told the bartender to make it with Grey Goose."

"That's cool," I said, taking a sip. "Something's coming. I know it is . . . but I also know I'm tired of him intimidating me. You don't have to worry about him fucking with you. He only seems to like to manhandle me."

She rolled her eyes. "Girl, act like you don't give a shit about the way he's acting. That's what I do. I'm here to have a good time, and I be damned if I don't have one." Candy raised her glass for a toast. "To a good time?"

"To a good time," I said, clinking my glass with hers.

Storm walked up on us before we had a chance to see him coming. "Ladies, you look nice."

"Thanks," we replied in unison.

"So, what was the toasting about? Can I join in?"

"Sure," Candy said. "We were just saying you have a lovely home and how off the chain this party is. We appreciate you inviting us."

"Thanks. I appreciate the compliment, but that's nothing to toast about." He looked back and forth at both of us as he spoke. "But this money you're about to earn is."

Candy and I looked at each other. "What are you talking about Storm?" I asked.

"I need y'all to dance. I bought the outfits and everything. They're in the back. Candy, you're really gonna like yours. You're gonna be a topless cowgirl." He smiled.

"Dance?" I asked in panic.

"Yeah. You got a problem with that?"

The few sips of alcohol must've brought about the old me because I snapped. "I'm not taking off my clothes for these niggas."

"Excuse me?" Storm asked, stepping closer.

Candy intervened. "How much money we talking?"

"Wait a minute," he said, shushing me. "I need to see what the fuck Ivy talking about." He stared at me like he dared me to repeat myself.

"Stormy, I got this," Candy said excitedly. "If Ivy don't want the money, I'll take her share. Don't be bent out of shape if she don't wanna dance."

With a scowl on his face, Storm slowly turned his eyes to Candy. "You sure? I mean, these niggas came prepared to pay up. You do your damn thang, and I'm willing to bet you could make about three thousand dollars."

"It's on! Where's my stuff?"

Candy and Storm walked to the back of the house. When he came back, he announced Candy like she was a big-time showgirl.

"Gentlemen, may I have your attention please?" Storm asked just after turning the music off. "I know it's been a long time coming, but the entertainment promised to you is here. I hope you liked the food and are ready for dessert, 'cause this woman's got the pie, the cream, the milk, and the shake." The men all cheered. "So, without further adieu, put your hands together for Ms. Candy Cane."

Storm turned on a CD. Candy pranced out to the tune of "My Neck My Back" by Khia. She bounced her titties and shook her ass like dancing was going out of style. She went to the middle of the floor and made it her stage. When she bent over and made her ass clap, she had created a signature move that got her paid.

The men began to pile loot into her thong and even took turns sticking bills into her butt hole. She smiled and acted as if she was enjoying how they felt her up. She clapped her ass, concealing and revealing the rolled-up green bills each time her cheeks opened and closed. The booty-clap became an ongoing thing because many of the men seemed to want to see her do it.

After her ass couldn't take any more bills sticking out of it, she transferred money into the pouch attached to her waist. Storm restarted the song at least eight times before the men slowed up on the money they gave Candy, but she was completely nude with the exception of her pouch before everything was over.

The men all applauded Candy then one of them screamed out, "Stormy, put her on the house."

"Yeah," many of them seconded.

Storm was standing with his arm around Candy. He turned and looked in the direction from where he'd heard the first outburst. "What? Are you crazy?"

A nasty-looking fat man stepped up. "Hell naw we ain't crazy. Put that bitch on the house. We done gave her all our money . . . we can't afford to pay for some."

"Then, nigga, you ain't gon' get none," Storm said.

The man's clothes were too little and dripping wet from sweat. His face was drenched, too, and rolls of fat hung from under his shirt. "A'ight . . . how much?"

Storm looked at Candy then turned to the man and said, "How long?"

"Thirty minutes. That's all I need."

Storm laughed. "You ain't gon' last thirty seconds, but a'ight. It's gon' cost you a G."

For the first time, I saw panic on Candy's face. "Storm—" she started.

"Hush," he said, putting his arm around her neck then cupping her mouth with his hand. "So what you gon' do, man?"

The man went into his pocket then said, "Fine. One G."

"Big baller," someone yelled out.

All the men began to laugh. Candy snatched away from Storm. He seemed to be shocked. "What's your problem?" he asked.

"I didn't agree to lay down with anybody," she said.

"It's not an option. You don't make the decisions around here. I do. Now g'on back to that room where you changed. This man is waiting," Storm said, patting on the man's back.

"I ain't fucking nobody, especially not a fat, greasy, sweaty mutherfucker like him," she responded, looking at the man. "I didn't come here for this shit. I danced . . . that ought to be enough." Candy tried to walk away.

Storm grabbed her braids by the roots. Candy screamed. "I know this shit is tight ain't it," he yelled. "I'll pull all of these mutherfuckers out, ho. What makes you think you can talk to me like that?"

"Stormy, let me go," she hollered.

"I'ma let you go all right."

Storm began bashing Candy in the face, and the sad thing about it is none of the men would stop him. I remembered how she'd helped me, so I made an attempt to save her. "Storm, please. Stop. She understands now," I said, grabbing his arm.

He jerked from me and held Candy down on the floor with his foot. "Unless you want some of this, I suggest you back the fuck up."

I stepped back and silently prayed her beating would stop soon. When it was over, Candy still had to go into the back with the funky-looking man. The man seemed to have felt sorry for Candy and tried to renege on his offer, but Storm insisted a deal was a deal. "Either you fuck her or you don't . . . don't matter to me because you still gon' pay up. I don't take too kindly of mutherfuckers wasting my time," Storm told him.

When the man came out of the room, Storm made a

last offer to anyone else who wanted a round with me or Candy, but no one else was willing to give up the dough. After another twenty minutes passed, I sneaked toward the back to look for Candy. I found her lying facedown on a bed.

"Candy?" I called. She didn't move. "Candy, are you okay?" I sat on the bed next to her.

She rolled over and almost scared me. Her whole head was swollen and cut up. I felt sorry for her because she could barely open her eyes to see. She sat up on the bed, trying to be strong.

"Do you want me to get you some ice?" I asked, not knowing what to really do or say.

"No," she mumbled. "I need a gun. I'ma kill that son of a bitch." A single tear crept down Candy's face.

"You're gonna be okay. I'm sorry I didn't do more to help you," I said, hugging her. I almost cried.

"Un-un . . . don't worry about it. There was nothing you could've done anyway. But mark my words . . . that mutherfucker has to pay. You with me?"

I answered with no hesitation. "I'm with you."

Chapter 15

What Becomes of the Battered?

Candy and I didn't come out of that room the rest of the night. Surprisingly, Storm let us stay in there without objections. The loud music and laughter continued for hours. If the house would've been on fire, I wouldn't have known it. Despite the loud clanging and banging, I didn't leave the room for anything. I wanted to be by Candy's side. She was shaking like a leaf on a tree.

"I see now I can't hang with Storm," I said, rubbing her shoulder. "I'll end up dead."

"Not if you kill him first," she mumbled.

"The thing is, I don't know when he's gonna do something to really hurt me. He's good on one hand, and then he's bad on another. What other man you know can bring home his other woman and make his live-in girlfriend accept her? He set me up. He got me use to a lavish lifestyle then sprung you on me."

"I never thought I'd say this, but I'm sorry. I should've walked away when he made me an offer."

"What offer?"

"Money has always been my weakness. Even though I come from a wealthy background and can get money from my mom or my dad, I've still had an uncontrollable greed for money. And I don't know where it first came from."

"Well, we all have our weakness."

"Yeah, but I can see now that the deal Storm placed before me hasn't been worth it. I thought I could be the other woman, have fun, fuck him every now and then, and get paid. I never thought he'd turn out to be so brutal."

"Neither did I. But, somehow we're going to make it through this. I know we will."

Candy shared more with me about her background and her upbringing. She admitted again that Candy wasn't her real name, and that she and her sister had been living such a fast life that they felt it necessary to use aliases.

I shared much of my life with her as well. I was most surprised to hear she had an identical twin who called herself Sugar. I never would've guessed there was a Candy look-alike walking around out there somewhere. She seemed to be the most surprised to hear of how my mother was treating me instead of helping me. She grew up with a mother who would defend and help her children to the end.

"You know something, Candy?"

"What?"

"I've learned to never judge a book by its cover. I use to think of you as a slut who just didn't give a fuck. But, now I've grown to know the real you. You've got a heart in spite of the issues that developed over the years."

"I misjudged you, too," she said. "You've made some mistakes, but you're learning from them. You could've just given up on your kids, but haven't, and I admire your love for them."

I smiled. "I guess what my momma said about every-thing happening for a reason is true. I really need your friendship right now, and I believe you need mine."

"I do," she whispered. "My sister and I don't speak be-cause I did a dumb thing by sleeping with her boyfriend. I use to have her back, and she had mine, but I don't think there's enough money in the world to make her to speak to me anymore."

"Perhaps one day your sister will come around. In the meantime, just work on forgiving yourself. And try not to make anymore mistakes like that one. I'm focusing on what might lay ahead for me. I'm not going backward any-more. I can't do anything about my past, so it's time for me to look forward."

Candy and I talked until we were tired. There was a bathroom in the bedroom, so I retrieved as many cold-water towels as she needed. We cleaned her up and suc-ceeded with stopping the blood trail that ran down her head, nose, and mouth. She dressed in her original outfit, and then we fell asleep on top of the covers of the bed. I think we both slept with one eye opened for fear Storm would be in the room to raise more hell.

The next morning, Storm stepped into the room, wak-ing us up around 9:00. He startled me when he yelled. "Ivy . . . Candy . . . get up," he said.

We both jumped up like scared little puppies. He walked over to the bed then sat down. He stared at Candy as she wouldn't even lift her head to look at him—a scene that seemed so familiar to me. "All I want you two to do is be gracious to me. I know I have more money than the two of you, so I can afford to show my gratitude with loot, but neither of you can do the same. If I ask you to do me a favor, I don't expect to get any flack about it. I do far more than the average man would for a woman. If you don't agree, then leave me." We kept silent. He looked at me. "I don't expect to see you at the restaurant when I've said don't go there—" He paused then looked at Candy. "And I don't expect you to try to fucking poison me when things aren't going the way you think they should."

Candy and I were caught off guard. She looked up at him as best as she could with her swollen face. "Yes, that's right," he said. "I found those sleeping pills in your purse. I knew I shouldn't've slept that long, and I was determined to get to the bottom of what happened. You thought I wouldn't remember shit, but it all started coming back to me. You started me to drinking long before Ivy came home then instigated fixing more spiked drinks, so I wouldn't beat Ivy's ass. You saved Ivy, but I owed you one . . . that's why last night I made up for old and new.

"Let me tell y'all one more thing. Don't think for a second that I won't kill you then replace you. I care about you both, but I don't take care of bitches who'll bite the hand that feeds them." He was quiet for a few seconds then stood. "I'm heading out for a while, so when y'all get ready to leave, call me and I'll tell you how to lock up. You hear me?" We nodded then he turned to walk away.

I eased down the hall to see if he had left. I heard the door shut and lock then I went back to check on Candy. "Hey . . . he's gone," I said out of relief.

I looked at her face. She looked like Mike Tyson had gotten a hold of her. I tried not to let my expression show it, but he fucked her up much worse than he'd ever done me. I couldn't pretend she looked okay if I wanted to.

"Umph . . . that obvious, huh?" she asked, getting out of bed to look in the mirror. I didn't want to see her reaction to her bruises, so I turned away. "A sorry mutherfucker." Candy was clearly upset.

"I know," I said with my back still turned. "He's gonna get his one day."

"Yeah . . . one day sooner than he thinks." She headed out of the room.

"Where're you going?"

"To have a look around. Why? Is that okay with you?"

"A look around for what? Are you crazy? I got busted trying to be nosy at the restaurant. Little did I know he had surveillance set up in every corner. Don't get caught snooping around."

"I've been here before. The only surveillance he has here is set up outside. I'm not worried." She disappeared down the hall.

My nervousness wouldn't let me think about looking around the night before, so after remembering I hadn't fully seen the house, I decided to check it out. I began in the living room then scoped every inch of the house. I wasn't surprised at Stormy's taste because he knew how to hire the right people to hook things up. I discovered that in addition to all the things Storm had told me about his house, it was also equipped with hardwood floors, crown molding, a plasma TV over the Jacuzzi, and stainless-steel appliances, including the microwave. And that's not the half of what I saw. This nigga really knew how to do things up big.

When I headed back down the hall toward the bedrooms, I heard Candy calling me. "Ivy, where the hell you at?"

I ran toward her voice, which came from another bedroom. "What's up? Are you okay?"

She was kneeling in front of a dresser with several pairs of Storm's jeans and a few sweatshirts scattered around her. As I got closer, I could see she was counting money. She looked up at me. "Can you believe he hides his green in his pants pockets in the drawers? He tried to cover the pants with sweatshirts." She had a smirk on her face. My eyes bulked. "I've counted what's in two pair of pants, and it adds up to eight thousand dollars."

"Naw . . . it can't be that much." I was in total disbelief.

"All of his pants have money in them—two grand in each pocket. There's at least eight pair of pants between all of the drawers. If he's put the same amount in each pair, we're thirty-two thousand dollars richer."

"Now wait a minute. Look who's sounding stupid, Candy. You know Storm's smart enough to know what he had in those drawers before he left."

"Duh . . . yeah, I know that." She kept spreading the money like a deck of cards.

"Then you must have a death wish, and I don't want no part of it." I began to walk away.

"Wait," she screamed. "We won't take anything today. He'll probably be throwing another one of his little parties soon, and all I ask you to do is keep him and his friends occupied. I'll get the money. Considering how much company he keeps, he'll never know who or what hit him."

I hesitated. "I don't know, Candy. I'm supposed to be getting myself together for my kids' sake, not creating situations that can get me killed. I'm already caught up in a twisted situation just hanging out with Storm as it is."

"Well, we'll talk more about it when the time comes. I say we hit him. It'll be worth it. We've got to get something out of getting our asses beat. I know splitting thirty-two thousand dollars isn't a lot, but it's more than we've got now. Hell, I bet he even got more stashed around here somewhere. I plan to hit him for as much as I can whether you help me or not."

I sighed intently. I stared into her battered face and remembered how Storm had abused me. The thought of him gagging me in front of his boys came to mind, and then I could feel my blood boiling. "Count me in. That mutherfucker thinks we're toys, but let's show him that Mattel ain't made shit that can compare to us yet."

Chapter 16
Work Toward Plan B

A week went by after Storm's party. I couldn't just sit around the house, so I used my salary/allowance money to get the car fixed. The transmission was messed up, so it cost me fifteen hundred dollars, including labor and parts. Since Storm would only let me and Candy use his Lexus when he got ready, I figured, I'd make things happen for myself. Storm didn't know it, but I had opened two savings accounts—one for my children and one for me. The way I had it figured, I only needed to put up with his stuff for six more months, and then I could be on my own, especially with what Candy had in mind. We were going to rob Storm blind.

From what I could tell of Storm's mood, he thought the first party went well. I suppose his friends and peers all deemed him right to jump on Candy the way he did. Not only did they not help her, they kept right on partying after the attack. Candy was being pretty strong about it though. She kept coming around and even spending the night as if nothing happened. She had her mind set on getting what we could out of Storm before we bailed out, and I was all for it.

I had mentioned Jaabir to Candy just about every day. She knew I thought a lot of him, so I shouldn't have been surprised when she called the restaurant to give him my number. I hadn't seen her all day, so I should've known she was up to something. Jaabir didn't waste any time giving me a shout.

"May I speak to Ivy," he said just after I answered.

"This is Ivy," I responded in a surprised voice. He sounded so formal, I didn't know who he was.

"Ivy, this is Jaabir."

My heart pounded. "Jaabir? You don't sound the same over the phone. How'd you get my number?"

"A woman by the name of Candy called me and said you might like to talk to me." There was silence between us. I didn't know what to say next. Jaabir spoke up before I could. "I've missed seeing you. Where've you been?"

"Um, I've had to take some time off. I've got some is- sues, and I need to get things straight in my life before I can return to work."

"Oh, I see."

"But, just so you know, I've missed seeing you, too." We paused again. "So, tell me what's been going on around the workplace?"

"Not much. Just me doing what I do. You know I love to cook, and if you let me, I'll show you some of my skills some time."

I smiled like a flattered schoolgirl. "Okay. That sounds nice. It'll be the first time a man has ever cooked for me."

"Well, if my prediction is right, it won't be the last time either."

I had to clear my throat on that one. "Is that right? You're just that confident that I'll like your cooking?"

"Yep. I'm just that confident. Just tell me when."

I had to think carefully about meeting Jaabir. The last thing I wanted to do was get either one of us killed. "To be perfectly honest, I don't see having much time for the next two weeks," I lied.

"Two weeks? Oh, boy. Sounds like you're even busier than when you would come to the restaurant every day."

"I told you I've got a lot going on."

"No, you said you've got issues," he stated.

"Right. Same thing," I responded.

"Anything I can do to help you work through your problems?"

Oh how I wish, I thought. "No. I'm a big girl. I should be able to get things under control soon."

"So what do we do in the meantime?" he asked. "I'd like to stay in touch. May I call you, so we can talk and get to know each other until our first official date?"

"Sure. I'd really like that. So, how about looking at your schedule, then tell me when to set our date."

"I'm the head chef. I can set my schedule any way I want. How about you let me know when you're ready?"

Jaabir and I chatted a bit longer then he gave me his phone number. When we hung up, I began dancing out on the patio. My back was turned when Storm stepped outside.

"What are you so happy about?" he said, startling me.

"Oh . . . um . . . I just talked to my kids. It was good to hear their voices."

"Hmm. I bet," he said, placing his hands around my waist. "Why don't you come in and give me some?"

"Now?"

"Yeah, now. You've got a better time in mind?"

"Not really. I was just thinking that since you just got in you might want something to eat."

"I do—you," he said, kissing me on the neck, pressing his stick against my leg. "You know we haven't made good love—like we did when we first hooked up—in a long time. C'mon, let's go," he said, pulling me into the condo, and then into the bedroom.

Storm and I did the six-nine for nearly half an hour. He couldn't believe how wet I was getting. "Damn, girl. I know it's been a while, but I can see you really miss daddy, don't you?"

"Mm-hmm," I said, moaning.

"Come sit on top of daddy. Show me how much you miss this."

I climbed on top of Storm and rode him like a wild bull. He bucked me back, taking care of me like old times. It was just too bad that it wasn't him that I was making love to. According to my mind, I was in bed with Jaabir. Thinking of him kept me sane, but the only problem was that Storm kept telling me how good I was and how he'd missed me working my ass. I was aiming to please myself, not make him want more of me.

I had to screw him for two hours before he was ready for an extended break. "Go run some bathwater for us," he said.

"How about a shower? That way we could wash each other and have more room."

He nodded. As soon as we jumped into the shower, he wanted more. I didn't think of Jaabir because I felt like shit. I wanted the whole scene to be over. Storm managed to release although I was dry. He left me weak and sore.

I washed him then washed myself once he got out. After drying off, Storm stepped back into the bedroom and asked me about Candy.

"Ivy, where's your bitch-ass friend?"

"I don't think I have one of those," I responded.

"Hmph." He pulled a shirt out of the drawer. "You know who I'm talking about."

"No . . . I really don't."

Storm pulled his shirt over his head then looked at me. I continued to lotion myself as if I didn't know he was staring. When I finally looked up, he rolled his eyes. "Candy . . . where is she?"

"I don't know. I hadn't spoken to her today."

"Oh, so now y'all don't talk every day anymore? What's up with that? I thought y'all were like ace-coon-boon—tighter than tight."

"We get along," I said matter-of-factly.

"You're trying to make me out to be stupid. Look . . . I don't give a shit about how close y'all are. Hell, I introduced the two of you. You don't have to try to make me think your friendship with her is less than what it is."

"Storm, I don't know what you're getting at. All I said was that I hadn't heard from her today. You may not believe that, but it's the truth. Would you like for me to call her?"

"Do what you feel, Ivy. You don't have to call her. I just asked about her, that's all."

Storm left the room. I picked up my cell then called Candy to let her know Storm was asking about her. She said he hadn't called her in a couple of days, and she hadn't tried to touch base with him either. I found that very odd.

"What's up with that, Candy? Something going down between you two that I don't know?"

"Naw . . . he just knows I know he's full of shit."

"Okay, you're always finding out his dirt. What's up now?"

"Ivy, he's married," she said. My mouth flew open. "That son he told you about—the one he's never brought around—is mothered by his wife."

"What? Get the fuck out of here," I whispered. "Where's the wife?"

"They recently separated. She took the son and moved to Mississippi with her parents."

"Candy, how do you know all of this shit?"

"You know I'm from Nesbit, Mississippi, right?"

"Yeah. I remember you told me that."

"Well, I went to visit some relatives, so I stopped by my old beauty salon to get my braids washed and set with rods. While I was under the dryer, I kept hearing this lady repeat Storm's name. I slid my head slightly from under the dryer so I could hear her better. She went on to say she and her husband, Storm, had a beautiful home in Memphis on the river, and that she and her son would be back home soon. She said their separation was temporary and that Storm had been telling her she should come home because he missed her."

"What the fuck—" I said, cutting myself off. "Does he know you've found this out?"

"Yeah. When we talked a couple of days ago, I asked him how was Debra, and if she was still coming home soon. He sounded like he was ready to choke. He cleared his throat a few times then said they hadn't discussed her return."

I couldn't believe how Storm could be so inconsiderate of his family. He had me and Candy—his other women—in that house. I wrapped up the conversation with Candy then got off the phone.

Storm stepped back into the room. "So, she couldn't resist telling you, huh?"

I looked at him for a minute. "Why?"

"Why what?" he asked.

"Why me? Why Candy? You'll be back with your wife soon, right? Why do you need me?"

"I don't need you." He paused. "But I do want you. My wife walked out on me."

"Yeah, but was that before or after she found out about your double life?"

"You mean about you or the drugs?"

"Both."

"She doesn't know about you, but she's always known about the drugs. She was game until she realized how much fun I like to have. You and Candy were just supposed to be my toys, but you've become more than that."

"You've got a funny way of showing your love, Storm. You only beat our ass every chance you get."

"I've only touched Candy once, and she deserved an ass-whippin' for putting that shit in my drink. I could've gotten killed."

"She was trying to save *my* ass from getting killed."

He stepped to me then kissed my forehead. "I get angry, but I wouldn't kill you. You should know that." He sat on the bed next to me.

I felt a little more relaxed about having the conversation about his wife with him. He didn't seem like he was going to bark or bite. I got up then put on a pair of jeans and a long-sleeved, fitted top. It had a V-cut, exposing most of my cleavage. Storm watched as I enhanced my chest and neck with glitter lotion. "So are you mad at Candy for telling me?"

He laughed. "I probably should be, but no. I'm not mad." He walked over and stroked my back. "Are you happy now?"

"Yes, very," I said, exiting the bedroom, heading for the living room. He followed me.

"Good. Now as for the wife thing, you shouldn't worry. She and I aren't getting back together any time soon. If I thought we were, I wouldn't be begging to hold on to you."

I picked up the remote then turned around to face him. "You're not begging me," I said, turning on the television.

"Yes, I am. I'm sorry I can't get on my knees, but please

know that me following you around the condo, rubbing your back, and being nice is my form of begging."

I didn't mean to, but I laughed at him. He laughed, too. I looked in his eyes and saw the Storm I use to love. He seemed kind and gentle again. He leaned over and kissed me. For the first time in a long time, I didn't mind kissing him back.

"You gon' watch TV all day, or are you gonna get out and do some shopping?" he asked over his shoulder as he walked away. I was still flipping channels when he returned. "Ivy, I know you heard me," he stated firmly.

"I heard you, Storm. I'd love to go shopping, but I don't have any money right now."

"What do you mean you don't have money? Didn't I just give you a paycheck? One you didn't earn?"

"Yes, but you forgot I have to pay child support. Most of my money went there," I lied.

"I know you're lying, but whatever. Here. Go do your damn thing, but stay out of trouble," he said, peeling off several hundred dollar bills.

"What? What kind of trouble do you think I'd get into?"

"Ivy, you know I'm not dumb by a long shot. Just stay on the up-and-up. That's all I'm gonna say."

I wondered if Storm was hinting that I might try to go to the restaurant. Since getting Jaabir's number, I didn't care if I ever went to the restaurant again.

He gave me the money then bent down to kiss me again. We tongued like we'd been away from each other for a while. The thing that broke our kiss was a shocking revelation on the news.

"The body was found last night around eleven o'clock," the female reporter said. We both stared at the screen. A body bag lay near the opened trunk of an Impala. "The man known to this neighborhood as Snowball has been found dead in the back of his trunk. A woman had complained of a stench coming from the car you see over here," she said, pointing, "and as you can see by the orange sticker on the window, the car has been abandoned for quite some time—"

Click. Storm turned the television off. Then turned to walk away.

Chapter 17
Make You Proud

Then next day, Candy came over to chill with me for a while. She and I had become more like sisters, and she even accepted that I didn't want to be sexual with her. She had skills and could please me just as well as Storm, but since she didn't come with the equipment men have between their legs, I felt I might as well be with a man. I've heard of the strap-ons some lesbians use, but being sexual with a woman just wasn't my desire. I didn't know what we'd do if Storm asked for another threesome, but I figured we'd just have to cross that bridge when the time came.

We were sitting around watching television when Candy brought up Jaabir. "So, when's the first date?"

"What first date?"

"Jaabir. And by the way, you're welcomed."

"Oh, Jaabir. I'm sorry. I guess I should've thanked you by now," I said, reaching to hug her. "Thank you, Candy. I can't even tell you how happy I was to hear from him."

"Yeah . . . yeah . . . yeah, how about starting with when the first date is. Or, has it already happened?"

"No. I'm not trying to get me and that man killed," I whispered, looking around.

Candy looked around, too. "What's wrong? Why are you whispering? I thought Stormy left already."

I continued to whisper. "He did, but sometimes he appears as quickly as he disappears. I would hate if he stepped up to the door and heard what I'm about to tell you."

"Well, tell me. You've got me curious now."

"I don't know if I told you, but when I got caught eavesdropping on Storm at the restaurant, I heard him plotting to kill someone."

Candy gasped. "Are you serious? You just thought you heard that." She shook her head.

"Yes, I'm serious, and I know what I'm talking about. The meeting he told you he was having while forcing me to give him head . . . it was about murdering that dude Snowball."

"Oh, shit! I just heard about that on the news last night. He was found in his trunk."

"Shhh . . . yeah," I whispered. "So, there's no telling how Storm would react if he found out about me and Jaabir."

"I know you're scared, but I thought we both agreed that we wouldn't let Storm be the death of us. That nigga got a wife, chicks on the side, businesses, a house, cars, and then some. Do we have to continue letting him dictate how we live? It's your thang . . . do what you wanna do. How would he find out?"

"You forget no one at the restaurant knew about me and Storm. Jaabir could go back bragging about us, and trust me, the word would spread."

"Then you just have to tell Jaabir you're a private person and you don't want your business in the streets. Simple as that."

"A'ight. I hear you. I ain't feeling you, but I hear you."

"Girl, I'm telling you . . . we can be better players than Storm is. Besides, we're on a mission, remember? In six months, Storm won't even know we still exist. By then, you and Jaabir will be happy, together somewhere on vacation with your kids."

"I guess you're right, except I don't know about taking my kids around him then."

"Whatever. I know you get my point though. Now call the man and set something up."

I did as Candy said. I picked up my cell and made a much-needed phone call. I went into the bedroom and closed the door. Candy was my lookout, so I felt comfortable speaking freely.

Jaabir sounded so sexy when he answered.

"Hello, Jaabir?"

"Hello, sunshine. How're you?"

I took a deep breath. "I'm fine. So you knew my number when you saw it on the caller ID, huh?"

"Yes, I did, but I'm also in tune with your lovely voice. It's good to hear from you."

"You make it sound like we didn't talk yesterday."

"Whenever I hear your voice, I get a brand-new refreshing feeling in my stomach. You know what I'm talking about?"

I smiled, thinking of my own butterflies. "Yes, as a matter of fact, I do. Listen, I was just thinking . . . I know I said I'd like to wait a while longer before we go on our first date, but do you mind if I retract that statement?"

"Are you trying to make me smile?" he asked. I didn't respond. "Well, if you are, it's working."

I laughed. "Good. How soon can you be free?"

"Is now too soon?"

"Yes," I said, laughing. "Try again."

"Well, tomorrow's a good day."

"Tomorrow will be fine for me, too. Hold on. I need to get a pen so I can get your address."

"How about I pick you up?"

I knew I couldn't let him pick me up from my place. I took my chances on the first thing that came to mind. "Uhmm . . . no, Jaabir. You stay at home and get dinner ready. I can drive myself."

"Oh . . . okay, well let me know when you're ready to write."

I put him on hold then went to retrieve my purse. I took out a small steno pad and wrote down the directions. We talked for a little bit longer then agreed we would see each other at 7:00 the next evening.

I went back into the living room. Candy had just stepped back into the condo with the mail. "I thought you were looking out for me. What the fuck were you doing outside?"

"Relax. I just stood out for a bit, thinking that if I saw him pull up, I'd go over to the truck and distract him so you'd have more time," she said. "I saw the mailman while I was out there. Here," she said, handing me a letter.

I took the envelope. "What's this? Everything is in my name, but I don't pay the bills here."

"Well, it doesn't look like a bill to me."

Candy was right. The piece of mail was not a bill. It was a letter from my brother. Tears came to my eyes as I stared at the envelope. "It's from my brother." My voice cracked.

"Really?" Candy hesitated as she watched my emotions turn from ecstatic to tearful. "What's wrong, Ivy? Aren't you glad your brother is contacting you?"

"I am, but I'm also afraid he's saying something like stay away from my children. I called and been over to my mother's house a few times since court over a week ago, trying to visit my kids. I just know my mother has Kerry brainwashed, and I don't want this letter to be him telling me to stay away."

Candy patted my back. "Well, how else are you gonna know what the letter says unless you open it?"

Candy took my hand then led me to the couch. After dropping a few tears, I tore the seal from the envelope. Candy patted my back once again. "You can do it," she said.

Candy sat patiently, awaiting my next move. I had to get myself together before unfolding the paper. I wiped my face then took a few deep breaths before reading the letter in silence.

Dear Ivy,

I've missed you, and so have your kids. They ask me about you all the time. I just tell them you're doing fine and that they'll hear from you soon. I'm sorry our mother is so hard on you, but at the same time, I understand her frustration and stubbornness. She wants more from you, and so do I.

You looked great in court. I regret not giving you a hug and telling you how proud I was to see you on your feet. I think grasping that you're really doing okay was a shocker for me. I was a little skeptical about how you managed to be doing so well so fast. But, since then, I've realized that if the judge doesn't have an issue with it, then everything must be legit.

I'm proud of you, sis. You've come a long way since the fire at the apartment. I know I turned my back on you when you needed me most, but I just couldn't stand the thought of you lying to me when all I want to do is help you. I know you say you weren't lying, and perhaps I didn't let you finish explaining, so since you're blood, I think you deserve another chance. I love you, Ivy, and I don't want anything else to come between us.

*Besides, you're about to be an auntie soon.☺Rita's due
in another month or so. You've had three children, so you
know how that is. The doctor will tell you one date, but babies have plans of their own. We don't know the sex yet. We
wanted to wait and be surprised during delivery. I hope
you'll be there, too. You know my cell number, and I haven't
moved. My door has now been reopened. In the meantime,
take care of yourself.*

> *Much love and always your li'l brother,*
> *Kerry*

My heart was overwhelmed with joy. When I started crying again, Candy was confused. "So is it bad news?" she
asked.

"No. He says he misses me and my children do, too."

I cried until my eyes were swollen. Candy held and
rocked me.

"Are you gonna call him?"

"I guess I should, huh?"

"Yeah . . . I mean, you never know. He just might be sitting around waiting for you to call."

I looked at the clock. "He might be getting ready to
take his nap before going to work—"

Candy cut me off. "Why are you making excuses?"

"I am? I don't know. Well, okay. Here goes—" I said, dialing the number.

"Hello," Kerry answered, sounding tired.

"Hi, Kerry. It's me, Ivy."

"Thank goodness you called. I've missed you, sis," he
said, sounding relieved.

"I've missed you, too, li'l bro. We'll talk some more. Go
ahead and get some sleep. I know you've got to be at work
in a bit."

"Listen, I'm sorry—"

"Kerry, don't be," I said, interrupting him. "You had to

go with what you thought was best. The good news for both of us is that we still love each other. I'm just glad you've touched base."

"The kids want to see you. Momma doesn't know about my letter to you, so I'll sneak them out to see you."

"Kerry, they'll probably tell."

"Well, maybe if we happen to be in the same place at the same time . . . you know?"

I smiled. It felt good to know he'd still go out of his way for me. "If you insist. I just don't want to be the cause of things going bad between you and Bessie Mae."

"Everything will be fine. Your children miss you, and I can't in good conscience keep them out of your reach."

"Li'l bro, I can't tell you how you've made my day. I won't hold you. You have my number on your caller ID now, so get some sleep. Call me any time you want."

"I will. Love you, Ivy."

"Love you, too, Kerry."

Chapter 18
Oh, How We Deceive

I put on a pair of jeans and an off-the-shoulder sweater. I wasn't sure if Jaabir and I would go anywhere after dinner at his place, but in case we did, I would be comfortable for the fall coolness that came at night. Storm wasn't at the condo when I left, but he met me as I was leaving the parking lot.

He stopped his truck then leaned out the window. "Where're you headed?" he asked.

"I told you I talked to my brother yesterday. He invited me over for dinner," I lied.

Storm stared at me. "How long do you plan to be over there?"

"Not long."

"You planning on seeing your kids while you're over there?"

"It's possible. He didn't tell me if he had them tonight. I don't know—maybe he's going to surprise me."

Storm stared again. "I'll see you later on."

I waved then drove off. I watched my rearview mirror,

making sure he didn't try to follow me. I hurried onto the interstate, then drove over to Jaabir's house.

His neighborhood was clean and quiet. Though it was dark, I could tell his lawn was neatly manicured. I got out of the car then headed up the driveway. Jaabir met me halfway. He kissed me on the cheek then escorted me into the house.

"Braids, huh?" he asked, pulling on a few strands.

"I know I look different with so much hair, right?"

"You look beautiful."

"Thanks," I said, smiling.

"Did you have trouble getting here?"

"No. Not at all. You give good directions."

"I'm glad to hear it. I was worried you might miss the second turn. The streets in this neighborhood can be confusing at night, especially since many of them share the same forename."

"I noticed that. Why would they name them all Redbird? Redbird Lane, Redbird Cove, Redbird Place, Redbird Circle . . . you think they ran out of Redbirds?"

We laughed as he escorted me to the couch. The smooth sounds of Grover Washington Jr.'s sax were flowing from Jaabir's speakers. I began to sway to the music. "Hey, what do you know about those sounds?" he asked. "You're just a baby."

"You can't be more than thirty yourself, and I know more than you think I know."

"Oh yeah? Well, for your information, I'm thirty-three. And I'm willing to bet you a dollar you don't know whose sound that is."

"Okay . . . bet! That's Grover Washington Jr., and considering that the song that just went off was 'Blues for DP' and the one playing now is 'Soulful Strut,' I'd say the CD is *Grover Washington Jr.—Prime Cuts: The Greatest Hits 1987–1999*. Now whatchu know about that?"

Jaabir smiled and nodded. "Impressive. So I take it you like jazz, huh?"

"That would be correct." I smiled.

"Who introduced you to Grover?"

"My brother, Kerry. I'm not sure how he got into jazz, but he has a massive collection. I can expect to hear Grover Washington Jr. and some other jazz artists any time I ride in his car or visit his home. I use to own a few great CDs before losing everything in a fire."

"I'm sorry to hear that." He reached into his pocket. "I guess I owe you a dollar."

"Save it. Since you were kind enough to go through the trouble of fixing me dinner tonight, I'll let you keep your money." I winked and flashed him a huge smile.

"Well, relax while I go check on things." I watched him as he disappeared into the kitchen.

The aroma was tantalizing. I wanted to get up and follow the smells, but I shook the urge and just waited for Jaabir to return.

"Would you like to have a look around?" he asked, carrying a tray of grilled chicken on skewers.

"Well, I would, but now that you've set this irresistible tray in front of me, I think I'll wait."

He laughed. "Oh, it'll be here when we get back. C'mon." He pulled me up then led me through the house.

Jaabir's decorative taste was masculine and reflected his religious beliefs. I noticed a copy of the Quran displayed in just about every room. I also spotted a couple of prayer rugs during my tour. I couldn't resist questioning him as we chatted over the appetizer and a glass of wine.

"Jaabir, forgive me for asking, but I take it that you're Muslim, right?"

"You don't have to ask for forgiveness, sister. Asking questions is the only way we can truly find out about something we want to know. The answer is yes. Now what gave me away?"

"Well, I kind of thought you might be because of your name. And since coming into your home, I've seen a few things that pretty much confirm it," I said, nodding then taking a sip of merlot.

"Problem?"

"Excuse me?"

"Is there a problem with my religion?"

"No . . . no . . . I was just curious."

"So, where do you go to church?"

"Well, I believe in Jesus Christ."

"I didn't ask you what you believed in. I asked you where you attend church."

I felt embarrassed. I swallowed my last bite of chicken then sighed. "Sorry," I said, reaching for my wine.

"Sister," he said, grabbing my hand, "I don't want you to be sorry or embarrassed by anything you say to me. I'm Jaabir—the same guy you use to smile at and sometimes talk to when you came to work. I respect who you are, your knowledge or lack thereof . . . whichever is fine with me. What you don't know, I will teach you. I'm patient like that." He smiled and stroked his thumb across the back of my hand.

"Okay. Well, I don't attend church at the moment, but I plan to go back soon."

"Really? You ever thought about joining the Nation of Islam?"

I frowned then immediately regretted it as Jaabir's facial expression changed to disappointment. "No. I've never thought about it because it's never been introduced to me."

"That's a fair answer. I'll accept that."

"Right now my mother is bringing my children up as

Baptist." He looked surprised. "Oh, I guess I should've told you by now that I have three children."

"Sister, you don't look like you've had three children. And why does your mother have them?"

"It's a long story, Jaabir. I'm sure we'll get to talk about it one day, but let's just leave it at I'm fighting to regain custody of them. My mother is the reason you saw me so upset in my office that day."

"Oh . . . well, we don't have to talk about it now. We'll come to know a lot about each other as we continue to be friends. Just know that I'm a good listener, and at times, I can offer great advice."

"Thanks, Jaabir. I appreciate that." I set my glass on the coffee table. "I want to ask you what your name means."

"How do you know it has meaning?"

I shrugged. "I just know that every Muslim name I've come across has a special meaning to it. So, what does yours mean?"

"It means comforter or consoler."

My eyes grew large. "Were you born with that name?"

"Yes. Why?"

"From what I can tell so far, your name fits you perfectly. You've been nothing but comforting and consoling since day one."

"Thank you, sister. And if you don't mind, I'd like to call you Zahrah."

My eyebrows rose. "Zahrah," I pronounced. "Why? What does that mean?"

"Because from what I can tell of you, you're a flower," he said, gripping my hand. "You represent beauty . . . a shining star—a far cry from being like a poisonous green leaf in my opinion."

I might've blinked a thousand times, trying to fight back the tears that burned my eyes. "Jaabir, you have such a beautiful spirit . . . I don't know if I could get use to someone as nice as you. If you knew where I've been—"

"Where you've been isn't important to me. I only care about where you're going," he responded, tapping my forehead with his finger.

He got up to check on the rest of the food. When he returned, he invited me to the dining room table. I sat anxiously awaiting the main course. Jaabir placed a delicious-looking plate in front of me, which was dressed with stuffed grilled salmon, garlic mashed potatoes, and green beans. I couldn't wait to dig in.

Jaabir said he couldn't eat the plate he fixed me because of his spiritual beliefs, so he had some more of the grilled chicken skewers on his plate along with vegetables.

"How did you get to be a chef when your faith doesn't allow you to eat certain foods?" I asked.

"You'll come to find that Islamic men are known for doing what we have to do to survive. I happen to love cooking, and it also provides a healthy salary. I can't change your beliefs—at least not tonight," he said, laughing, "but in the meantime, you'll never see me put impurities into my body."

I shrugged. "So, what's inside the salmon?" I asked just before putting another forkful in my mouth.

"Shrimp, crabmeat, and brie cheese. How does it taste?"

The food was so good, I couldn't talk. "Mm," I mumbled, chewing rapidly.

"Slow down," he said, laughing. "There's more for seconds if you want."

I managed to clear my mouth, but not for long. "Good, because I just might have to take you up on that offer."

We finished dinner then sat on the couch to chat some more. "What do you do in your spare time, Zahrah?"

I almost forgot that he was talking to me. My new name

was going to take some getting use to. "Oh, um . . . well, I like to shop."

"As most women do," he said teasingly. "But seriously . . . do you have another hobby? Do you read, play chess, or work out?"

I frowned at all of his suggestions. "Jaabir, everything you just named are hobbies men like."

"I beg to differ. I know several women who like to read. Are you telling me that you don't?"

I shook my head. "I guess I've never been introduced to a book that could hold my attention."

Jaabir got up and went over to his built-in bookcases then returned with a book. "You've said twice tonight that you need someone to initiate things for you. Let me be the first to introduce you to reading. Here's one I think you'll find entertaining and educational at the same time. It's set back in time, but promise me you'll give it a try. I think you'll be glad you did."

I took the book from his hand then glanced at the cover. Besides the lime-green color that outlined the paperback book, the young girl in the picture caught my attention. "*In Search of Satisfaction* by J. California Cooper," I said, reading the title aloud. "You've read this?"

"I sure did. It's the only fictional paperback book I've read more than once."

"Sounds deep. I'll make you a promise: I'll give it a try."

"Great. That's what I wanted to hear."

"Now tell me what you like to do. I take it you're a reader, a chess player, and you work out."

He laughed. "Yes, I do all of the above, but what I really enjoy the most is riding my motorcycle."

"You have a motorcycle?"

"Yes. You wanna see it?"

"Sure."

We got up then went into his garage. The moment he turned on the light, his shiny red and black bike seemed to wink at me. "Wow," I said, stepping closer to the motorcycle. "How long have you had it?"

"A year, but this is actually my second Ninja. I sold the first one to get this one," he said, rubbing the seat. "How about we go for a ride tonight?"

"Who me? Ride on this thing?"

"Yes . . . it'll be fun. C'mon."

"I'm sorry, Jaabir. I don't think I could enjoy myself on one of these," I said, pointing. "I don't have on the right top. The ride will probably be too windy, plus I'm not really a fan of high speed."

"Well, listen. How about I get you one of my long-sleeved sweatshirts to go under your jacket, and then I'll take you more on a low-speed ride."

I laughed. "You're silly. There's no such thing as a low-speed ride, but you almost make it sound tempting."

"Are you really scared, or is there something else going on with you?"

He confused me. We stared into each other's eyes for a minute. "Jaabir, I'm really scared."

"Don't be," he said, cupping my hand. "I want you to trust me. If you know there's no such thing as a low-speed ride, then trust that I'll create one—just for you."

I caved in like a wimp. "Okay, Jaabir," I sang, staring into his eyes.

He retrieved a sweatshirt, and then we were off. He did just what he said. People seemed to be staring at us as we cruised the streets of Memphis, never picking up speed of more than forty miles per hour. I held on to his waist for dear life. I'm sure he threw his bike into shock, traveling for an hour at such a low speed. Despite my previous precautions, I enjoyed myself.

"That was great," I said, taking off my helmet after we returned to his house.

"See. I told you. Maybe next time you'll let me increase the speed by five miles per hour."

"Hmm . . . at the rate you're going, you might just talk me into ten more miles per hour."

"Well, that wouldn't be a bad thing." We laughed our way back into the living room. "More wine?" Jaabir asked.

I looked at my watch then noticed it was ten-thirty. I wasn't ready to leave, so I figured what could half an hour or so hurt. "Sure. I don't mind if I do," I responded.

One glass turned into another and then another. Two hours later, I woke up to my cell phone vibrating on my hip. I glanced at the caller ID and noticed it was Storm. I debated whether to answer it then decided against it.

Soft music was still playing, but I didn't see Jaabir anywhere. I stepped into the hallway and headed toward the room he'd said was his bedroom. When I got in there, he was rising from his prayer rug. He turned and noticed me.

"Hi, Zahrah."

"I didn't mean to disturb you," I said, leaning on the door frame.

"You didn't disturb me. I was finished. Did you get a good nap?"

"Yes. I actually did. I'm going to head home now."

He walked closer to me. "You've had quite a bit to drink. You shouldn't be driving. Besides, it's late."

"Thanks, Jaabir, but I'll be fine."

I started toward the living room to retrieve my purse. My cell began to vibrate again. I noticed it was Storm. I wanted to answer, but my first mind kept telling me not to deal with him right then. *What if he knows I haven't been over to my brother's house?* I thought. *Don't answer him now. He might need time to cool off.*

"You got everything?" Jaabir asked. "The book I gave you, too?"

"Yes, I've got it in my purse." I walked toward the door then paused. "On second thought, Jaabir . . . I am feeling tired. If you don't mind, can I sleep on your couch?"

He shook his head. "Nobody sleeps on my couch. I have a guest room you can have for tonight."

I smiled. "Thanks."

Once in the bedroom, Jaabir offered me some night clothes and towels. "Here's a T-shirt you might find comfortable, and in case you want to use the shower in your room, here are some towels."

"Wow. You're too kind. Thanks, Jaabir."

I couldn't resist utilizing my temporary space and freedom he'd offered me. I went into the shower and turned the water on. Steam filled the bathroom pretty quickly before I had a chance to get in. Once in, I tilted my head back and let the hot water dance on my scalp and drench my braids. I had just removed my head from under the water when I heard Jaabir enter the bathroom.

"Jaabir," I called.

He opened the glass shower door and stood nude, staring at me. He looked so damn sexy with his dreads pulled back and off his shoulders in a ponytail. His eyes seemingly wanted approval to join me. I nodded then he hesitated no longer, stepping into the dense steam. He grabbed my towel and soap then washed me gently from head to toe. He took the soap bar then bathed himself. I stood patiently, awaiting his next move.

He put the soap back into the holder then met his lips with mine. He examined my body with his hands as he kissed me nonstop. I took the opportunity to be touchy-feely with him, too.

His arms were hard like bricks, and his chest was solid. His abs felt like steel, but the scary thing was that his dick did, too. I gasped then looked down. I kept playing around with it, trying to figure out if it was real. Not only was it hard, but it was bigger than anything I'd ever had. When I traced my eyes back up toward his, he had a look of lust in them.

"I want you," he said. "May I have you?"

Lord knows I wanted to have him, too, but I couldn't help feeling I shouldn't be so willing after only one date. Part of working on a new me was to grow and learn from previous mistakes. I worried that having sex with Jaabir so soon would be a detrimental move toward having a meaningful relationship. I hesitated before answering him.

"I'd like to, Jaabir . . . but . . . but . . . I don't want you to think less of me afterwards."

"Never," he said, kissing my fingers.

I sighed. "I can't sleep with you tonight Jaabir. Wouldn't that make me a whore?"

"No," he said, fondling my breasts.

I looked into his eyes. "What would it make me?"

"Mine." His soapy hands continued to knead my breasts.

"Do you have condoms?"

"Yes."

Aw, hell, I thought. *Who am I kidding?* "Then I'm yours." I kissed him then rinsed myself.

Jaabir turned off the water then opened the shower door. When I got out and went into the bedroom, I heard my phone vibrating on the bed. I picked it up, turned it off then put it on the dresser. Jaabir walked up behind me then dried me off. He led me to sit on the bed then asked me to lie back. I stared at the muscle between his legs and noticed there was no condom.

"Where's your condom?" I asked.

He produced a condom from the nightstand drawer then set it on the bed next to me. "Relax," he said, pushing me back.

He spread my legs then surprised me as he made his wet, warm tongue explore my insides. Given how much pleasure I was experiencing, I doubted seriously that he was only using his tongue, so I rose a bit to watch. I was shocked to see that his fingers had nothing to do with the pleasure I was getting. His hands held my thighs apart as he snaked his tongue in and out of me, around my clit and then back inside me again, traveling deeper into me with each repetition.

"Aaaahhh," I moaned. "Aaaaahhh, Jaabir, you gon' make me cummmm," I screamed as I climaxed.

He wouldn't stop, causing me to climb to the head of the bed, penning me. I clamped my legs over his head, yet he still wouldn't stop. I squirmed and squirmed until I was hanging headfirst off the side of the bed, yet he still wouldn't stop. Jaabir seized the opportunity to lick me more, sliding his tongue into my ass. I thought I was gonna do my first backflip off the bed, but he had me, and I wasn't going anywhere.

By my third orgasm, Jaabir finally cut me some slack. I lay on the bed weak and limp. He turned me over then put on the condom before working himself into me. He filled my walls and damn near touched my back as he repeatedly thrust himself into me. He sexed me for about an hour, which was about fifty-nine minutes too long for a man of his stature as far as I was concerned. But, if it had to be anybody, I was glad it was him. He didn't have to worry. I knew if Storm didn't kill me first, I would be back.

Chapter 19
The Morning After

Morning came quicker than I had wanted. My time with Jaabir had been refreshing, and it felt good to have him hold me through the night. I eased out of bed then went to the shower. I stood under the water nearly thirty minutes, thinking about how much I wanted Jaabir. I thought about how wonderful it would be to claim a caring man like him. He was very attentive to my needs, be they sexual or otherwise. I felt safe with him, and I felt like I could love him, but I had a serious problem—Storm. I knew that even if Storm and I separated, there was no way I could live happily with Jaabir. As soon as Storm found out, he would make life hard for us. He'd say I had been screwing around with Jaabir all along.

When I got out of the shower, Jaabir sat up in bed. "I didn't know you had gotten up," he said.

"Yeah . . . I'm pretty sensitive to light. The sun peeped through the blinds and tapped me on the forehead." I laughed.

Jaabir smiled. "Got time for breakfast? I make a mean omelet."

His offer was tempting, but I knew I needed to leave. I picked up my phone then turned it on. After noticing the time, I had to decline. "Um, actually, I should get going. I promised a friend of mine I'd meet her this morning, and I need to get changed," I lied.

"Well, if you insist. I sure wish there was something I could do to change your mind. I don't have to be at the restaurant until noon."

My phone began to vibrate. I looked at the caller ID and noticed it was Candy. "No . . . sorry . . . she's calling me now. Excuse me a minute," I said, pressing the talk button. "Hey, girl, what's up?"

"You," she said.

"Not really, but I'll explain on my way," I responded.

"You need to get your ass home, Ivy. I'm worried for you."

"That's cool," I said, trying to play off my conversation with her. "I'm on my way now. I'll hit you back in a minute." I closed the flip on my phone then turned toward Jaabir and shrugged. "I wish I had more time, Jaabir, but maybe you'll let me come back and make it up to you."

He smiled. "You bet I will," he said, getting out of bed. "Just let me help you get dressed."

After sliding on my jeans, Jaabir helped me put on my boots. I was in awe at his kindness. "I still don't understand why there's no lucky woman in your life."

"Perhaps I've been waiting on you," he said, zipping up my boot.

"That's sweet of you to say, but I'm serious. Why in the world is a loving man like you single? Or is there someone in your life you haven't told me about?"

He stood, walked over to his dresser then pulled out a pair of sweats. He put one leg into his pants then looked at me. "That's a long story. You'll have to come back when you have more time for me to share it with you."

"Isn't there a short version? I'm curious. Where is the woman in your life?"

He slid a T-shirt over his head then stood in front of me with his hands on his hips. "I wish I knew her whereabouts. I still love her, and I probably always will, but it's time for me to move on," he said, pulling me off the bed.

We headed toward the front door. "Jaabir, you're leaving me hanging here. What are you talking about? Who is this woman?"

He stopped before we were outside the door, squeezed my hand then pulled it to his lips and kissed it. "Since you must know, we were happy together for three years then she met a woman who became a negative influence by introducing her to crack cocaine." He looked down and sighed before continuing. "I struggled for a year, trying to help her get clean, and then she up and turned to the streets. She use to come back here from time to time, asking for food and money, but I haven't seen her in almost two years now. Her family says she's still alive, but I never see her."

We walked toward my car. "I'm sorry to hear about your loss, Jaabir. I can imagine your pain feels like the death of a loved one."

"You're right. Sometimes I think I would be better off knowing she was dead. At least, I wouldn't have her well-being on my mind so much." He kissed my hand again. "Enough about that—I said it's time for me to move on. I think I've found someone to move forward with." He smiled.

I reached and threw my arms around his neck. We hugged for several minutes then I gave him a soft peck on the lips.

"That hug was heartfelt. This won't be your last time seeing me, will it?" he asked pleadingly.

I raised my eyebrows. "Are you kidding me? I had a wonderful night with you. You cooked for me, took me on a thrill ride, and then rocked my world before I went to sleep. What woman wouldn't come back for more—" I cut myself off, remembering the love of his life still hadn't returned. "I mean . . . I'll be back."

He looked weary. "Zahrah, are you sure?" I dropped my head, thinking I should tell him about Storm and me. I wanted to be honest with him, considering he'd had his heart broken before and didn't need to get caught up in my mess. He called out to me several more times. "Zahrah . . . what's wrong?" he asked.

I inhaled the morning air then released an intense sigh. "Only death will keep me from here," I replied.

He smiled and let out a chuckle, seemingly relieved to finally get a response. He pulled me back into his arms. "Glad to hear it, Zahrah . . . glad to hear it."

I stepped back from our embrace then kissed his lips again before getting into my car. He watched as I drove off. As soon as I was out of his sight, I called Candy. "Candy, what's up?" I asked just after she answered.

"Bitch, are you crazy?" she snapped.

"What? Huh?"

"Don't what and huh me. Stormy is gon' beat the fire out of your ass when you get here."

"Are you at the condo?"

"Yeah, I'm here. Stormy called me over to his house last night because he had his son, and he wanted us to meet him. We watched movies pretty late then I got his key and came over to the condo to sleep."

"So, where is Storm now?"

"He's on his way. I suggest you get your ass home before he does."

"Don't worry. I'm on my way."

When I pulled into the parking lot and saw Storm's truck, I prayed for mercy. I couldn't get out of my car before talking to God. I knew Candy was there, but with it being so early, I knew this would probably not be one of the times when she could save me.

I stuck my key into the door then put on my acting face. I pranced into the condo like nothing was wrong. No one was in the living room, so I headed for the kitchen where I heard dishes being dropped into the sink.

"Good morning, all," I said, turning the corner.

"Morning," Candy said.

I noticed a young boy sitting at the table. "Well, who do we have here?"

"Ivy, this is my son, Terrance Daniels. We call him Teddy," Storm said, running his hand down the boy's coal-black, wavy hair, which was pulled back into a ponytail.

He looked like a young Storm. The close resemblance was amazing. If I didn't know any better, I would've said Storm birthed Teddy all by himself. I didn't see a thing on the boy's body that didn't look like Storm.

"Teddy, I'm Ivy. How are you doing?"

"Fine," he said rather short.

He sat, staring at the floor as if he didn't want to be there. I tried to think of some questions that would make him feel comfortable. "Are you hungry?"

"I've already eaten."

"Well, good. I'm starving. I hope you saved me something to eat."

"Isn't this your house?" he asked.

"Yeah. Why do you ask?"

"Then you ought to know if you've got something to eat in there," he responded, being sassy.

Storm squeezed his shoulder. "Teddy, c'mon now, man. Lighten up. Ivy's just a friend. Ain't nobody here tryna take your momma's place."

I fixed me a piece of toast. "So, how old are you, Teddy?" I asked.

"Ten. I'll be eleven January second."

"Well, that's not far from now, young man. What're you gonna do for your birthday?"

"I don't know. I'll probably get my dad to take me to Las Vegas or something."

Storm nearly choked on his juice. "Man, what are you gonna do in Vegas?"

"I don't know, Dad. But, there's got to be something a kid can do there. You're the man, Dad. You can figure it out."

I buttered my toast then excused myself from the kitchen—bad decision. Storm followed me into the living room.

"Hey," he said. I stopped and waited for him to raise his hand. "Where were you last night?"

"I told you I was going to—"

Storm interrupted me. "Think . . . before you speak. If you lie to me, the consequences will be severe. Now finish."

I didn't know what Storm might've known, so I struggled with finishing my statement. "I, um . . . I . . . I um—"

"Hey, Dad," Teddy interrupted, walking into the living room. *Whew! Saved by Mini-me,* I thought. "Candy was telling me about this new arcade place. Can we go?"

Storm never took his eyes off me. "Yeah, but give me a minute," he answered.

"Aw, Dad, let's go now," Teddy whined.

Storm fussed. "A'ight. Go get your stuff, man." Teddy walked off then Storm turned back to me. "This ain't over."

Storm and Teddy left the condo. Candy came out of the kitchen and shook her head at me.

"Thank goodness that kid was here or else your ass might've been grass," she said.

"Yeah, tell me about it." I rolled my eyes. "He asked me where I was last night, but I don't know what to tell him."

"Why?"

"'Cause he acts like he knows something. I wonder if he knows where my brother lives. Perhaps he knows I wasn't over there."

"I doubt it. Even if he does know something, your ass needs to deny, deny, deny. You better not confess the truth. He's probably gonna beat your ass anyway it goes, so if it comes up again, lie between every slap. Don't own up to shit."

"Yeah, you're right."

"Oh, and the party is tonight at Storm's house."

I was shocked. I didn't even know if I was ready for another one of Storm's parties. "Damn. That was quick."

"I told you he likes to keep a lot of people around. You're just getting hip to what all he does. So are we ready? He wants us there by eleven o'clock."

I sighed. "I guess I'm as ready as I have to be."

"Hold up. You're not getting shaky on me, are you?"

"I'll admit, I'm nervous as hell, but I want this money, so I say let's do this."

Candy gave me a high five. "That's what I'm talking about."

Chapter 20
Show Time

Storm told us where he had left some money in the condo for us to get dolled up for the party. Candy and I went to buy me a costume. After perusing a few lingerie shops, we went to Party City and ultimately decided on a Catwoman costume because it would take longer to get out of, giving Candy more time to disappear with the money then make it back to Storm's house.

I bagged my outfit then pinned my hair up so that I could easily fit the hooded part of my costume over my head when the time came. Candy and I selected the music we thought best then she showed me a few moves to drive the men wild. We practiced for nearly an hour then I showered and put on my favorite pair of Baby Phat jeans and a fitted sweater top that cropped above the navel.

"You look great," Candy said then whistled.

I laughed. "Thanks, girl. You do, too. That sequin belt looks good with that spandex dress."

"Thanks," she said, rubbing the belt. "I kinda thought so myself."

We jumped into my car then headed toward Storm's house. Candy asked me to take a detour about three streets over from our turn.

"Look," Candy said, pointing as I drove, "here's the spot where I told you I would be dropping the money off until later," she said.

"Candy, that's a place of business, and it's closed. How will you be getting in there?"

"This is Tony, my friend's recording studio, and it's close enough to Storm's house so I'd get back quick. I told him I needed to get in late tonight for some studio time. He gave me the key. Girl, he thinks I can sing," she said, stroking her throat. "He knows talent when he hears it." She laughed. I shook my head then drove off. "Anyway, I might have to make it up to him later, but right now all that matters is I have the key. There's no alarm code to have to figure out, and there aren't any surveillance cameras."

"What if he goes to the studio in the morning and finds the money?"

"He won't. He doesn't open the studio on Sundays. I'll have our dough and his key back to him before Monday."

"Okay, let's do this." We tapped our fists together.

When I pulled up to Storm's house, Candy slowed me down. "Wait," she said. "We shouldn't park where he can see our car. I'm gonna have to crawl out of here to avoid surveillance, so go down a bit and park in front of those cars up there."

"Good thinking."

We walked up the street to Storm's house and rang the doorbell. A man was standing at the door, apparently waiting for visitors. He opened the door immediately after the first ring. We walked into a crowded, noisy house of men.

All of them seemed to be drinking, and when Candy and I walked in, they raised their glasses to us, screaming cheers.

"Which one of us is gonna lay down with these mutha-fuckers," I whispered.

"Well, hopefully it won't come to that tonight. You just make sure you shake your ass long and hard enough to keep them distracted from what I'm doing. If you can do that, I'll step up to go in the bedroom."

I took a deep breath. "Okay," I said, sighing.

Storm stepped over to us. "What's up, ladies?"

"We're cool," Candy said. I seconded her comment.

"C'mere. I wanna holla at you." He led us to the bed-room where Candy and I slept last time. "So, y'all know the business, right?"

I spoke up. "Storm, I'm dancing tonight. Candy had her turn already. I wanna make the loot this time. Plus, she's already agreed to stand down this go 'round."

He looked at Candy and she nodded. He placed his hand on my shoulder. "I guess the men will be excited to see something different tonight, so that's not a bad idea. Well, the floor is all yours, kid. Are you ready?"

"I've got my outfit right here," I said, pulling it out of the bag.

"Cool. You've got music?"

"Right here," Candy said, handing him the CD.

"A'ight. Ivy, send Candy to tell me when you're ready." He bounced out of there, seemingly happier than a six-year-old with a lollipop.

I got dressed then said a prayer. I had opened the bed-room door and heard the roaring of the men. I knew I would need protection from above to get me through.

Storm made his fancy announcement then I began a se-ductive Catwoman routine to the tune of "I'm in Love with a Stripper" remix. I looked at Candy, and she was be-hind a group of men, trying to remain low-key. I just danced without taking off anything the first time the song played. The men all cheered me on. By the time the song repeated, I pulled one of the men onto the floor with me and used him as a pole. When the song said, "she climbing that pole and she . . ." I was up and down the man like a snake.

The crowd went wild. Even Storm seemed shocked by my skills. He winked and gave me a thumbs-up. I laid the man down on the floor then rolled my stuff all over his face, avoiding his lips. He kept trying to lick me, but I didn't want his tongue to touch me. I didn't know where his tongue had been, and for all I knew, he had herpes in his mouth or something. After having my way with him, I was on to the next man who flashed Ulysses or Benjamin at me.

The song played about three more times, and I was out of everything except for my thong. My braids had come down and swung freely as I continued my routine. I had money hanging from my pouch, my thong, and in my hands. I began to get nervous because I hadn't seen Candy yet. I wanted to ask Storm to hold my money, but I was afraid he would wonder why Candy hadn't helped and notice her missing, so I danced on and on.

Storm started the song over then yelled, "Final time."

I still didn't see Candy, and I panicked because the men wanted me to take off my thong. I began collecting the money from my thong then out of nowhere Candy appeared to help me. I felt so much better. Once she had all my money in hand, I took off the thong then rolled all over the floor, pretending to be masturbating. I was relieved to finally hear the song go off. Storm coerced the crowd into giving me a second hand. Some of them threw more money at me. I happily picked it up then headed to the bedroom with Candy.

Even with the door closed, I could still hear the men

roaring. I had put on quite a show. Candy even complimented me.

"I taught you a little something, and now I believe you got me beat with shaking whatcha momma gave ya." She laughed. "I think I came back just in time. One more pop-shake like that, and your ass would've been up for auction. Did you see how surprised Storm seemed at you?"

"Yeah, I saw his face. He even threw me a thumbs-up. He's gonna want me to do this shit again . . . I just know it."

"Well, you can't deny that it pays well."

"Shit, I'm just glad no one asked for VIP privileges," I said, making quotes with my fingers.

"I know that's right. Let's keep our fingers crossed." Candy spread the money on the bed and began separating it by like bills.

I helped her. "Damn, these niggas don't mind breaking off some loot, do they?"

"That's why I volunteered last time. Hell, I've seen how much cash they spend when they party," she said, waving a stack of fifties.

"Mmph . . . mmph . . . mmph." I shook my head. "This is a lot of money, but nothing compared to what our total balance is for tonight, right?"

"Right," Candy said, licking her fingers to make sure the money wasn't sticking together as she counted.

I waited for more response, but Candy was focused as she counted. "So?" I asked.

"So what?"

"So . . . how did it go?"

"Oh, I ran into a few minor issues, but everything worked out." She spoke rather quickly.

My heart began to pound. "A few minor issues? What kind of issues? Were you able to get the money?"

"Yeah, I got it."

"Did anybody see you?"

"No. You had them niggas wrapped up. Nobody saw me going or coming. Don't worry. We're straight."

I felt a bit of relief since she was confident, so I continued to help count the money. By the time we had all of the money separated, Storm busted into the room in a rage.

"Get y'all asses out here now! Some muthafucker done robbed me, and I want everybody in one room until we finish viewing the videotapes."

Candy and I looked at each other in shock. I grabbed the jeans I came over in then began to put them on. Storm stepped back into the room, screaming. "Now, got-damnit. Ain't nobody safe until I find my muthafucking money."

I had to go into the living room with just my jeans on. Candy stood next to me, shaking. I really became nervous, too. "What happened?" I whispered. "How did he miss the money so fast?"

"I don't know," she whispered back.

"You said there were problems. What kind?"

"He had locked his bedroom door, so I had to pick it. I tried to close it back, but it wouldn't close all the way since the lock was broken." She hushed when a man was shoved near us by one of Storm's boys.

Storm came through yelling. "I don't wanna hear a muthafucker breathe. Don't let me see anybody's goddamned mouth moving. My boys are viewing the tapes, and then they're going on the grounds to look for anything suspicious. Nobody's leaving until my money reappears. And I ain't talking out of the side of my neck either. I mean that shit."

My heart was beating so loud, I thought it could be heard in the next room. We were all bunched up in the living room while Storm paced, waving his gun, and waiting for some type of reply. He had plenty of backup, too. Four other men waved guns around and watched people.

I feared Candy had been caught on surveillance, trying to get out.

I thought about what my brother would think once he found out about my true lifestyle and how I got killed. I wondered what he and my mother would tell my children about me when they got old enough. I didn't want to die—not that day, and not for being stupid.

An hour later, Drake and Bling stepped into the living room, shaking their heads. "What's up?" Storm asked, frowning. "Don't tell me you still ain't seen shit . . . I'm telling you . . . we gon' be here 'til doomsday until my money shows up or we find out what nigga broke into my room. What's up?"

"Nothing on surveillance, boss," Bling said. "But we found something you need to see. Come out here for a minute."

Storm instructed his men in the living room to hold things down then went outside. My heart rate picked up even more. "What is it?" I whispered to Candy. She shrugged then grabbed my hand and squeezed it.

I wanted to cry, but I couldn't because tears would've surely been an admission of some kind of guilt. Candy began to bite her nails, something I'd never seen her do. I wondered what had she done. She seemed awfully nervous to be the same woman who was extremely confident just over an hour before about having not been seen by anyone.

When Storm returned, he had several pieces of his clothing in his hands. He dropped them then waited for Drake and Bling to step over and grab a man sitting on the couch. Storm smacked him across the face with his gun. The crowd grunted. I jumped, damn near pissing on myself as I saw blood splatter across the couch.

"Where the fuck is my money?" he asked the man.

The man was dazed. He didn't seem coherent, but Storm grabbed him by his collar and yelled at him some more. It took the man a minute, but he finally responded. "What the fuck are you talking about, Storm? Why'd you hit me like that, man? I don't have your money."

"Oh, you wanna play dumb?" Storm taunted. He thrust his fist into the man's stomach. "Huh?" He hit him in the face. "You wanna play dumb?"

The man could hardly speak. "Storm . . . I swear . . . I don't know what you're talking about. You know I never left here. I was here . . . watching the show with everybody else. C'mon, man. Let me go."

"All I want is my money. If I don't get it, you gon' pay with your life. If you didn't take it, tell me who did."

The man pleaded. "I don't know. Storm, I swear. I don't know."

"Everybody, get the fuck out." Storm had turned a shade of red I hadn't seen before. "Now!"

Candy ran to the back room. I didn't know if Storm wanted us out of the house or not, so I followed Candy. She met me coming up the hall. "I've got all the money you made tonight. Let's go," she said, handing me a top and my coat.

"Where's my shoes?" I asked.

"Fuck 'em. We've got to go," she whispered.

When we headed back through the living room, everyone was gone except for all of Storm's boys. The man was on the floor, motionless while Storm repeatedly played kickball with his head.

I didn't say a word until we got into the car. I waited until I looked in the backseat and all around us to make sure no one was near. I began yelling at Candy.

"What the fuck happened? Where did those clothes come from?" Tears streamed down my face.

"I couldn't sit in the room and empty those pockets, so I went outside. I wrapped one of Storm's socks around each knee and elbow so I could crawl, but I couldn't take all of the clothes with me. I had to ditch 'em. That man's car happened to be unlocked. I didn't know Storm would miss his money so soon. I was just trying to cover our asses as much as I could."

"*Oh my God,* Candy," I screamed. "That man is good as dead, you know that?" She looked panicky. I continued to scream. "*Oh my God!*"

Chapter 21
Unexpected Backfire

Candy and I had trouble sleeping. We were in the room we shared with Storm, lying across the bed. We woke up every time we thought we heard a noise, be it loud or soft. For the first time since I'd known her, Candy showed some real emotions. She cried in between dreams. Every time she turned over, she'd begin sobbing and apologizing for the harm she'd caused the innocent man.

"I should've just left the clothes spread across the lawn. I didn't know they would look on the floor of his car," she cried in her sleep.

I patted her back, then shed a few tears myself. My gut feeling told me that Storm wouldn't let the man live, but I could only hope for the best.

Candy and I were up before sunrise. We sat in the living room, watching a Lifetime movie, wondering where Storm was and if he'd come to the condo any time soon. Once the movie went off, it was 6:00 in the morning. I changed the station and stopped when I saw the weatherman giving tidbits of what was to come with the weather.

"Stay tuned for more weather details. Heather . . . now back to you," he said.

"Thanks, Ron. And now for our top story this morning," Heather said. "A man was found dead downtown near the Mississippi River around three o'clock this morning. Police say it appears the man had been severely beaten and shot execution style before being placed into his car then pushed toward the water. The car had apparently stopped rolling, leaving the front end submerged halfway into the river when police discovered it a few hours ago—" she continued.

When news cameras flashed shots of the car partially underwater, Candy started crying. "That's the car, isn't it?" I asked.

She couldn't talk, so she nodded. I turned off the television and sat, rocking her. "C'mon now. We've got to stop all this crying before Storm comes in and catches us," I pleaded. "Please, Candy. I don't want him to see us like this. We've got to be strong. I've already told God how sorry we are. We've just got to work on being strong, okay?"

She stopped sobbing then began wiping her face. "Turn on a comedy or something. I've got to get this off my mind," she said. "You're right. The last thing we need is for Storm to see us looking guilty."

"I've got about fifteen thousand saved in the bank, but even after we split what we stole from Storm, it won't be enough to bounce. Besides, we've got to stick around a while longer anyway because we've got to make sure we don't look guilty about anything."

"I know. Let's chill. The perfect opportunity will come, and we'll know when the time is right."

I nodded then turned the TV back on. Around 8:00, I began to develop an appetite, so I went into the kitchen to fix breakfast. Candy fell asleep on the couch.

Fifteen minutes later, I heard someone entering the

apartment, and I knew it had to be Storm. I went to peep at him. He looked disoriented as he stood over the couch, watching Candy sleep. He looked up at me then nodded in a "good morning" type of way. His son stepped into the condo and spoke.

"Hi, Ms. Ivy," Teddy said, closing the door behind him.

"Good morning, Teddy. I'm making breakfast. Are you hungry?"

"No, ma'am," he responded.

"Storm? What about you?"

"Naw. I'm good."

Candy finally woke up after she heard us talking. She sat up on the couch, trying to shake off her sleep.

"Y'all slept in those clothes last night?" Storm asked.

"Yeah. We fell asleep watching TV," I said, heading back into the kitchen.

Storm followed me then sat down on one of the stools at the breakfast bar. I poured him some black coffee. "Thanks," he said after I handed it to him.

"You're welcomed. How are you doing this morning?"

"I'm all right . . . I guess." He looked dazed.

"Wanna talk?"

"Not really. Do you?"

I put down my spatula and turned off the sausages. I walked over and put my arms around him. Surprisingly, he hugged me back and kissed my forehead. I figured I better act like I cared about what happened the night before, so he wouldn't get any suspicions about me or Candy being involved.

"You scared me last night. I've seen you angry before, but you were in a rage."

"I can't accept people fucking with my money, Ivy."

"I'm not saying that you should, baby. I was just worried about you. Candy and I were hoping you'd come over so we could take care of you," I lied.

"Hmph. That would've been nice. Maybe tonight, li'l sexy," he said solemnly.

Storm looked like something was bothering him. I wondered if he had a conscience about having something to do with that man's murder. "You don't look good," I said. "Something else bothering you?"

"Yeah. I wish I could tell you what it is. Truth is, I don't know what's bothering me. I just feel something ain't right."

"Now you're really scaring me. What are you saying?"

"I'm saying that usually when I feel like this, either there's a snake around me and/or some dirt is about to go down."

I didn't know what else to say. His comments made me nervous. I began to fear there was a loophole in me and Candy's scheme and that Storm would figure out our guilt. He'd never expressed insecure feelings before, and I wondered if his instincts were tied to me and Candy's deceit. I took my arms from around him and headed to the stove.

"Gotta get these sausages out of the skillet before they're too greasy to eat," I said.

I fixed two plates then called Candy in to eat. She came into the kitchen looking sluggish. Storm noticed her demeanor, and he didn't seem to like it too much. "Damn, kid. You look like shit," he said.

She slowly turned her head toward him. "Gee, thanks," she slurred.

"What's up? I don't remember ever seeing you look so down," he continued to question.

"I'm cool," she replied. "Just tired." She shook her head as she sat at the table.

I added my two cents. "I just think you're getting two old for all these late nights, kid. I already told Storm how we tried to wait up on him. Didn't we?"

She nodded. "Mm-hmm."

I set a cup of coffee in front of her. She poured a couple of packets of Sweet'n Low in it then began to stir it in what seemed like slow motion. Storm got down off the stool then walked over and stood over her. Candy never looked up. The whole scenario made me tense.

"Candy, wake up," I screamed.

"I wanna know what the fuck is wrong with her," Storm said, staring at Candy. "She doesn't look sleepy to me. She looks depressed. What the fuck has she got to be depressed about?"

"Storm, she ain't depressed," I quickly said. "She hit the vodka bottle too hard last night while we were waiting up on you."

He never looked at me. He just kept staring at Candy as she sat slumped at the table with one hand up to her head. Teddy walked in, sniffing.

"Ms. Ivy, did you make an extra sausage? They sure do smell good." He smiled and rubbed his stomach.

"I sure did, Teddy. Hold on. Let me get you a plate."

I pulled two more plates out of the cabinet then handed one to Teddy. I walked over to Storm then nudged him on the arm with the other, hoping to take his focus off Candy. "Here," I said. "You might as well sit down and eat, too."

My cell began to ring in the living room. Storm finally looked up at me. "Is that your phone?"

"Yeah, I'll get it." I set the plate on the table then headed for the living room.

Storm followed me. "No. Let me get it," he said, pulling me back.

My heart almost jumped out of my chest. I had logged Jaabir's number into my phone as TOOKIE, trying to disguise his number. I knew even if the caller ID didn't reveal who was on the other line, Jaabir's voice would be a dead giveaway. I prayed he wouldn't ask to speak to me. Storm picked up my phone then stared at me as he answered.

"Hello," he said. "Hello . . . who's there? Hello," he continued to say several more times. "I said who is this?" He paused then closed the flip then walked toward me.

I was about as scared as a man sitting in the electric chair, awaiting execution. I tried to control my breathing as I nearly let my nerves succumb me. Storm had the same evil look on his face that he did the day he nearly ran me over in the street. When he stood over me, I had to keep my composure because I felt faint.

"Who was it, Storm?" I asked in a calm tone.

He tilted his head then frowned even more. "I don't know. Why don't you tell me, Ivy?"

I wondered if the person had said anything to Storm. I played it off. "Storm, how would I know? You were the one who answered the phone."

"Who did you give your number to? Last I remember, only me and Candy were calling this cell."

I shook my head. "Right, but—" I was interrupted by my phone ringing.

My heart dropped in my stomach. Candy came into the living room, looking at me with worry on her face. Storm stared at the caller ID. I attempted to shame him into giving me the phone. "Storm, let me answer it," I said pleadingly. "Why do you bother with me if you don't trust me? Besides, Teddy is in the other room. Don't make a scene." I reached for the phone, but he slapped my hand down.

"This is the same mutherfucker calling back," he said, looking at the screen. "I guess he figured he had the wrong number the first time. Let me see if he'll talk now." He pressed the talk button then put the phone to his ear. "Yeah," he screamed. There was a short pause then Storm screamed some more. "Nigga, who the fuck are you?"

I thought I was going to pee on myself. I waited for Storm's next response, but instead of him saying something, he calmly handed me the phone. I stood still, thinking he was about to tag me as soon as I answered the call. I looked at Candy then back at Storm. "You want me to answer it?" I asked.

He nodded. "It's for you."

Teddy walked into the room. Confident that Storm wouldn't hit me, I answered the call. "Hello?"

"Big sis, are you okay? That dude sounds mean," Kerry said.

I wanted to break down and let the praises go up. "Kerry," I said with excitement. "What's going on, li'l bro?"

"Just hollering at you. What's going on at your place? Is that your boyfriend screaming like that?"

I wasn't ready to tell Kerry about my lifestyle, so I played off his concern. "No . . . no, nothing like that." I looked up and saw Storm escorting Candy and Teddy back into the kitchen so I began to speak more freely. "No, Kerry, he's Can—I mean, Stephanie's man. You remember the girl who came to court with me?"

"Oh . . . yeah, I remember her."

"Yeah . . . her. That's her boyfriend. She's over here, and he thought he was answering her phone. That's all."

"She better be careful about a dude like that. If that's your friend, you should warn her. I'm serious. That dude sounds like trouble."

"I hear you. I'm going to talk to her." I took a seat on the couch. "So how's Rita, the mommy-to-be?"

"She's good. I don't ever think I've seen anyone more excited to be pregnant." We laughed. "She seems to enjoy every bit of it. We just moved into our new house, and I finished decorating the nursery yesterday, so she's sat in the rocking chair, rubbing her stomach and reading to the baby at least five times since then."

"Whoa . . . she's got it bad," I teased.

We laughed some more then caught up on the latest happenings in our lives. I told him more lies about my so-called career as an event coordinator, and then I told him more lies about not dealing with any men. Kerry seemed to be extremely impressed and more importantly, proud of me. I didn't have the heart to tell him the truth about how messed up my life really was. He'd always been the one person who I cared about what he thought of me.

After we played catch-up, I took the opportunity to ask about the kids. "So, what's up with my babies? What has Robin been up to?"

"I learn something new every time I see Robin. She's taking Spanish in school now, and she updates me with her latest vocabulary—in Spanish of course—every time she sees me."

I laughed. "That's my girl. Now what about my boys?"

"What can I tell you? They're just boys, I guess. But, listen. I'm going to pick them up from school tomorrow. I try to give Momma a break every now and then. How about you meet us for a couple of hours or so?"

I was stunned. I wasn't sure I'd heard him right. "Huh? Meet you and the kids?"

"Yes. I'm sure they'd be excited to see you. You don't have anything planned already, do you?"

I was dumbfounded. "No . . . no, not at all. And even if I did have plans, seeing my children would certainly be enough reason to cancel. Are you sure you wanna chance making Bessie Mae angry?"

"Look. Stop with the Bessie Mae stuff. She's your mother no matter how much you don't want to admit it. Anyway, I'm going to tell Momma I'm taking the kids to Chuck E. Cheese's for dinner and games. I'm just not going to tell her that you'll be there."

"Aren't you worried that one of the children will tell her? Kids let things slip, Kerry."

"I'll just have to explain to them the importance of not letting their grandmother know you were there."

"I don't know how you're gonna make them understand that, but okay . . . if you say so."

"The worse that could happen is they tell Momma, and she'll never trust me to pick them up from school again. I don't mean any harm, but I can live with that." He laughed. "Now do you want to see your children tomorrow or not?"

"Yes . . . yes . . . I want to see them, Kerry."

"Cool. So what time do you get off tomorrow?"

"Huh? Oh . . . get off work? Um, well you know I'm my own boss basically, so you just let me know what time you'd like to meet, and I'll make it happen."

"Okay. I should have them all around three-thirty. How about we meet at Chuck E. Cheese's in the Hickory Hill area around four o'clock?"

"Kerry, you don't know how you've made my day," I sang into the phone. "Thanks so much, li'l bro. I can't wait to see you all."

"Me, too, big sis. Me, too."

We agreed again on the time and place then said our good-byes. I was so excited that I started jumping up and down when I closed the flip on the phone. I was ready to share my good news with everyone. I turned the ringer off on my phone then put it on the coffee table. Just as I was about to head into the kitchen, I bumped into Storm's chest.

"Oh, excuse me, Storm. You scared me," I said, holding my chest. "I didn't see you standing there."

He grabbed my arm. "What were you jumping up and down about?"

"My brother invited me to hang out with him and my children tomorrow when they get out of school." I looked at his hand on my arm. His grip was beginning to irritate me.

"And . . . where are you going?"

"To Chuck E. Cheese's." I tried to move, but he still had my arm too tight.

"Which one?" he asked, tightening his grasp.

I sighed. "In the Hickory Hill area . . . now let go of me," I screamed, jerking from his grip.

Candy and Teddy came running into the living room. Storm looked at Teddy then stuck his arm out, inviting him near. "What time do you get out of school tomorrow, son? Ms. Ivy's going to Chuck E. Cheese's. We thought you might want to go."

I was ready to scream at Storm again. How dare he invite someone else to intrude on my time with my children? I was about to let him have it, but Teddy fixed things for me. "Dad, I thought you knew I'm too old for Chuck E. Cheese's. That's a kid's hangout. Now if she's going to Jillian's then let me know. Jillian's has the big boy games." Teddy walked back into the kitchen.

I tried to go behind him, but Storm took a hold of my arm again. "If I find out you're lying to me, it's on," he said through clenched teeth. He dropped my arm, swinging it as if it was a rag.

I stood near the kitchen entrance, massaging my arm. He bumped me, knocking me into the wall as he went past me. He could act a fool if he wanted to. Knowing I would see my children the next day had me on cloud nine—a high I hadn't experienced in a long time. Not even a bull like Storm could bring me down.

Chapter 22

What's a Woman to Do?

Candy had gone the day before to retrieve our money from her friend's studio then took it somewhere safe. She and I met up Monday morning at my bank to deposit some of it. We agreed that since we had thirty-two thousand dollars, we should make gradual deposits. We took five thousand dollars in to see how receptive the bank would be. I made out the deposit slip then stepped into the line. When I got up to the counter, the woman smiled, took my bills then counted it all in front of me. She handed me a deposit receipt once she was done then I was on my way.

"That was fairly easy," Candy said as we walked out.

"I didn't think we'd have any trouble, but I wasn't sure. Now we know we shouldn't hear any flack or be asked a billion questions about our deposits being too large, so let's do the rest of the money in five more increments."

"I agree. And that's perfectly fine with me," she said.

"Are you sure you want me to hold on to all of the money?"

"Yeah. I still haven't been able to straighten out my

credit history with the bank, so it's better if you have it. Every time I try to open an account somewhere, my banking history shows up. Nobody will let me open an account."

"Do you think your mom will open one in her name for you?"

"I thought about asking her, but really I don't want her to know my business," she said, opening the car door.

I stood on the driver side. "Oh, you're right. I forgot about that. She'd have access to the account with her name being on it. She'd probably question what's going on after she sees your transactions, huh?"

"You got that right. My mom is one nosy bug."

Candy got into the car, but just before I got in, my ex-boyfriend, or should I say, ex-trouble-maker, Gerald, popped up in my face. He grabbed my arm, scaring the shit out of me.

"What's up, Ivy?" He smirked. "Miss me?"

Though frightened, I refused to show it. I boldly snatched my arm from him. "Did you follow me here?"

"Naw. Guess we use the same bank."

"Bullshit, Gerald. Since when have you kept a job and learned how to put away money?"

"Since you dropped my ass. Hey . . . at least something good came out of our breakup, huh?"

"What do you want, Gerald?" I asked, frowning.

"You," he said, pulling me into his chest. He tried to kiss my lips, but I turned my cheek. "What's d'matter? Don't you miss me?"

Candy called out to me. "C'mon, Ivy, let's go. Who is that?"

"Coming," I answered. I pried his arms from my waist. "Excuse me, Gerald, but my friend and I have some business to take care of."

"Ivy, I went to jail because of you. The least you could

do is give me a little of your time. C'mon, now, baby. I miss you," he said, placing his hand on my shoulder.

He stared and smiled at me, apparently awaiting a reply. I stared back, noticing he still had the same velvety chocolate skin I once licked daily as well as those perfectly kissable lips I use to love so much. I smiled back at him.

"Sorry, but I don't miss you, Gerald." I winked at him. "Have a nice life."

I got into the car and drove off. Candy wanted to know the scoop on Gerald, so I told her the whole story of our rocky relationship before the fire and the final breakup. She told me how she was planning on getting a new car with some of the money we stole from Storm, but that was gonna have to be a gradual thing. She no longer had a job, so her suddenly having a new car would raise an eyebrow for Storm. She'd been asking him to let her drive his Lexus, but I guess that was too much like right, because he always declined her. He'd tell her that I could take her where she needed to go.

We stopped at the McDonald's around the corner from Candy's apartment. We both ordered a McGriddle breakfast combo with a Coke then sat in front of her apartment talking and eating.

"You think that Storm will ever find out we were behind the stolen money?" Candy asked.

"Not if we have anything to do with it. Once we make all the deposits, neither of us has to ever talk about it again. It'll be just like it never happened."

"Yeah. You're right. I just wish we had gotten away with more. The little bit we stole was hardly enough to eat on . . . let alone live comfortably for a while."

"Hey, but at least we got something out of him. I believe it was you who said we had to make him pay. We have to have something to show for our unethical time with him." I reached to slap a high five with her.

"I know that's right. I'll see you later. Have fun with your kids today," she said, getting out of the car.

"Thanks. I appreciate the well wishes. I plan on enjoying myself. I'll call you later tonight."

"A'ight. Take care." She closed my door then headed into her apartment.

Time seemed to be creeping slowly as I anticipated meeting with my children. I tried everything to make the day go by faster. I washed and roller set my braids, repainted my toenails, and played solitaire with a deck of casino cards Storm had brought home one night, but despite all of my time-consuming activities, 4:00 just wouldn't come fast enough.

I decided to take a nap around 1:00. I woke up to my cell vibrating on the bed next to me. When I looked at the caller ID, it was Jaabir. "Hello," I answered.

"Zahrah?" he asked.

It was good to hear his voice again, but I wasn't sure I needed to be talking to him. Unknowingly to him, I was filling his life with as much danger as I was mine. "Yes, it's me, Jaabir. How are you?"

"That's my question for you. I've been worried about you. Why haven't you called me?"

"It's only been two days, Jaabir. You sound like I've been missing in action for several months," I responded teasingly.

"Well, honestly, that's what it feels like. I mean, after the other night, I had hoped you'd at least stop by the restaurant so I could see your lovely face."

He sounded so sweet. "I apologize, Jaabir," I said with a heavy heart. I decided I should try to come clean with him. "Maybe it was a mistake for us to make love the other night. I kinda feel like I've been leading you on."

"I don't understand." There was a long pause. "Zahrah, are you there?"

"I'm here, Jaabir. And please . . . call me Ivy. You put an unbelievable amount of guilt on me when you call me Zahrah."

He cleared his throat. "Ivy . . . I'm sorry. Of course, it's never been my intent to make you feel anything other than good about yourself. Please help me understand what I've done. Do you not want to see me anymore?"

I sighed heavily. "I do. I mean, I wish I could be with you for always. My life is just so screwed up right now, and I have no right bringing you into it like this."

"I'm still lost. I don't feel you've brought me into anything. Before this conversation took a turn, I was actually feeling great about having heard your sweet voice answer the other line. I'm pretty confused now, and you don't seem to know how to clear things up."

"Jaabir, I don't know what to do."

"Ivy, I don't know what's going on with you, but considering the way I'm feeling right now, it doesn't matter. I won't call you anymore. Have a nice day." He hung up.

I sat up in bed ready to bawl my eyes out. I looked at my cell for what seemed like forever, trying to decide if I should call him back. I remembered what happened to the man who Candy accidentally involved between me and her shit. His life was gone, and no matter how I wished I could bring him back, I couldn't.

There was no doubt in my mind that Storm would hurt Jaabir if he found out about us. Jaabir's blood would be on my hands. How could I live with that? I was pretty sure that I couldn't live with it, so I ultimately decided not to call him back. I lay there reminiscing on the night I'd had with him before drifting back to sleep.

When I woke up, it was after 3:00. I jumped up to get dressed. I pulled out some blue jeans, a rose-colored cashmere sweater, and some denim boots. After taking a brief shower, I dried off then brushed my teeth and made up my face. It's a wonder I still had braids because I nearly yanked them all out as I quickly snatched out each roller. I switched the contents of my Coach bag to my denim Nine West hobo bag then was out the door.

The closer I got to Chuck E. Cheese's, the more nervous I became. It had been over six months since I'd last seen my children—the longest amount of time they'd ever been away from me. I wondered how they were going to react when they saw me. There was no telling what the woman who birth me had told them about me, and I feared they wouldn't be happy to see me.

I pulled into a parking spot then went inside the restaurant. I looked all over for Kerry and the kids, but there was no sign of them. It was 4:00 on the dot, so I figured I should have a seat because they were probably running a few minutes behind. There was a vacant table facing the door, so I decided to sit there. The restaurant was fairly quiet, considering it was a playland for children. But, then again, it was a weekday, so most kids were probably at home doing homework.

Once 4:15 rolled around, I became a little worried. I wondered if Bessie Mae had learned what Kerry was up to and had put a stop to his plans. I stood and began to pace the floor. After about five minutes putting wear into the rug, I noticed Kerry and the kids coming through the door. The children all had on khaki-and-white school uniforms. They didn't seem to notice me as I stood awaiting their arrival.

Kerry stopped the children halfway to where I was standing then pointed in my direction. "Look over there, Dillon. Who is that fine woman standing right there?"

Not only did Dillon's eyes widen, but Zachary and Robin looked surprised, too. "That's my mommy," Dillon screamed. He broke away from Kerry and ran toward me.

Robin and Zachary tied for second in the race to greet me. I had to take a seat in order to absorb all of the love they gave me as they each planted kiss after kiss on my face. I didn't want our moment to end. Kerry watched as my children continued to size me up.

"Mommy, I like your braids," Robin said.

"Thanks, pumpkin. Would you like to get your hair braided, too?"

"I can get my hair like that?" she asked excitedly.

"You sure can. But, of course you have to ask your nanna first. If she says yes, I'll give Kerry the money to take you, okay?"

"Oh, wow. Thanks, Mom."

The boys were taking turns giving compliments, too. "Mom, how did you get your nails like this? Are these real diamonds?" Zachary asked as he traced his finger over my nail tips.

"No, sweetie." I laughed. "They're called rhinestones. They just look like diamonds."

"They're pretty, Mommy," Dillon added.

I pulled them all in for another group hug then it was time for me to pay compliments. "Robin baby, you're getting so tall. Soon, you'll be looking me eye-to-eye. I'm just going to have to enroll you in modeling school."

"Wow, you mean I'm going to be a supermodel?" Her mouth was rounded into a perfect *O*.

"Yeah, sweetie. I mean if that's what you want to be. You certainly are pretty, and my guess is, by the time you're a teenager, you'll be even more beautiful." She hugged my neck, squeezing me until I couldn't breathe.

"That's enough, Robin," Zachary said, prying Robin's arms from me. "You're going to hurt Mom."

"Sorry, Mommy," Robin said.

"No problem, sweetie." I stroked her hair then looked

at my boys. "Your brothers are my little men, and they just like to protect me. That's all. They'll protect you, too, as you get older."

Kerry interrupted. "They already do. You should see Zachary taking up for his sister at other people's houses. They all like to play and have fun, but Zachary and Dillon keep an eye out for their sister."

I smiled and nodded. "That's really good to hear. Very good to hear."

"Now fellas, do you mind if I get a hug from your mom—my sister? It's been a while since I've seen her, too."

"I thought you said you saw her in court," Zachary protested, clinging to me.

Kerry laughed. "I did, but it still seems like a long time ago. Now do you mind?" Kerry picked Zachary up then set him down off to the side of me.

"Hey," Zach screamed.

We all laughed. I stood then put my arms around my brother's waist. He bent down and placed loving kisses on both of my cheeks. "It's so good to see you again, sis. You look good, too."

"Thanks, Kerry. I've been waiting for this moment," I said, squeezing him tighter.

"What? To see me again?"

"Yes, and to have you hold me like this. You know I love your hugs. You make me feel like everything is gonna be all right."

"Well, it is. You know that, don't you?"

"If you say so."

He pulled away from me. "Wait a minute. Don't you answer me with that tone. In six month's time, Momma is gonna come around and things will be back on track with both of you and with your children. Look at me and tell me you believe everything is going to work out for the best."

I hesitated. I wanted to ask him to help me to get away from Storm, but I feared disappointing him with the news of having another no-good-ass man around. Kerry believed I had finally made some sound decisions for once in my life, and while he was proud of me, I didn't want to ruin it.

"Everything is going to work out for the best, Kerry," I said not even believing my own words.

Kerry smiled. "Now that's more like it. C'mon, let's feed these hungry kids and beat them at their own games."

"Nuh-un, Uncle Kerry. I'm gon' beatchu," Dillon screamed.

Kerry shook his head then laughed with all of us. We ordered two large pizzas—one cheese and one pepperoni. I ate so much, I was embarrassed at myself. Kerry laughed at me, saying I probably had a build-up from starving myself, trying to keep my tiny figure. He was far from the truth. It just felt good to be around him and the kids and be worry-free, even if it was for a short time.

Although I felt like curling up in a chair after eating so much, I still managed to drum up enough energy to run loose with the kids. I even took off my boots and climbed through the play bins and jumped around in the colored plastic balls. Kerry laughed at me, swearing I was a big kid at heart.

Three hours came and went. The kids and I were heartbroken to have to say good-bye to each other. Kerry assured them that he'd get us back together soon, but his promise did nothing to alleviate the pain I felt. The children moped all the way to the car. As they got buckled in, Kerry had the little talk with them about not telling their nanna about our time together, and they all agreed. We'd just have to see if they could keep their word.

I leaned into the car and gave all of them big kisses.

"Mommy," Robin said.

"Yes, sweetie?"

"Nanna still says you don't care about us."

"Nanna is just unhappy, sweetie. She doesn't mean what she says."

"So, have you found our knight in shining armor?"

I was surprised Robin remembered our last conversation. I looked at Kerry as if he could help me answer. He shrugged then turned away. I kissed Robin's forehead. "Not yet, sweetie. But, even if I don't, I'll always love and take care of you. I promise."

"That's enough, Robin," Kerry said. "We need to go."

Looking into their sad faces tore at my heart, and I wanted to break down right then and there. I held onto my composure—that is until Kerry's car was far out of sight.

I got into my car and cried like there was no tomorrow. I couldn't even muster up the strength to drive away from the parking lot. I felt alone, and I didn't want to go back to the condo. I had a full tank of gas, so after calming down, I figured I'd just drive around and do some sightseeing. The whole while, I had the children on my mind and wished things could be different for us. I was turning twenty-seven in a few months, but I still hadn't accomplished anything I could be proud of other than a high school diploma. I cried some more.

Jaabir crossed my mind. He always lived up to the meaning of his name, and I felt I needed him more now than ever, but I had messed things up with him. *Call him anyway, Ivy,* I said to myself. *The worse he can do is not answer or hang up without hearing me out.* More tears rolled down my face as I desperately dialed the numbers of Jaabir's cell.

"Hello," he answered in a low, sluggish tone.

I swallowed then tried to clear my throat. "Jaabir, it's Ivy."

I could hear him shifting as if he was trying to sit up to

listen closer. "Ivy, what's wrong? You sound upset. Are you okay?"

"No," I said just before breaking down again. "I'm not okay, Jaabir."

He sounded very concerned, but I didn't know why, considering the way I had treated him earlier. "Why? What's wrong? Ivy, where are you?"

"I'm near East Memphis." I sniffed.

"Are you at the restaurant? I just left there."

"No. I'm not at the restaurant, but I'm not far from there. I'm having a bad evening and . . . and . . ." I couldn't find the words to continue.

"And what, Ivy? Don't stop now. You've got me worried."

I began to cry. "Jaabir, I need you." I paused to cry some more. There was silence on the other end of his line, but I sensed he was still there. "Please," I continued. "Please, Jaabir. I need you right now. In more ways than one."

"Ivy—" he started, but I didn't let him finish.

"Jaabir, you've been more than kind to me. I want nothing more than to have you in my life, but—"

"But what, Ivy? Why do you do that? Why can't you just tell me what's going on with you?"

"Because I don't think you'll understand."

"Try me."

"I can't," I screamed then cried. When I calmed down, my voice was a whisper. "I can't talk about it right now." I wiped my face.

"Then you're right . . . I probably won't understand. And I don't understand how you say you need me. What's the real reason you called me, Ivy?"

I sighed. "The real reason I called you, Jaabir, is just what I said before: I need you. I just had a wonderful time with my brother and children, but now they're gone. All I have left is memories . . . just like I have with you. I feel like I lost your friendship earlier in the day, and now I don't know what to do to dismiss this yearning to be near you again." There was a long pause before I spoke up. "I guess you don't have to do anything about the way I feel, and maybe I should just be happy that you even listened to me."

His sigh was intense. "Ivy, I want to be sure that the next woman I'm with won't run out on me like the last one. If you're having issues, I want to help you with them or else go through them with you. You think you can let that happen?"

"There's so much to know about me, Jaabir."

"That's not what I asked you. Answer my question."

I thought hard before I could answer. Just when I was about to speak, Jaabir tried to bid me good night. I stopped him before he hung up. "Wait, Jaabir. I can do that."

"You can do what, Ivy?"

"I can share my world with you, be it good or bad."

"Fine. Then if you still need me, you know where I live. I expect to see you in less than an hour." He hung up before I could say anything else.

Chapter 23

Roulette Is Gambling

Jaabir and I had a wonderful night together. Not one time did my cell phone ring while I was with him, which led me to believe Storm had other things going on with him. Had he been at the condo, he would've been calling me off the hook, trying to find out where I was. Candy obviously hadn't been to the condo either because she hadn't bothered to find out what I was up to.

I awoke to a heavenly aroma floating out of the kitchen. I got out of bed then opened one of Jaabir's dresser drawers to find something to wear. After slipping on one of his jerseys, I cleaned up in the bathroom then let my nose lead me toward the tantalizing smell. I found Jaabir slaving over homemade pancakes, turkey sausages, and eggs.

"Morning, sleepyhead," he said, turning to notice me. "Did you sleep well?"

I placed my arms around his waist then kissed his lips. "Yes, I did. Thanks to you, I truly did."

"Oh, I didn't do all that much."

"Hmph. Well, I'm curious to see what you can do when you do a lot."

He smiled then set his fork on the stove. "Give me those lips," he said, kissing me with more passion than I can ever remember.

Our embrace lasted until we heard the grease from the sausages popping in the skillet. "You better get those before a fire is started."

"I know that's right. Have a seat at the table. Everything is almost ready."

I thought about checking my cell, but then decided I'd rather not spoil my good mood by finding out Storm had been trying to reach me. I'd only worry about what he was going to do when I got home, so I figured I'd save the worrying until after my time with Jaabir was over.

We chatted over breakfast and even talked about what our future would be like. Jaabir started the subject, and he wouldn't let me back down from it.

"I'm just wondering, Ivy. Do you see us having more children or are you closed to the subject?"

I cleared my throat then sipped on my juice. I definitely hadn't considered having more kids. Three was more than enough in one household. Besides, I still wasn't sure how things would end up for me. I had to get out of the damaging situation with Storm before I could determine what a future with Jaabir would be like. I set the glass on the table then cleared my throat again.

"You can't answer me, can you?" he asked solemnly.

"Jaabir . . . I . . . I just . . . well, you kinda caught me off guard with this one. I have three children already."

"And I don't have any. What's d'matter? Your tubes tied or something?"

I wanted to lie and say yes, but something wouldn't let me. I'd already been withholding enough from him as it was. "No, my tubes aren't tied."

"Then I presume you're still able to have children, right?"

"Jaabir, we're still learning things about each other. This

relationship is too new to be talking so heavily. Why are we on the subject of kids already?"

"Honestly . . . having children is important to me. If I only have one, I'll be grateful."

"Don't you think you could grow to love mine?"

"Oh, I'm sure I would. I also would like to know the joy of seeing a little one I helped create run around, looking and acting like me. Anything wrong with that?"

Despite his argument, my mind hadn't changed. "No. I understand where you're coming from. I just . . . I—"

"You know what. Time will aid your decision. As a matter of fact, we need to be together more. Once you fall in love with me, you'll be more than willing to have my child for me."

"Really? You're that confident, huh?"

"Yes, really. I'm just that confident. As a matter of fact, would you like to go to a cabin with me this weekend? Gatlinburg, Tennessee, is nice. I think you'll like it. It'll be a great spot for us to have quality time and get to know more about each other."

"I've heard of Gatlinburg, but I've never been there."

"Then say yes. If you don't love me by the time the weekend is over then I'll cut you some slack." He smiled then couldn't refrain laughing at himself.

I laughed and shook my head, but I understood Jaabir was dead serious. It would take some time for me to be willing to have another baby. Hell, my youngest was wiping his own ass and fixing his peanut butter sandwiches. It would take some strong love to make me have another child for anyone.

"I'll go to Gatlinburg with you. Sounds like this is going to be an interesting weekend."

"Oh, you don't know the half. I'm gon' make you love me." We held hands and laughed some more.

Jaabir had to be at the restaurant at noon, so we left his

house at the same time. Storm still hadn't called me, but neither had Candy. I called Candy to see if she could give me a heads-up on what Storm was up to.

"What's up, girl?" I said just after she answered.

"Not a lot. Whatchu been up to?"

"Just leaving Jaabir's place. I was wondering if you'd seen Storm."

"You're just leaving Jaabir's house? Ivy, tell me you didn't spend the night with that man again."

"Okay. I won't tell you that I spent the night at Jaabir's house again." I laughed.

"You're a mental case. You know that, right?"

"I'm not crazy."

"Any time you keep pushing Storm's buttons the way you do, I'll say you're a basket case. Ain't no way in the hell I would've been just leaving this morning. The sex can't be worth the ass whipping you gon' get when you get home."

"Are you at the condo?"

"No. And I'm glad. I just hope he doesn't kill your ass."

"Well, how do you know he's there? He hasn't even called me this morning. I might just play it off and say I just left the condo before he got there."

"Whatever. You just need to think of something quick."

"Hey . . . get this: Jaabir and I are going to Gatlinburg this weekend."

"Bye! I'm about to hang up this phone on you. *Bitch,* you gon' do what? Now I know the mutherfucker's got you sprung. What kind of dick is it? Tell me now, 'cause I don't want none. A dick that can make you play roulette with your life is dangerous as hell. You're crazy, and I don't know what else to say."

"Well, I'll be home shortly. I'll call you this afternoon if I'm still alive."

"Cool, but you need to try to live at all costs because you got some of my money tied up in your bank."

"Bye, girl," I said, laughing into the phone. I hung up before she could say anything else.

By the time I made it home, Storm's truck was indeed parked outside. I was praying that he had Teddy with him, so he wouldn't have a chance to beat my ass. I took a deep breath before going inside.

Storm was sitting on the couch flipping channels on the television when I walked in. He looked me up and down then spoke. I spoke back then nervously walked over to sit next to him. He kept his eyes glued to the television as he began to question me.

"Where've you been?"

Aw, shit. Here it goes, I thought. "I told you I was visiting with my kids, baby. Did you forget?"

"That was yesterday. I'm talking about where were you last night and this morning?" He kept flipping the stations.

I was frozen. I was afraid to lie, but at the same time, I knew I'd get hit or even killed if I told the truth. I remembered Candy had said I should deny, deny, deny. I decided lying was my best option. "I spent the night with my brother and kids."

He turned to look at me. "Oh, really?" he said deepening his voice. I was afraid to respond. "Well, I hope you had a good time because that's the last time you're going to be spending the night away like that."

"Huh? Storm, those are my children. Why would you keep me from spending time with them?"

"You've got a place. Just tell me when they'll be here, and I'll be certain to stay away."

I remembered my weekend. "But, Storm, baby . . . my brother invited me to vacation with them this weekend."

He frowned and stared at me with a blank look on his face. I hated when he made his eyebrows look like they were one. "Where are you going?"

I hesitated. "Huh? Not far."

"Not far isn't a place, Ivy. If you can't tell me where you'll be, then you're not going."

I had to think fast. "Well, my brother's wife, Rita, is pregnant, so we can't drive far. So she—"

"Just tell me where, Ivy," he interrupted. "I didn't ask you about your brother's wife. I just want to know where."

"I'm trying to tell you, baby," I said then paused. "We're going to Hot Springs, Arkansas. Rita and I are going to get massages while Kerry and the kids explore the town. You know they got those museums down there."

Storm lifted the remote then flicked the television off. He stood then headed toward the bedroom. Before he got out of sight, he turned back to look at me. "Have a nice time."

I couldn't believe how easy that was. I wanted to pinch myself. Not only had I managed to lie my way out of an ass whipping, but I had succeeded in making him understand that I was going to be away for the weekend. I was dying for Storm to leave so I could call Candy and tell her the news.

"Guess what," I said just after she answered the phone.

"What?"

"I'm going out of town with Jaabir this weekend."

"Uh . . . and so you're going to tell Storm you'll be where?" she asked in a duhlike tone.

"I've already handled that."

"Really? Storm said you could go? You must've told one hell of a lie."

"I told him I'm going to be with my brother. He didn't say much except that I could go."

"Girl, I'm scare of you. You better be careful. If Storm is calm, he might have something up his sleeve."

"Naw. I just think he has other things to worry about or something. I don't know. I'm just glad to be getting out of Memphis for a minute."

"So where're the two of you going?"

"Gatlinburg," I said, grinning from ear to ear.

"Get out of here. Girl, he's taking you to the mountains? Damn, I wish I could find a man to care about me like that. What's your secret?"

"I don't have a secret." I laughed.

"Bitch, don't lie. Karrine Steffans needs to move over because I'm about to call you the next Superhead up in this mutha—"

"It ain't like that," I said, cutting her off.

She laughed. "Well, g'on, girl. Do your damn thang. I ain't mad atcha. I just wanna grow up to be like ya."

"Mm-hmm. Anyway, I gotta go pack."

"Girl, it ain't the weekend yet. Slow your roll."

"I know, Candy. I'm just so excited. You have to be with a man like Jaabir to understand how I feel."

"Actually, after listening to you, I can understand. And I was just teasing about that Superhead, shit. You're a beautiful person, inside and out. Storm is a fool, but Jaabir has enough sense to recognize your worth."

"Aw, Candy, that's so sweet of you to say."

"It's the truth, Ivy. G'on start your packing. All I got to say is, have enough fun for me."

"No doubt," I said just before hanging up.

I clasped my hands together then squeezed tightly. I looked up toward ceiling then spoke out loud. "Thank you. Finally, someone who will love me. Thank you."

Chapter 24

Only Once in a Lifetime

Time had come for me to meet Jaabir so we could go to Gatlinburg. I let Candy drop me off at his house so she could keep my car. Although she still couldn't understand how I had managed to pull things off, she was very excited for me.

All week long I had been reading the book Jaabir loaned me. I was only a few pages from being finished with it, and I couldn't bear leaving it. It was pretty interesting, and I understood how he figured I would enjoy it. In my opinion, many of the characters were in search of satisfaction, and obviously Jaabir knew I was, too. Though the events of the novel were set way back in time, I could see myself and some other people I knew in the story.

Jaabir drove as I finished the final pages of the book. When I closed it, he grabbed my hand. "How was it?"

"Wonderful. I don't know how to thank you. This book has so many of life's lessons in it. I can't wait to tell my friend to buy it. By the way, I appreciate you letting me read yours, but I think I'm going to buy my own copy."

"You liked it that much?"

"Yes. I just may have to be like you and read it again." I smiled.

Jaabir squeezed my hand tighter then lifted it to kiss it. "That's what I wanted to hear. If this is the end result every time, then I guess having to introduce you to something isn't necessarily a bad thing." He smiled.

We continued to discuss the book as well as some non-fiction titles he wanted me to try. I was game for anything he suggested. We had a six-hour drive ahead of us, so we utilized the time to ask the things we hadn't before. I told him about the situation that led to me losing my children to my mother, and I even told him about Candy. However, I conveniently left Storm and the threesomes we use to have out of the equation. They were a couple of experiences, that's all, and those occurrences meant nothing more to me. I knew I wasn't a lesbian, so I felt no need to discuss how close Candy and I had really been.

As we got closer to our destination, we began to see signs referring to the area as the Smoky Mountains. The ground had about two inches of snow on it for as far as I could see, but the roads were paved and safe for traveling. When I noticed we were about to stop, I became more excited about the weekend. I still couldn't believe Jaabir and I were going enjoy each other's company for two whole days.

I stayed in the car while he went to check us in. He got back into the car smiling. "Hey there," he said.

"Hey you. Why are you looking at me that way?"

He cranked up. "Just admiring your beauty. That's all." He began to pull away.

"I thought we were here. Where're we going?"

"To our cabin. It should be right around there," he said, pointing and driving with one hand on the steering wheel.

Once he parked, my jaw dropped. I got out of the car and stood, staring at what appeared to be a two-story log cabin. It was huge, like something I'd only seen on television before. I was speechless.

"Ivy, you okay?" Jaabir laughed as I stood motionless.

"Are we in the right place?"

"Yes," he replied, removing our bags from the car.

I went over to help. "But, isn't this place too big? It looks to be about two stories. What do we need with all of this space?"

"It's two stories, but the bottom part, which you can barely see from here, is the game room. You'll see once we go inside. C'mon."

"Game room? Wow, that sounds nice."

"Oh, it is. You'll see. I haven't vacationed in this location before, but I did in a similar one about four years ago. Now pick up your jaw, so we can go check it out."

I elbowed Jaabir as I carried our grocery bags. He laughed at me some more then headed to the cabin door. Cold air met us as we entered. "Gosh, you'd think they would've come by and warmed the place up for us."

"Well, we're operating on fireplace heat only, so I don't think leaving a fire unattended would've been the wisest thing to do."

"Huh? Well, what about each room? There can't be a fireplace in every room."

"Why can't there be?" Jaabir said, staring seriously.

"Un-un. No," I said, setting my bags down and looking around. "Jaabir, you're kidding."

He laughed heartily. "Yes, I'm only kidding." I hit him across the arm. "Ouch," he said, rubbing his arm. "Listen . . . don't worry about staying warm. There're plenty of ways for us to get heat."

"Mm-hmm. I can imagine." I walked up to him then placed my hands around his waist. "I've wanted you ever since the first day you walked into my office."

He stroked my braids. "Would you believe I've wanted you ever since, too?"

"Yeah. You confirmed it when you stared at my short skirt."

He smirked. "You didn't know I was looking."

"Um-hmm. You didn't know I knew you were looking."

We rocked in each other's arms for several long minutes—until I became too cold.

"You're shivering," he said. "Let's get this place heated up."

Jaabir started the fireplace while I put up the groceries. After the heat began to do its thing, I went over to stand in front of it for a while. He went to the kitchen to start dinner. The whole cabin became lit with a mixture of smells ranging from oregano to pineapple. I'd had enough with standing out of the way. It was time to at least have a taste.

"What are you doing in my kitchen?" Jaabir asked.

"Hey, something smells too scrumptious. You've got to at least let me have a sample," I said, reaching for the large spoon on the counter.

Jaabir caught my hand. "My . . . aren't we impatient. Just hold on for me a few more minutes. Everything is almost ready."

I stepped closer then slid my tongue into his mouth. Our tongues tangoed for a good minute before we let up for air. "Yes, everything is almost ready," I said, placing his hand between the crotch of my pants.

"C'mon, now. Stop that, girl. Good thing you're wearing pants."

"Why? Are you afraid of accidentally adding my special sauce to your ingredients?"

He laughed. "Oh, you are so nasty and bad, too."

"Yeah, but even when I'm bad, I'm good."

We both laughed then kissed again. "Now get out of here," he said. "I'll be in there when I'm done, all right?"

"All right, baby." I headed to unthaw my feet.

I placed a blanket in front of the fireplace then took off my socks and boots to allow the heat to caress my toes. The cabin was quiet with the exception of crackling of the fire and the clanging Jaabir made in the kitchen.

"Next year we aren't going to come here in November. It's too cold," I yelled.

"Winter is the best season to be here, baby," he yelled back. "We'll be fine tonight. You'll see."

"Whatever," I said, wiggling my toes in front of the fire.

About thirty minutes later, Jaabir came out of the kitchen and set two plates of spaghetti down on the blanket in front of me. "Shall we eat in front of the fireplace?"

"Sure," I said with excitement.

He left then returned with garlic rolls and a bottle of wine. He kissed my forehead, graced the food, then took my fork and fed me the first bite. I giggled like a school-girl in love. I sensed Jaabir liked seeing me so happy.

We finished eating then went down to the game room. There was a pool table, a pinball machine, an electronic dart game, a chess table, and a large flat-screen television with a PlayStation2 hooked up to it.

"Now how'd it get so warm down here?" I asked.

Jaabir pointed to the heating unit. "I ran down here and turned it on while you unpacked."

"Good thinking."

"Do you shoot pool?" he asked.

"No, but I bet you can teach me."

Jaabir smiled then set up the table. After three games of pool, we gave the dartboard a try. I learned something new about myself—I could throw darts. The electronic board kept score, and I beat Jaabir three games to one. He swore he let me win each time, but I knew better.

"Now, why would I let little biddy you beat me?" he teased, stepping toward me.

I began to back up. "Let? You've got it twisted. You didn't let me do anything. I won 'cause I've got skills."

I had taken one too many steps backward and ended up with the pool table in my back. With nowhere to run, Jaabir was able to press his weight against me, pinning me between him and the table. "What now?" he asked.

I raised his shirt then began kissing his chest. "Let me go," I said between pecks.

"Un-un," he moaned. "You're going to have to do more than that."

With that said, I unzipped his pants then pulled them down. "It's on," I commented. He was hard as cement. I slid to my knees then took great pleasure in taking him into my mouth.

Jaabir leaned over the pool table, trying to support himself as I continued to make him weak. He hissed and moaned my name over and over, turning me on like fire. I swallowed him deep then came up for air. "I love you, baby."

Jaabir seemed shocked and turned on at the same time. He let out a loud moan. "I love you, too, Ivy." His movements became rapid, pumping in and out of my mouth, until he exploded. "Oh, oh, ooooooo!"

He leaned over the pool table, then I slid from under him. "I'll go get you a warm towel," I said. "Be right back."

After cleaning myself up, I returned with Jaabir's towel. I reached to hand it to him, but stopped in my tracks when I noticed he was butt naked. "C'mere, lady," he said, stroking himself and motioning with his finger.

I wanted to run, but since the distance between us was only about eight feet, I skipped to him. He picked me up then placed me on the pool table. I removed my sweater as he slid my pants and panties off. I lay panting as he smoothed his hands all over me, from head to toe.

He climbed on top of the table then kissed me like he never wanted to let me go. I had chills running all over me—not because it was cold, but because Jaabir was taking me to another level. I never knew a kiss could make me come until then. My body didn't jerk though. Instead, I experienced a slow yet steady arousal until kissing him became difficult because of panting. He slipped his hand between my legs to discover a heap of moisture.

Jaabir smiled. "Don't worry. I won't let it all go to waste."

When he stepped down and began to lap me, I could barely stay put. I reached behind me to grip the table for support. Before I knew it, I climaxed again. Jaabir had my mind gone to someplace beyond this earth—must've been heaven.

Just when I thought I wouldn't be able to take anymore, Jaabir climbed on top of me and began to sex me like he couldn't get enough. The more he stroked me, the deeper he went. I thought we'd break the table, and I prayed not to have burns on my back from the vigorous friction. I could've sworn Jaabir read my mind because suddenly he calmed down and began to do a slow grind. When I reached my third climax, he came with me.

I was happy to see Jaabir removing a condom when he got up. I didn't remember him putting one on, but the fact that he did let me know that not only did he love me, but he respected me.

We were heading back upstairs when we heard a knock on the door. I looked at Jaabir, wondering who could be visiting just after midnight. He shrugged then insisted I go into the bathroom to shower while he answered the door. I felt uncomfortable, so I kept the bathroom door cracked so I could eavesdrop. I couldn't hear who Jaabir was talking to or what they were saying, but I became more relaxed when I heard him shut and lock the door.

I hurriedly turned on the shower and jumped in. I'd

only been bathing about five minutes when Jaabir joined me. "Who was at the door?" I asked.

"The property manager," he said, lathering himself.

"Really? What did he want at this hour?"

"He said my credit card didn't go through. I gave him a different card and told him to come back and see me in the morning."

"Gosh . . . he couldn't wait until daylight to talk to you about payment?"

"I guess not. Good thing I brought another card or else he would've put us out."

"Oh, that would've been messed up," I said, hugging him. "But then again, we've had a great time already. Don't you agree?"

"I do, but I haven't gotten enough yet." He puckered, inviting me to his lips.

Once we got out of the shower I went into the bedroom to put on the sexy black negligee Candy had picked for me. Jaabir dried off then put on a pair of boxers. "I'll be in the living room."

"Aren't we going to bed?" I asked, rubbing lotion on my arms.

"That's a likely decision, or we could hold each other in front of the fire and chat a bit more. Who knows what talking could lead to?"

I headed into the living room to find Jaabir snoring on top of the blanket close to the fireplace. The room was only lit by the fire. I walked over to Jaabir and noticed he was lying on top of what seemed like a billion red rose petals. I gasped. As soon as I kneeled to grab a handful, Jaabir jumped up.

"Boo," he screamed.

My heart raced. "Oh, shit . . . shoot, you scared me."

He laughed. "I'm sorry. I shouldn't've frightened you like that, but it was hard to resist."

"Now see if I would've had a bad heart, you would've killed me."

He pulled me on top of him. "I'm not trying to kill you, baby. I just wanna love you."

"So, I take it the property manager didn't sweat you about your credit card, huh?"

"Actually he did, but he also took care of this surprise for me, too," he said, running his fingers through the rose petals.

"Hmph. What am I gon' do with you?"

"Make love to me . . . again," he said, sliding his tongue into my mouth.

Before I knew it, we'd made love three more times throughout the night. Though he'd worn me out, I was having a tough time sleeping. I had a lot on my mind. I got up to fix another glass of wine. When I returned, I sat on the blanket and watched Jaabir as he slept peacefully next to me. *I have to find a way to be happy with him forever,* I thought. *God help me.*

Chapter 25

Never Mess with a Hustler's Pride

A knock came on the door, waking me from what felt like only a catnap. I looked around and noticed the sun was up, sending bright rays through the cracks of the curtains. Jaabir and I hadn't bothered to leave the living room all night, so we lay naked under a blanket. He lifted his head and squinted at me.

"Somebody's at the door, baby," I mumbled.

"That's got to be the property manager again," he said groggily. "Will you get my credit card from him, baby?"

"Okay." I rolled over and pulled the cover off of him then wrapped it around me. Jaabir sat up and frowned. "I won't open the door all the way, baby," I said, giggling.

I cracked the door then peeped out. "You can hand the card to—" *WHAM*.

The door flung open, busting me in the face, knocking me to the ground in the process. By the time I collected myself, I looked up to notice Storm and his entourage standing over me as well as Jaabir while he sat up in front of the fireplace. Storm stood with his hands on his hips, shaking his head at me. I looked over in time to see Drake bust Jaabir's head with the butt of his gun. "*Asa lama lakem,* my brotha," Drake said.

Jaabir fell limp onto his side. Drake grabbed a handful of Jaabir's locks then stuck the gun to his head. I screamed for mercy.

"Oh . . . oh . . . please . . . nooooo," I cried. "Storm, please. Drake, don't kill 'im."

Storm leaned closer then stung me with a powerful slap to the face. "Shut the fuck up," he demanded. "Close the door, man," he told one of his other boys.

I was scared shitless, but I knew I needed to protect Jaabir's life at all cost. "Storm, let 'im go," I begged, looking at Jaabir who had blood running down his temple. He seemed to be too hurt to be afraid. "Please . . . I never told him anything about us, Storm. He didn't know a thing . . . I swear."

"That's a damn lie," he huffed. "I found out about this muthafucker pushing up on you a long time ago. I told him you were mine, and I told him to leave you alone—he was warned."

I couldn't believe my ears. Jaabir had as much responsibility for putting his life in danger as I did. Tears flooded my face as I stared at him. "Why? Jaabir, why did you risk your life to be with me?"

He panted. "Something about you," he said. "I'd risk my life again and again if I had to."

"Well, mutherfucker, your wish is my command," Storm shouted. "Drake, take his ass out in the woods and cut off his dick. Bring it back to Ivy since she loves it so much. Wait on me before doing anything else. I want to be the one to cancel his punk ass."

"Noooo," I screamed. Drake and another man dragged Jaabir's naked body out into the cold as if they couldn't hear me pleading with them. "Don't do it. Please, Storm. Stop them. Pleeeeeease!"

Storm stood, displaying no emotion as I continued to beg for Jaabir's life. He shook his head. "You've got two minutes to get dressed and gather what you want to take with you." He turned to Bling. "She's got one minute after that to be in the car waiting for me. If not, shoot her in her leg. Maybe she moves better with a limp," he said sternly.

"A'ight, boss," Bling answered. Storm left out, and then Bling turned to me. "Get your shit, Ivy, 'cause I really don't wanna have to shoot you."

Needless to say, I was in the truck quicker than a flash of lightning. I swooped up my clothes and purse then got dressed in the truck. Bling watched my every move.

As soon as I finished dressing, I heard a loud gunshot come from the woods behind the cabin. I sat up in the truck to look out the window. About a minute later, I saw Storm and Drake heading toward the truck. Jaabir wasn't with them. I stretched out on the backseat and cried.

I heard Storm tell Drake and the other two men to head on back to Memphis. He said he'd pay them once they get to his house. Storm gave Bling the keys to his Hummer so he could chauffeur us home.

I didn't think the ride to Memphis would come to an end. There were three of us in the truck, and although Storm sat in the backseat next to me, I felt lonely and empty inside. All I could do was look out the window and cry. I knew I had put Jaabir's life in grave danger by dating him, but I also hoped I could continue seeing him without Storm ever finding out.

I never would've guessed Jaabir already knew about Storm. He was a brave soul—just to be with me. *He really thought a lot of me,* I thought, gazing out of the window. *He truly cared for me. But now he's gone . . . because of me he's gone.*

A gloom came over me that I could compare to no other. After about four hours of riding and staring out the window, I turned to look at Storm. He had a blank look on his face, but it was not the regret I had hoped to see. I felt sick to my stomach and felt that since Jaabir was dead because of the brief relationship he had with me, I didn't deserve to live either.

I quickly slid closer to the door then opened it. Call me crazy, but I wanted to jump. The truck was moving about eighty or ninety miles per hour, so it was hard to hold it open. The lines in the pavement went by rapidly as I looked down, trying to get the courage to take a leap. I could hear Storm yelling in the background, but in my state of mind, he sounded far away.

"Ivy, what the fuck are you doing?" he asked. "Yo, Bling, pull over! I think this crazy woman is trying to jump." Storm grabbed me around my waist.

"Let me go," I screamed. "I gotta do it . . . I gotta jump."

Storm's grip was firm as he held on to me until Bling could come to a complete stop. Storm reached around me, closed my door, then grabbed my waist again. I cupped my eyes and cried until I felt weak. The car was quiet with the exception of my moans and sniffling. I guess Storm just didn't know what to say. He kissed me on the top of my head a few times. Maybe that ounce of affection should count for something, but I just wasn't feeling it.

I knew Bling was probably turned around in his seat, watching me. I confirmed that he was once I looked up. I could also see we had pulled over into the emergency lane. I tried to pry Storm's hands from me.

"Let me go," I cried. I fought hard to get away.

"Ivy, why are you doing this?" he asked.

"He's dead. He's dead because of me. You should just kill me, too. I don't need to live either."

"That's a lie. You've got a lot to live for. Your kids want to be with you, remember?"

I was angry. I leaned back on his chest then looked up, screaming into his face. "You don't give a fuck about my kids. You don't give a fuck about me. Let me go. Why are you trying to hold on to me? After I'm gone, you can get any woman you want. Hell, you even still have Candy. You don't need me."

"Do I need you? Maybe not . . . but believe it or not, I do love you."

"Please . . . Storm . . . whatever. I hear you. Just let me go. I can't take no more—"

He pushed me away. "No more what, Ivy?" he asked, cutting me off. "So now you wanna die because of some nigga you ain't known long?"

"It doesn't matter how long I knew him," I screamed, pounding my fist into the palm of my other hand. More tears fell. "The time we spent together was priceless. That nigga as you say knew how to talk to me. He got inside my mind and found out who I am and what I'm about. He knew how to show me he cared for me."

"And I don't, huh? I just pay for muthafucking condos, put money in your pocket—money you don't even earn, and I make sure your every want is taken care of. Do I not do that?"

"Yes," I said, nodding. "You do very well at throwing money at me. Your money speaks much louder than you do. And to tell you the truth, you can just shut the fuck up, so your money can keep on talking. If it wasn't for your loot, I wouldn't have shit to do with you."

SMACK! I knew it was coming. I didn't even flinch.

Storm looked as if he could kill me. "You better watch your damn mouth. Don't forget who you're talking to."

"Stormy Daniels . . . yeah, yeah, yeah, I remember. Anything else?" I looked him straight in the eyes. He gritted his teeth, but I wasn't backing down. I had a death wish, so I taunted him. "You wanna hit me again, don't you? Well, what are you waiting for? Hit me." He sat still with his chest heaving. "Hit me, damnit. Don't just sit there looking stupid. I'm begging you to do what you do best. Now c'mon and hit me. As a matter of fact, pull out your gun and leave me on the side of the road, dead. I can't live with knowing I cost Jaabir his life."

Storm's voice was calm. "You didn't," he said. I looked at him, but I couldn't speak. He continued. "I let him go."

"What?" At first I was surprised, but then I realized Storm was just trying to shut me up. "No . . . no . . . I don't believe you," I said, shaking my head. "You're just trying to pacify me. It won't work."

"Ivy, I let him go. When we get home, ask Drake. He'll tell you. Now sit back so we can go."

"I don't have to ask Drake anything. You're a liar, and you're evil. I heard the gunshot. I'm no fool."

"Fool or not . . . sit your ass back. We've got to roll. Bling, push on, man. Try to drown out all this goddamn sobbin' and shit as best as you can. I am. She can jump if she wants to." He turned to look at me. "You got some ID on you, right? 'Cause if you jump out, we ain't stoppin'. Maybe somebody'll pull over to help you. We ain't even slowing down. Shit, I'm ready to get back home. I got a damn headache, fucking with you." Bling started driving. Storm pulled out his cell and began pushing numbers.

"Who're you calling?"

He just looked at me as if I hadn't said a word. "Hello?" he said into the receiver. "Who is this?" He paused. "Nigga, put Candy on the phone." He paused until she was on the line. "I'm not going to even ask who that was answering your phone. You and Ivy are some ungrateful little wenches. Anyway, I was just calling to tell you to be over at the condo in two hours. Yo' friend is on her way home, and she's gonna need you. I ain't gon' stay over today. I might end up doing something to hurt her." On that note, he hung up.

When we made it back to the condo, Candy was pulling into the driveway at the same time. My eyes were swollen, and I began to cry some more. As soon as I stepped out of the truck, Candy ran over to me. She reached for me and hugged me tight. "Are you okay?" she asked.

I shook my head. "He's dead, Candy. Storm killed him."

"Oh no, Ivy. I'm so sorry." She looked as if she wanted cry, too.

Storm got out of the truck then tossed my purse at me. "Stay your ass in the house. Don't let me find out you left here today."

Candy threw her arm around me again then escorted me into the condo. I lay across her lap and bawled until I began to throw up. My mind was all messed up. Candy tried to get me to eat something, but I couldn't. I felt like wasting away. Although she fussed at me for moping, she also cried with me a few times.

"Have you still been getting direct deposits from the payroll at the restaurant?" Candy asked.

"Yes. Why?"

"I'm wondering if we should forget making more money and just go ahead and bail. We have one more deposit to make. I say we total up what we have then split it."

"But, my children—what about court in a few months? How do I just walk away from my kids?"

"Ivy, perhaps it's time you explain to your brother

what's been going on with you. Do you trust him not to tell your mom?"

"I don't know. I mean, he won't give me away, but he'll definitely be disappointed in me for not being honest from the get-go."

"Well, would you rather he be disappointed in you or crying over you at your funeral? I hate to say it, but Storm is way out of control. I can see him killing us or vice versa. Ivy, it's time to go."

I nodded. "Let's make the last deposit on Monday. After that, I'll have a talk with my brother. I hope he'll fuss a bit then be over it."

"I'm sure he will."

We heard Storm turning the key in the door, so we hushed. He walked over to the couch where we were sitting. "You still mad at me?" he asked in a sarcastic tone. I just stared at him with no response. "Well fuck you then. I don't give a shit."

Candy interrupted him. "I thought you weren't coming back here today."

"I changed my mind. I am allowed to do that, right? If not, just let me know. I kinda thought since I pay the bills here, I'm allowed to show up when I want."

"I didn't mean any harm, Stormy," Candy said.

He turned his attention back to me. "Speaking of change . . . you've got some balls, girl. I'm gonna have to cut 'em off. Never again will you disrespect me like you did this weekend. Believe that." He started toward the kitchen then headed back to me. "And to tell you the truth, I think I ought to kill that brother of yours . . . just so he won't be around for you to tell another lie about vacationing anymore."

I jumped up in Storm's face. "Don't you talk that way about my brother. You better not lay a hand on him," I yelled.

"And if I do?" He towered over me. I remained silent. "That's what I thought—nothing. Sit your frail ass down." He pushed me down, practically into Candy's lap. He headed into the kitchen.

"Chill out," Candy whispered. "Remember his day is coming."

Chapter 26
And the Drama Continues

Monday morning, Candy and I headed down to the bank to make the last deposit of the money we stole from Storm. Although still sad, I was in a better mood than I'd been the past few days. Losing Jaabir damn near took my life, too. I was determined to get out of my funk because I needed to live for my children's sake.

Candy and I were on our way out of the bank when Drake stepped to us. We were totally shocked to see him, and I even became paranoid that Storm was with him.

"Ladies, ladies, how are we doing this fine morning?" he asked.

I smirked. "Where's Storm, Drake?"

"In his skin I suppose," he responded, holding the bank door open for us to exit.

"Did he have you follow us?" I questioned further.

"Nope. I'm here on my own free will."

We began to walk toward my car. Drake kept pace with us. "W'sup, Drake?" Candy asked.

"You," he simply stated then turned to me. "And you, too, Ms. Ivy."

"What do you mean?" I asked.

He looked around before he spoke. "How about the two of you step over to my truck? I have something to show you."

Candy and I looked at each other. She seemed to have the same hesitation in her eye as I did. "Hell naw, Drake. G'on leave us alone."

"Suit yourself, but if I were you, I'd follow me to my truck. I'd want to see this," he said with a sinister smile on his face.

"Ivy, maybe we should see it," Candy said.

I had begun to feel sick. "A'ight, Drake. You've got two minutes."

He motioned his hand. "This way, ladies."

We walked with him to his truck, which was parked in the back of the bank lot. Drake opened the truck door then clicked the remote to the DVD player. There, playing before our eyes, was a clear shot of Candy inching back onto Storm's property, wearing one of his shirts around her knees as she crawled out of the camera's view.

My heart sank. Candy stood with sheer panic in her eyes. Drake laughed at our distress. He took the DVD out of the player then stuck it in his inside coat pocket. "See, something told me to go back and review the whole film. I knew there had to be something caught on tape. I had a little time on my hands last night, so I decided to use it wisely."

I cut him off. "How much do you want, Drake?"

"Ah . . . money. See, money is of no object to me," he explained. "I wouldn't bribe you ladies for money. What kind of man would that make me?"

"Cut the bullshit, Drake. What do you want?" I yelled.

"Well, a few hours of your time here and there oughtta do."

"What?" Candy frowned.

Drake raised an eyebrow then stepped into Candy's face. "For the next six months, your asses belong to me. I wanna be fucked when I call you, how I want to, and wherever I want to. After the six months is up, we can negotiate on me giving up all copies of this recording. Do I make myself clear?"

At first I could see Candy's chest heaving, but then a sudden calm seemed to take over her. "Sure, Drake. I don't see why we can't get started today. I'm sure you could use a good blow job right now."

He threw his head back and laughed with an evil tone. "Now I know why Storm loves you hoes so much. You're so fuckin' obedient—gotta love it." He stroked Candy's face. I looked in her eyes and could tell she wanted to cringe. He continued. "Follow me over to the Chandelier Motel on Lamar Avenue. Nobody will expect us to be over there. I'll get the room, and once you see me go inside, get out the car and come in. The door will be open."

"Fine," she replied. "Do you mind if we stop at a corner store first? I need to get some condoms and some douche. I didn't expect to be having sex this morning, so I'm not as fresh as I'd like to be."

He nodded. "Freshness is important," he said, getting into his truck. "Follow me. There's a store not far from the motel."

"We're right behind you," she said.

Candy and I walked over to my car. Once we got in, I questioned what the hell she was thinking. "Okay, so what do we do now? I don't want to be screwing this man left and right. And why the hell did you have to encourage him to have sex with us today and right now?"

"I got this," she said with a stone face. "Don't worry about it. You don't have to do anything. I'll take care of him."

The store was only a few blocks away from the motel

Drake led us to. Once we saw him go into the room, we got out of the car. "You don't have to take everything off," Candy said. "Just strip down to your panties and bra to get him excited a little bit."

"Okay, but I hope he doesn't get ticked off about me not participating."

"He won't. I'll make sure of that. Oh, and don't take off your shoes or touch anything because these type of motels are dirty."

"Then where the hell am I supposed to set my clothes?"

"I'll find a place to set mine then you put yours on top of mine."

Candy knocked on the door with her knuckles. Drake came to the door, irritated. "I thought I told you to just come on in."

We stepped inside and he locked the door behind us. "Drake, wasn't there any other place we could've gone?" I asked.

"Maybe next time, but this was closer, and I knew no one would recognize us over here." He walked over to me. "Ms. Ivy, girl, you just don't know how long I've been dreaming about you ridin' this thang."

I looked at Candy for help. "Um, Drake, you get to have a taste of me first," she said, stepping over to him. "I've been wanting you for a while, but I was worried you'd tell Storm."

"Well, get out of those damn clothes." He turned to me. "You, too, Ivy."

It didn't take Drake very much time at all to get undressed. He stretched out on the bed and watched Candy and me. We were wearing skirts so all we had to do was step out of them and pull our tops over our heads. After she placed her clothes on the table, I set mine on top of hers. I stood, looking like a hooker in my bra and panties and boots. Candy was completely nude. When she went to the bathroom to douche, Drake stepped to me and began sticking his tongue in my mouth. I went along with it, but I prayed Candy would hurry up. His beard and mustache were rough on my face.

"Hey, give me some of that," she said as she reentered the room.

Drake turned to her then began tonguing her. I played along like I was interested by rubbing him through his boxers. He didn't have much to offer, which was probably some of the reason he felt eager to blackmail me and Candy for sex. I should've known the poor man wasn't getting any when he opted to have sex over our money.

When his pecker rose to the occasion, it couldn't have been more than four inches long, yet he swore he was hard. "Well, bring it on then, daddy," Candy said. She hopped on the bed in a spread-eagle position.

Drake stood in front of her stroking himself and moaning. "Oh, shit . . . look at that thang. That bitch is fat. Damn, Candy . . . I didn't know your shit was juicy like that."

Candy stuck two fingers inside herself then put them in her mouth. "Mmm . . . she tastes so good. And guess what, Drake . . . no calories."

He laughed. "Good because my big ass don't need any more calories today." He stuck his fat tongue out of his mouth and made it snake in the air.

"Damn," Candy screamed. "C'mere. Bring that shit right here." She stroked between her legs.

"C'mon, Ivy," Drake called.

I walked over and sat on the bed. I watched Drake stick his tongue into Candy like he was trying to find her womb. I looked over at her for guidance on what I should do. She motioned with her fingers that I should talk.

"Damn, you eatin' up all her stuff, Drake," I said.

"Mmm-hmm," Candy moaned.

"That's right," I chanted. "Make her come, Drake. She wants to come." He reached for my hand then placed it on the back of his head. I guessed he wanted me to push his face into Candy's stuff, so that's what I did as I chanted some more. "Mmm-hmm. Eat it good, so she can fuck you right."

"Oooo," Candy said, moaning. "I wanna come, Drake. Please make me come." She began grinding her hips into his face.

He seemed to enjoy tasting Candy's juice. His head didn't stop bobbing and making circular motions until she climaxed then released.

"Climb on top of her, Drake," I said.

"Un-un . . . she gots to get on top."

"Oh, it's like that, huh," Candy stated. "Well, no problem. You want me to tie you up, too?"

"Hell naw. I'm kinky, but not that kinky."

Candy went into her purse and grabbed the box of condoms and something that looked like a flask. Drake looked at her like she was crazy. "I like to take a swig of vodka every so often in the middle of fucking. I hope you don't mind."

He shook his head. "Whatever floats your boat."

"Cool." She placed the flask on the nightstand then turned to me. "Ivy, I put your pack of Black and Mild in my purse. Go ahead and relax. Light you one up until it's your turn to ride him."

Candy was talking out of the side of her neck as far as I was concerned because she knew I didn't smoke. She kept giving me this weird look, so I decided to just follow her lead.

I went into her purse then pulled out the pack of Black & Mild and a lighter. I lit the cigar then took a puff. Candy nodded at me, which let me know she was pleased that I had done as she suggested. "You don't have to put them back into my purse. I'm going to smoke one when it's your turn to let Drake feel you," she said.

I placed the lighter and the pack of Black & Mild on the nightstand. Candy began to moan as she grinded on top of Drake. He sounded like he was about to explode after about two minutes. "Slow down," he whined. "Slow down, damnit. Slow the fuck down."

"A'ight . . . a'ight," she said, laughing.

Despite her slowing down, Drake came less than two minutes later. Candy got off him then went into the bathroom. Drake looked spent, and his little pecker laid over like it was retarded. He huffed and puffed like he had done all the work. He couldn't seem to open his eyes. "Just give me a minute, Ivy," he said. "I'ma take care of you, too."

When Candy came back, she was wearing her bra and panties. She noticed Drake's eyes were closed, so she motioned for me to get dressed. I eased into my top and skirt. Candy went to the nightstand then picked up the flask. Drake opened his eyes momentarily. "Whatchu doing?" he asked.

"About to smoke me a Black and Mild and have me a drink while I watch you wear Ivy's ass out," she answered. He never bothered to look past her at me.

He grunted. "Yeah, but she gon' have to wait a minute. I'm talking about you. Why you got on your underwear?"

"Oh, I thought you were through with me. If you want some more, daddy, you can get it."

Drake's breathing was still heavy. Candy lit a Black & Mild then took a few puffs. She looked over at me then looked me up and down. I was fully dressed with my purse on my shoulder. Candy turned back around then opened the flask. Just when Drake opened his eyes again, she dashed most of the contents of the flask into his face.

He seemed stunned and apparently his eyes burned because he squirmed as he held his face. She hurriedly emptied the rest of the contents on him and the bed. Then pulled the receipt from the grocery bag and set it afire. Before I could say anything, she had already tossed the burning paper in Drake's face. I watched his beard and hair go up in flames.

He opened his mouth to scream, but the flames had taken his breath. He tried to roll around on the bed to put the fire out, but Candy defeated him when she set the plastic grocery bag on fire then tossed it onto the bed. The fire began to spread quickly.

I wanted to scream, but I knew better. I stood, paralyzed and in shock. Candy slipped on her clothes faster than I had ever seen anyone get dressed. Then she went into Drake's coat and stole the DVD. She grabbed my hand then led me to the door, opening it with her sweater in order to avoid fingerprints.

We walked quickly to my car. She told me to get into the passenger side, so she could drive. We managed to get out of there before the fire got out of control and before anyone noticed us.

We were halfway home before I could speak. "Candy, I didn't know you were gonna kill him," I screamed.

"Well, I didn't have a choice. In fact, we didn't have a choice. That muthafucker was gonna have his way with us then rat on us when he got ready. I didn't trust him."

"What type of alcohol was that? He went up in flames quick."

"That was lighter fluid. I didn't need to douche. I was buying time to figure out how I would kill his ass. I got the lighter fluid and the Black and Mild at the store."

"You didn't think to clue me in on what you were doing?" I argued.

"Hell, no, because my mind was made up. You would've tried to talk me out of it, and I just didn't see any other way out of the situation. He had to go, Ivy."

"Damn . . . damn . . . damn. Shit, just won't get any better. Everything is so twisted. I want away from this madness," I cried. "I don't want this life no more. I want out."

Candy continued to drive in silence. I don't know how she did it, but she had turned into something stone cold. My only hope was that she didn't turn on me.

Chapter 27

Things Just Won't Get Any Better

The next day, Storm came over to the condo in the afternoon. I was sitting on the floor in front of the couch, eating popcorn, watching a *Good Times* marathon on cable TV. He didn't see me when he first walked in. "Ivy," he yelled. "Where are you?"

Once he stepped around the couch, he looked down at me then I waved. "Over here. What's up?"

"What're you doing on the floor?"

I shrugged. "I dunno. Just felt like sitting on the floor."

He plopped down on the couch. "I've got some—"

"Shh," I said, pointing at the television. I picked up the remote then turned up the volume. "Kid—" I clapped once—"a dyn-o-mite," I said, mimicking J.J. on *Good Times*. I laughed, but Storm didn't seem amused.

"Ivy, I'm trying to tell you something."

I turned the TV down then got up to sit on the couch with him. "Go ahead. What's up?"

"I don't know if you've been watching the news, but the man who was set on fire in that hotel room on Lamar was Drake."

I pretended to be shocked. "What? Storm, what are you talking about? When did this happen?"

"Yesterday."

"Is he dead?"

Storm nodded. "He's gone."

I slid closer to him. "Oh, Storm, I'm so sorry to hear that. Are you okay?"

"I'll be all right. I'm not gonna lie—I'm gonna miss Drake."

"I can imagine," I said, kissing him on the cheek. "What in the world was he doing at a motel on Lamar?" I frowned.

"Well, that motel is known for the hooker-type activities that go on over there. Apparently Drake went over there with one, but she got bold and killed him. Why? Nobody knows. His wallet and money was charred, but they were all still there."

"*Mmph, mmph, mmph* . . . poor Drake," I said, still pretending to be shocked and sad.

I stood to go to the kitchen. "Where're you going?" Storm asked, pulling on my arm.

"To the kitchen. My glass is empty," I said, holding it up. "I'm just going to fix me some more Crystal Light."

"That can wait." He pulled me down on his lap then kissed my lips. "Besides, after that big-ass bowl of popcorn you ate, it doesn't matter how light the crystal is." He laughed. "You can wait." Storm kissed my lips again then slid his hands down my stomach and into my pants.

"Stop it," I said, trying to get up. "I'm thirsty. Now leave me alone."

He held me tightly. "C'mon, now. I just told you my friend was found dead, but you're acting like you don't even care. You're supposed to be comforting me."

I conjured up enough strength to get out of his grasp. I turned to look at him. "I don't mind comforting you, but sex isn't the best way. Why do you men always think sex is the answer to everything?"

"My friend is dead. I just feel like being close to you. What's wrong with that?"

"Storm, if I thought you just wanted to be close to me, I would be all right with that. You were sticking your hand down my pants."

He stood, and I took a step back. "You think you gon' live in my place, let me take care of you, and not give me any?"

I rolled my eyes without saying a word. I picked up my glass then started toward the kitchen, mumbling with my back to him. My cell began to ring on the coffee table. I turned around just in time to see Storm picking it up. I started back toward him.

"I can answer my phone," I yelled. I reached for it, but Storm held it high so I couldn't reach it.

"Who the fuck is Kerry?" he asked.

"That's my brother . . . now give it to me."

"Your brother, huh? I'll find out." He pressed the talk button. "Hello," he answered. There was a long pause as Storm listened to someone speak on the other end. I watched his face go from hard and angry to soft and humble. Then, with no further dispute, he passed me the phone. "Someone needs to talk to you," he said.

I snatched the cell from him. "Hello," I answered, masking my irritation. At first all I heard was someone whimpering, "Hello? Who is this?"

"Ivy, it's Rita." She sniffed.

"Rita? What's wrong?" I thought maybe she was in labor since about it was a week or so past her due date. She kept crying, so I became worried. *God, please don't tell me she miscarried the baby,* I thought. "Rita, talk to me. What's wrong?"

"Kerry," she cried. "Kerry . . . he's . . . he's dead."

"What?" I screamed. "What? No, no, no, Rita, no . . .

please tell me you're lying." Her sniffling and whimpering went into a full-fledged holler.

A nurse took the phone from her. "Hello," she said. "Is this Ivy Jones?" I could hear Rita crying in the background.

"Yes, I'm Ivy. Where's my brother? Put him on the phone." I began to sob uncontrollably.

The nurse paused before she spoke. "I'm sorry, Ms. Jones. Your brother was pronounced dead just a few moments ago. I'm so sorry." Her voice cracked. "We did all we could."

"What happened?" I cried. Storm put his arm around me.

"He was playing basketball at a gym this morning when his heart failed. His friends provided CPR as quickly as they could, and we worked on him for over an hour. There was just nothing we could do. Your family is here at the hospital now."

"Which one—"

Storm took the phone from me. "Go get ready. I'll find out which hospital."

I fell on my knees and begged God to wake me up from such a horrible dream. My brother, the only family besides my children who loved me, couldn't be dead. What was I going to do without him? I never thought I'd ever have to live without him. I lay on the floor, sobbing and feeling like my world was gone.

Storm kneeled to lift me up. I sat up then looked at him with rage. "Don't touch me," I said, swinging at him. "You wanted to kill him. You didn't want me to have my brother. Don't touch me."

Storm's face was very humble. "I never meant those words, Ivy. I didn't want to kill your brother. I said that just to make you angry." He pulled me into his chest. "I know how much your brother meant to you. I'm so sorry this has happened. Please believe me. I'm sorry, Ivy."

I cried into his arms because I didn't know what else to do. He comforted me for a few minutes then helped me get ready to go to the hospital.

When I walked into the emergency room, the first person I saw was Bessie Mae. Her head was buried in her lap. I looked around some more and discovered Rita pacing the floor with a flood of tears on her face. I went over to Rita. When she looked up and saw me, she cried in my arms.

"Where is he?" I asked.

"They're taking all the tubes and everything off of him so we can see him."

I began to cry again. Storm was there rubbing my back. "I still can't believe this. He was supposed to live to see his baby born."

"God had other plans, Ivy. I feel so selfish right now, because I want Kerry here with me." We held each other for quite a while. She broke our hug then pointed at my mother. "You should go talk to her. She needs you right now."

I walked over and sat next to Bessie Mae. She hugged herself tightly as she rocked and cried with her head down. I put my hand on her shoulder then squeezed it. She looked surprised to see me. She dropped her head again and continued to rock. "Who called you?" she asked.

"Rita," I murmured. "She must've gotten my number out of Kerry's cell because that's the phone she called me on."

She looked up then rolled her eyes. "Why are you here? There's nothing you can do for him now. He's gone. My son is gone." She began to wail. "Ain't nothing nobody can do for him. Not even me."

I felt sorry for her, but I was in pain, too. "I still want to be here. He was your son, and he was my brother. I loved him. I still love him."

"Oh, why don't you just go?" she screamed. "You never did anything except break his heart time and time again."

"That's not true," I said, standing. "Kerry and I loved each other. One of the last things he told me was how proud of me he was. Ask Rita. She'll tell you."

Storm came and put his arms around me. "Do you want to leave?" he asked.

"No." I jerked from him. "I'm not going anywhere. I'm family, too. I ain't leaving until I see my brother." She stood then turned her back on me. "Bess—" I stopped to correct myself. "Momma," I called. She turned around. "Let's not argue. This is the wrong time. We need each other. Rita needs us, too. All Kerry ever wanted was for us to get along. Can we at least try?"

She stared at me like I was crazy, but when I walked over and put my arms around her, she melted like butter. I could hardly hold her up. "What am I gon' do without you, Kerry?" she cried.

I rubbed her back. "We're all going to miss him, Momma, but I'm not going anywhere. I'll be here for you."

Rita joined the group hug and cried with us. We were interrupted by the doctor's voice. "Mrs. Reynolds," he called, "you and the rest of the family can go see your loved one now."

We all looked at one another then followed the doctor. Rita was on Momma's arm, and I had Storm holding me because I felt faint. I didn't know how I was going to make it through, but I knew somehow I was going to have to find a way.

Chapter 28
High Hopes

It was December—a month later—and I was still empty inside. Rita had given birth to a healthy, seven pound, fifteen ounce, baby girl six days after Kerry's death. Her doctor decided to induce her labor the day after the funeral because her blood pressure had gone sky-high. I was over to my mother's house when Rita called. I told Momma we had to get to the hospital quick. We made just in time for Momma to be her support person during delivery because Rita's mother lived in California and hadn't flown in yet. Rita named the baby Kerry after her father. Momma and I were very touched and also proud.

I woke up on my birthday, and for the first time ever, it just felt like another day. Candy had other things going on with a guy name Paul she'd met around the time I went to Gatlinburg with Jaabir. She didn't tell me much about him except that he was a personal trainer for the spa in her apartment complex, and that he was accepting of her bisexuality. Although I needed her around to lift my spirits, I tried not to deprive her of time with her new man because she was very understanding when I was dating Jaabir.

Without Kerry around to make a big fuss over me, things just weren't the same. Storm stayed out of my face as much as possible because he said it was tough watching me go through depression. He still came around periodically to check up on me. He did what he could to put some life into me, but all the shopping sprees in the world couldn't measure up to me having Kerry's arms around me just one more time.

Momma allowed me to have frequent visits with the children. She arranged for us to have another court hearing in April. She said she felt by then I should be ready to take on full custody. I didn't want to let her down, so I went to a different restaurant in Memphis called Silver Spoon to apply for a job as an event coordinator. I created a résumé, detailing my experience at Exquisites, and then went for an interview. The owner was impressed, so he hired me, giving me a healthy five-figure salary. It wasn't what Storm paid me, but at least I could hold my head up about it. My new position was scheduled to begin after the new year.

On Christmas day, Storm came in with a surprise announcement. I was in the kitchen making some bread pudding when he came in. "Hey, you," he said. "Something smells great. What is it?"

"Hey, Storm. I'm cooking bread pudding," I said, closing the oven door.

"When did you learn how to make bread pudding?"

"There're a lot things you still haven't learned about me, but I don't have time to teach you," I teased.

"Oh, so it's like that, huh? Whatever. I just hope that I don't get sick after tasting that thing."

I hit him on the arm. "You won't. Believe me, you'll be coming back for more."

"Yeah . . . yeah . . . yeah. C'mere. I wanna talk to you for a minute. Turn everything off because we need to have a seat."

My heart dropped. "What? What's wrong now?" Kerry's death had made me very paranoid.

"It's nothing bad. I just want to talk with you for a minute."

I stabilized everything then followed him out of the kitchen. "Ivy, you've had a rough seven months or so with me," he said, leading me over to the couch. "I feel like I owe you something for putting up with me. I love you, but I liked you more when you were li'l sexy. You don't seem to have that energy anymore."

"True. I'm twenty-seven years old, and I just feel like I should've accomplished something by now, or at least be on my way to some great achievement."

"Well, you know I've always been in a position to help you. And after careful consideration, I realized I need to just give you the condo." I looked at him like he was crazy. "I know the paperwork is already in your name, but technically, we had a verbal agreement that the condo belonged to me. I sold my cleaners and the club across the bridge." He handed me some documents. "This place is paid in full, and I want you to have it."

My bottom lip trembled as I racked my brain for something to say. All I came up with was, "Thank you."

"I appreciate you telling me you got a job, and I can respect your reason. Since day one, I've known you wanted to be a more responsible woman and mother. You'll have to keep up the property taxes, utilities, maintenance, and such, but now that you have a job you're proud of, you should be able to handle it."

"Wow . . . I'm speechless. I just don't know what to say. My children will be happy here."

"I'm sure they will. Your children are the other reason why I did it. I brought you here, promising to help you get them back."

"Oh, so now you have a conscience?" I teased.

"Yeah . . . brotha man's got feelings. Plus, I realize after Drake and your brother's death that life is too short to be mean. I'm trying to be a better person. I don't know how long it'll last, but at least I'm trying, right?"

"What about Candy? She's put up with your shit, too."

He laughed. "Candy's taken care of. I gave her some money to get registered for school. She says she's going back to college in the spring. She said she had some issues with her bank credit, so I gave her enough money to straighten that out, too."

"I can't believe she didn't call to tell me."

"I asked her not to. I wanted you to be surprised, too."

"I'm still surprised."

He patted my leg. "One of these days you're going to believe me when I say I love you. I can't be the man you need me to be—it's just not in me. I'm taking your advice to set you free, but I do love you, and that's not going to change."

I leaned over and kissed his cheek. "I love you, too, Storm."

He smiled. "That's good to know. So we're still friends, right?"

I looked down at the paperwork with my name on it, realizing how many thousands he'd spent to pay off the condo. "If you can continue to be the caring person you are sitting here in this living room, you've always got a friend in me."

He stroked my chin. "Merry Christmas, li'l sexy."

"Merry Christmas, Storm."

None of his kindness made me forget what he'd done to Jaabir, but he'd earned a softness in my heart that added him to my prayer list. Storm said he wanted to change, and I believed him. Time would be the true answer.

Chapter 29

No More Drama—Or So It Seems

Having a career with Silver Spoon was very fulfilling. I started in January, but by late April, I'd already received three bonuses and a pay increase. My check stubs were going to look great for court, which rolled around on me before I new it. I was in the bathroom getting dressed when Candy, Storm, and Teddy popped up.

"Ivy, where are you?" Storm called.

I stepped out of the bathroom wearing a black-and-white pinstriped Prada suit. "Whoo-hoo," Candy said then whistled.

"Do you think it's too much?" I asked, spinning around. "I don't want Momma and the judge to think I'm back to my old ways because they see me in Prada. I mean, I still love nice clothes, but this is the first designer outfit I've bought in a long time."

"Girl, you deserve to get what you want. You make a nice salary, so you've earned your shopping spree. Besides, they know you've been taking care of the kids since your last court date."

"Yeah, you're right." I looked at Teddy. He was pretty

quiet. "Teddy, what's up, man? I haven't seen you in a while. How's life treating you?"

"Good," he responded.

"Good? Is that all?" I asked.

Storm interrupted. "He means great. Hell, only spent two thousand dollars on his birthday party in January, now he's getting ready for spring break in Orlando."

"You mean *we*," Candy stated. "I don't care what y'all say. I'm going, too."

"You can come, too, Ms. Ivy," Teddy said.

"I just might do that. We'll see." I grabbed my purse then headed toward the door. "Storm, lock up for me, but when I get back, I'm gon' need your key. Since my kids are going to be living here soon, it won't look right for my friends to be running in and out of my place when they get ready."

"A'ight . . . a'ight. I can respect that. I'll get with you later."

"Peace," I said, closing the door behind me.

I stood nervously awaiting the judge's response as he looked over my paperwork. "So, Exquisites just didn't do it for you anymore, huh?" he asked.

"Well, Your Honor, I liked Exquisites, and I'm grateful for the experience I received working there, but Silver Spoon is a different and much better opportunity for me. I have more freedom for creativity now."

"I see," he said. "And what about your relationship with Ms. Reynolds? Have the two of you been working on the mother-daughter thing?" He smiled.

I looked over at Momma in the plaintiff booth. We both smiled. "Yes, Your Honor. Momma and I love each other very much."

He paused before making his final decision. "Ms. Jones, I only see one reason why I should postpone awarding custody to you." I gasped. "No, let me finish." My heart began to beat rapidly. "I would hate to interrupt the children's school year this late in the season. What I'd like to do is award custody to you, but I ask that the children are allowed to finish out the school year at their current schools. This might mean they'd have to continue living with Ms. Reynolds until then, and child support payments would still need to be made to her."

I was elated. "No problem, Your Honor." I turned to my mother. "I mean, if that's what you want to do, Momma."

She nodded then Judge Prather's decision was made. My children would be returned to me no later than the first week of June. We would have all summer to play and make up for lost time. I ran over and hugged my momma. She squeezed me tightly then kissed me on the cheek. I sensed she was just as pleased as I was at the judgment.

I took Momma out to lunch then started toward home. A man on a motorcycle flew past me, sending me on a trip down memory lane about Jaabir. Out of nowhere, the tears came. I remembered his smile, how good he made me feel inside and out, and how he taught me so much in so little time.

I pulled over and began to pray. After having a brief conversation with God, I realized my faith lay on a fence. My momma brought me up in two different denominations then once I was grown, I visited a nondenominational church and I sort of liked it. Then, Jaabir came into my life, and I liked so many things about the way he praised his Allah. *I need a prayer rug*, I thought. *I've got to find out where and how I want to worship, but in the meantime, I'll create my own corner with God in my home.*

I drove to a nearby carpet store and picked out a beautiful handwoven silk rug. I didn't expect it to cost a hundred dollars, but I didn't see a cheaper one that I liked. I put it in the car then headed toward home again. As I drove, I began to have flashes of how terrible my life was nearly a year before. Then, I remembered Jennie Brooks— the woman at the extended-stay motel who gave me five dollars. I turned the car around and headed there to see if she still worked there.

When I pulled in front of the motel, I didn't see anyone sitting at the desk. I got out of the car then went inside. The bell rang when I opened the door, but no one came from the back. "Hello," I called, looking around. "Hello," I called again.

The door behind me opened. "Well, hello there," Jennie said, stepping inside. "Lookie here. I ain't seen you in a month of Sundays. How're you doing, Ivy?" she asked, reaching to hug me.

"I'm doing great, Jennie. I had you on my mind, so I just dropped by to see you."

"Well, it's good to see you. I mean, you all sharp and everything . . . gurl, where you going looking so spiffy?"

"I went to court today. I'm getting my children back this summer."

Jennie's eyes grew wide. "Whaaaat? Shut cho mouth . . . are you serious?"

"Yes, they're really coming home," I said.

"That's wonderful, Ivy. This means you've really gotten yourself together. I'm proud of you." She hugged me again.

"Oh, Jennie, I've got something for you." I went into my purse and grabbed two bills. "Here's the five dollars I owe you," I said. "And here's the interest because I do realize it was long overdue." I handed her a hundred-dollar bill.

"Oh, Lawd . . . God is good. I sho was worried about how I was gon' pay my cell phone bill . . . now He done sent you in here. Lawd, I thank ya," she said, looking up in the air. "This here is right on time."

Jennie's reaction made me feel good. She helped me when I needed her, and I was more than happy to be able to give it back. We stood around laughing and talking for nearly an hour. We were interrupted by my cell phone.

"Excuse me for a minute, Jennie." I pressed the talk button. "Hello," I answered.

"Ivy, where are you," Candy screamed.

"On the other side of town. Why are you screaming?"

She started crying. "Oh God . . . oh no, Ivy—"

I was terrified. "What's wrong? Candy, stop screaming and tell me what's wrong."

"They tried to kill us, Ivy. I think he's dead—"

My heart dropped. "Who?" I screamed. "Who's dead? Storm?"

"No . . . Teddy. We were about to pull into Storm's driveway, but he stopped and asked Teddy to check the mailbox. Just when Teddy got out, some men pulled up in a black truck and started blasting at us. Me and Storm are all right, but they lit Teddy up."

"Are you at Storm's?"

"Yeah," she cried.

"I'm on my way." I hung up the phone then turned to Jennie. "I'm sorry, Jennie, but something terrible has happened. I've got to go, but I'll be back to see you soon."

"G'on, gurl. Sounds like your friend needs you. I'll see you some other time. You be careful, hear?" she hugged me.

"Okay. I will."

As soon as I got into the car, I broke down and cried. I knew once I made it to Storm's house, I wouldn't be prepared to say the right thing to him. He had been trying to get his life together then death entered his life in a cruel way. I had just seen Teddy earlier in the day. He was looking more and more like Storm and seemed proud to be around his dad. I just couldn't imagine him gone.

I made it on the street where Storm lived, but I couldn't get up to the house. Yellow and black crime tape kept me from being able to get closer. Candy spotted me talking to a policeman then came and got me. "She's family," she told the officer.

He let me through. As I walked toward the house, a loud feminine scream pierced my ears. Without anyone having told me, I knew the woman I saw sitting on the curb with several people hovering over her was Teddy's mother.

"She's been screaming like that off and on since she got here," Candy said, weeping.

"This is messed up, Candy. This is so messed up." I looked over at the ambulance. "Why are they still here? Please tell me Teddy's not dead." The truck's siren began to blare then it drove off.

"Looks like they're leaving now, but I don't know if Teddy's gon' make it," she cried.

"Where is Storm?"

She pointed to a police car. "They've got him in the car for questioning."

"Why? He was the one being shot at. He didn't do anything."

"I know, but I've been interrogated, too. Plus, I was told I need to go down to the station later for further questioning." She leaned on my shoulder. "Ivy, those men came out of nowhere. I was so scared. I can't explain it, but I just knew I was about to die."

I hugged her. I could only imagine how terrified she must've been. I should've known something bad would happen. I had never known a man in the drug game who could successfully retire after having been in the game for so many years.

"I wonder if the police will let me talk to Storm," I said.

Candy shook her head. "I doubt it."

I started toward the patrol car. "Well, at least they should let me look at him."

Before I we made it to the car, some policemen came and escorted Candy to a different car. I hugged her and told her to call me as soon as they released her. I stopped in front of the car Storm was in. I'd never seen him look so sad. He stared at me, but he didn't seem to have words for me. I wasn't looking for him to say anything. I just wanted to look into his eyes and have him know I was there.

The piercing screams came again. I turned and looked at the woman. "My baby," she cried. "Why'd they do this to my baby?" She ran toward me. I figured she was heading to the car Storm was in, so I moved out of the way. She began kicking on the door and screaming at him.

"You're going to get yours, muthafucker," she yelled. "My baby shouldn't have gotten caught in the middle of your shit. I've been telling you for years to leave that ruthless lifestyle alone." *Boom!* She kicked the door again. "Are you happy?" *Boom!* "Are you happy now, muthafucker? What are you gonna do if our baby dies?"

Storm sat shaking his head. Although he wasn't saying anything, his eyes said he was very sorry. He watched as her friends and family came to carry her off. I heard a woman mention they needed to get to the hospital. I blew Storm a kiss then headed to my car. I went home, rolled out my prayer rug in the corner of the bedroom then got on my knees. My mind was blown, and I needed help to keep from going into more depression. I couldn't see help coming from anywhere except from above.

Chapter 30

Can't Dodge What's Coming to You

I didn't get very much sleep the night before. I kept calling Storm's cell phone on through the morning, but it repeatedly went to voice mail. By 10:00 A.M., I still hadn't heard from him. Candy was released from questioning before midnight, and she came to spend the night with me. She kept waking up with nightmares, the same thing she did when she was upset about having caused that man's life the night of Storm's party.

By 1:00, Candy was up, looking for something to eat. I hadn't been to the grocery store, so went to the kitchen to make us some sandwiches. We sat quietly listening to the radio until we heard Storm coming through the door. Candy and I ran out of the kitchen to greet him.

I spoke, but he walked straight past me and into the bathroom. I followed him, but he locked the door. "Storm, are you all right?" I asked. He didn't answer. "Are you hungry? I'm making sandwiches." Still, no answer.

I started to worry, but I felt better after hearing the shower running. I heard him rambling around, then I heard the shower door close. Candy had a panicked look on her face also. "He's taking a shower. That's all," I said, trying to ease her mind.

We went back into the kitchen. We both seemed to be speechless. After sitting down to eat, Candy broke the silence. "Storm has done so much dirt in his time: Beat the shit out of you, beat the hell out of me, killed, ordered killings . . . I understand he's upset about his son, but how does he think he could live the type of life he lives and never get any of it back?"

I looked around to make sure he wasn't coming. "He's probably always expected someone to try to take him out," I whispered. "I imagine he never thought his payback would come in the form of someone doing harm to Teddy. He's got to be in so much pain."

"It hurt me to see Teddy lying there suffering. Ivy, I promise I'll never forget that little boy's face when he said, 'Dad, help me.'"

"Poor, Storm. He'll never forget that," I said then suddenly hushed when I saw him entering the kitchen.

Storm had changed into a different pair of jeans and a shirt. Candy got up to get him something to eat.

"I'm not hungry," he mumbled before she could touch anything.

"Well, I was just going to fix a little bite for you," she responded.

He shook his head as he took a seat at the table. "I don't want it. Just give me a drink of water."

Candy went into the refrigerator to get a bottle of water. I slid my chair closer to Storm then rubbed his back as I spoke. "Teddy," I said, clearing my throat, "is he um . . . is he—"

"He's gonna make it. He was in surgery for several hours, but he's gonna pull through."

I let out a sigh of relief then hugged Storm. "Are you going back to the hospital?"

He shook his head then sipped his water. "My in-laws don't want me there. That's my kid, but they're acting like I don't deserve to be there."

I didn't know what to say. I rubbed his pants leg. "I didn't know you still had clothes over here," I said, turning the conversation light.

"Yeah—in the guest bedroom. I'll get 'em later. If there is a later."

"Huh? What do you mean?"

"I know who shot Teddy. The whole incident was retaliation for what happened to the man who stole my money at the party that night. I'm going after them today."

Candy and I looked at each other. Her eyebrows met her hairline just like mine. "What?" I screamed. "Storm, if you know who those guys were, you should go talk to the police."

"You think I didn't," he yelled. "Woman, I talked till I was blue in the face. I dimed out everybody I thought could be connected to the shooting. Do you know they told me they'll get back to me once they get the evidence they need? Why not go and arrest the muthafuckers then find some fucking evidence?"

"Storm, you know shit doesn't work like that. We just need to be patient—" I said just before he cut me off.

"Patient my ass," he yelled, standing up. "My son is in the hospital in serious condition. Do you hear me? I don't have patience for a muthafucker who is bold enough to shoot at me and my family in broad daylight. I'm sorry, but I just don't."

Candy tried to speak up. "Stormy, you—"

"Shut the fuck up, Candy. I heard that shit you and Ivy was talking before I walked in here. Yeah, I've lived by the sword, but they always told me I'm supposed to die by the sword. No one, and I do mean no one, ever told me my son would have to be the one to pay the cost. Do you think

I would've continued living on that rugged path had I known that I would have to one day look my wife in the eye and tell her our son might not make it—shot over a beef some nigga on the street had with me? Huh? No. Teddy was *not* supposed to lie on the street bleeding like that."

Although I feared rejection, I walked over to him. I put my arms around his waist and held on tight. He threw his arms around me then caved in, crying like he knew no tomorrow. Candy walked over and joined us. She stood on the side and grouped her arms around both me and Storm. We must've been standing there for about fifteen minutes.

Once Storm was able to collect himself, he sat back down at the kitchen table. I sat next to him so I could continue to plead for his understanding. "You can't take the law into your own hands," I said. "That'll only make matters worse."

"I hear you," he said shortly.

"No, Storm . . . I'm serious. I don't want anything to happen to you."

He nodded. "I said I hear you. I'm gon' chill for now, but I can't stay in that house. I'm going to pack as many of my things as I can today 'cause once I'm gone, that's it. I'm selling that house, and whatever is left, the buyer can have. I just don't think I can live there knowing my son almost died right in front of the driveway."

Candy spoke up. "I'll help you, Storm. Do you have boxes?"

"No, but I'll get some. I guess I need to find storage space, too."

"Well, we'll both help," I offered. "You don't need to be alone right now anyway. Just let me finish eating then we can go."

He kissed the back of my hand. "Thanks, li'l sexy."

Candy was right. Storm had done a lot of dirt to us, and he was very lucky to still have us both willing to share his grief with him. As far as we knew, he was still wanted dead by the men who had shot at him the day before, but we stuck by him.

We left around 3:00 in the afternoon to find a storage unit and some boxes. After piling about twenty large, broken-down boxes into the back of a rental moving truck, we headed over to Storm's house. It had been a while since I'd been inside, but all the rooms were still very familiar.

The three of us chose which room we wanted to tackle. Storm told us what to keep and what we could leave behind. I started in the living room because it seemed like it was going to be fairly easy, considering his family photos were the most important thing to him. I wrapped all the frames with newspaper and stacked them tightly into one of the boxes. I went into the kitchen next and did the same thing with his expensive porcelain and china. The house phone began to ring as Storm stepped into the kitchen. He picked it up to answer it.

"Hello," he said then paused. "What's up, Debra? How're you feeling?" There was an even longer pause then I could hear a woman yelling when he took the phone away from his ear. When he put it back up to his ear, he began to argue back. "Debra, I'm not in no mood to hear all this shit," he yelled. "He's my son, too. Don't worry about the expenses. I'm gon' take care of everything tomorrow." He paused then put the phone on back on the charger.

"Everything okay?" I asked.

He hung his head low, pressing his chin into his chest. "No. Hell no. She hung up in my face." He shook his head. "I'm not going to be able to get through this if I wanted to. Debra's not going to let me. I guess she thinks she's the only one hurting." He had tears in his eyes when he looked up.

"Storm, I don't know what to tell you. I know this has got to be hard on both of you. I just wish this was all a bad dream."

"Yeah . . . me, too." He sighed. "C'mon, so we can finish."

Storm offered me several of his dishes and silverware, and he gave Candy most of his towels. By 10:00 we still hadn't finished loading the moving truck. From the looks of it, we still had two rooms to pack, but we were exhausted. Storm took off his clothes then stretched out across his bed in nothing but his underwear.

"Storm, what's up?" I asked. "We've still got work to do. I know you ain't quitting."

"No . . . I'm taking a break," he mumbled.

"Aw, c'mon, Storm. We're almost done. Don't stop now."

"Ivy, maybe we should take a break," Candy said, removing her shoes. "Hell, I'm tired." She stripped down to her underwear then jumped up in the bed with Storm.

"Oh, this is jacked up. I'm trying to get finished here," I responded.

"Well, finish then, superwoman," Candy teased. "You got this."

"Un-un . . . if y'all quitting, I'm done, too." I took off my shoes and climbed into the bed with them.

Storm reached over and turned off the lamp on his side of the bed. We were lying there for close to half an hour when I heard kissing noises. I reached over and turned on the lamp on my side of the bed to see what was going on. Candy and Storm were completely nude, and she was kissing on his chest. He looked over at me then slid his hand under my shirt to massage my breast.

Candy looked at me then tugged on my shirt. "Take it off," she said seductively.

My mind said no, but my body said yes. I got up, stripped out of everything then climbed back into the bed. Storm rolled over and began to kiss me like he did when we first got together. He stroked my side then lay back after Candy started groping between his legs. She took her other hand then began to knead one of my breasts. Out of nowhere, I became ill. I realized I didn't want what was happening.

I removed her hand. "I'm sorry," I said, getting out of bed. I put my clothes back on then began to pace. Candy and Storm sat staring at me. "I can't do this. I'll leave the two of you alone so you can finish." I started out of the room.

"Ivy, wait," Storm called. "You don't have to go. I'm not feeling this either." He turned to Candy. "Sorry, Candy. My head ain't right for making love. I promise I'll make it up to you later if you'll let me." She nodded then plopped down on the bed. Storm beckoned me. "C'mere, li'l sexy. Get some sleep." He patted the bed then turned over and threw his arm across Candy.

I was relieved that Storm was on the same page with me. If his son hadn't almost been killed the day before, he might've been trying to convince me to indulge with them. I didn't know what was on Candy's mind, but I had hoped she would get over the fact that I couldn't be sexual with her and Storm. I loved her as a friend, and she knew I didn't mind that she was bisexual, but I needed her to respect that I couldn't be down with her in bed.

Storm and Candy were snoring long before me. I was comfortable staying the night at Storm's because not only did he have an alarm system, but I also knew he slept with a gun under his pillow. Still, my mind was working over-time, trying to figure out how the rest of my life was going to go, so I couldn't get to sleep right away. An hour must've passed before I finally drifted off.

I felt like I had been sleeping for at least two hours before I turned over with my back to Storm. He was in the middle, and apparently he felt me moving, so he turned and threw his arm over my side. I cupped his hand on my stomach. That's when I heard it . . . the *click, click.*

All three of us sat up in the bed wide-eyed. I turned on the lamp and discovered Debra hovering over us with a gun. "Don't nobody fucking move," she said through clenched teeth.

"Debra, what're you doing?" Storm asked. He eased his hand under his pillow.

"Put your hand under there all you want, Storm. Your gun isn't loaded. I came by earlier while you weren't here and emptied it."

I looked at Candy. Her bottom lip was trembling, and she looked as if she was about to break down in tears at any moment. I tried to talk to Debra.

"Debra, it's not what you think," I said. "We're all just good friends—"

"Shut the fuck up," she yelled walking over to me, pressing the gun in my forehead. "You one bold bitch to be sitting up here trying to explain why you're in my bed nude with my husband and another bitch. Where the fuck did you come from?"

I began to shiver. Debra was clearly drunk and hurting. There was no doubt in my mind that we were all going to die. She backed off me. I looked over at Candy and noticed she had a flood of tears streaming down her face. Storm seemed pretty calm considering the circumstance. He just sat, watching every move Debra made. Before we knew it, Candy had made a mad dash at Debra, but Debra's reflexes were too quick. Candy was hit in the chest with a bullet before she could reach Debra.

I screamed and Storm hollered. "Shit, Debra, why'd you have to shoot her?" He got out of the bed to go over to Candy. I sat there and whimpered like a baby.

"Get your ass back into the bed," Debra screamed at Storm.

"She needs help," he said. "Debra, you're not thinking straight right now. Just let me call for an ambulance."

"You're not going to be dialing nobody. I'm going to do all the calling. Now get your ass back into the bed before I blow you apart."

Storm did as he was told. He sat up in bed on the side closest to where Candy lay. I could hear her wheezing on the floor, but I couldn't see her. I was afraid to try to look.

Debra picked up her cell phone then dialed a number. I think both Storm and me were all puzzled about who she was calling. "Hello, Mamie," she said. "Wake up. I've got something you need to see." She paused then continued. "I'm over at the house. I need you to see one of the reasons your son traded in his family. You spent all these years trying to tell me I wasn't being a good enough wife. You wouldn't listen to me telling you about his lifestyle . . . the drugs . . . the money . . . the hoes. Well, I've got him right here at gunpoint. He ain't going no fucking where until you get over here and see this." Again, there was a short pause. "I ain't gon' kill him yet, but if you don't hurry up, I will."

"Don't come, Ma," Storm yelled.

"Wait a minute, Mamie," Debra yelled into the phone. She looked at Storm. "Do you want me to blow your ass off right now?" He kept silent. "Shut up. I'm trying to hold a conversation wit cho momma." She stared at Storm briefly then got back on the phone. "Yeah, Mamie? I'm back. Like I was trying to say, you need to get over here quick. I already got one bitch on the floor over here dying. She needs some help . . . bad, so hurry up."

Debra closed the flip on her cell phone. "I can't believe you," she said to Storm. "Yo' bitch is over here on the floor, dying and you gon' yell for your momma not to come." She shook her head then turned to me. "Girl, I'll be sho 'nuff scurred if I were you. This nigga don't care 'bout y'all."

"Debra, you're going to be in a lot of trouble. I hope you know that," Storm said.

She shrugged. "The way I see it, I don't have anything to live for anyway. There's enough bullets in here for all of us. Why should I have to sit through a funeral for Teddy when I could just easily join him?"

"Debra, you're drunk," Storm said. "Just put the gun down, and then we can talk. I know I didn't do a lot things right in our marriage, but I've come around now. I'm sorry Teddy had to almost die for me to understand, but I know he wouldn't want you behaving like this right now."

"Blah . . . blah . . . blah . . . blah . . . yaddi . . . yaddi . . . yaddi," she sang. "Are you through? Huh? Nigga, are you through singing your sad song?" Storm remained silent. "Save it, 'cause I ain't trying to hear it."

We sat quietly, waiting for Storm's mother. I had wondered what she was like and if I'd ever get to meet her, but I certainly didn't know it would be under these circumstances. I kept praying for Candy as I could hear her breaths getting shorter. Debra had started whistling until she heard Storm's mother crying out. "Storm?" she called. "Are you okay?"

"Don't come in here, Ma," he yelled.

She stepped into the room anyway. "I called the police," she said, entering the room.

Debra turned around and aimed the gun on her. "Oh, did you really now?"

Storm dashed out of the bed then landed on top of Debra. They wrestled around on the floor for a while.

Storm yelled for me and his mom to get out of there. I grabbed his mom by the hand then started out of the bedroom. She screamed and cried for Storm as she ran. By the time we made it to the end of the driveway, Storm was yelling behind us.

"Ma, run! Get into the backseat . . . both of you," he said. We did as told then he jumped into the front seat. "Ma, where's your keys?"

She gave him the keys. He had just gotten the car started when Debra came running down the driveway. Storm began to back out, but then a sudden crash came through the windshield. I pulled Ms. Mamie down on the floor as bullets continued to fly. Debra fired several rounds. The car rolled into the neighbor's yard across the street. Once it hit their living room wall, it came to a halt.

The gunshots had ceased. I was afraid to come up for a peek. Ms. Mamie seemed to be losing her mind. She was screaming for dear life. I opened my eyes and saw flashing blue lights, so I looked up. The police were there, and they had Debra at gunpoint. Her gun was on the ground, and her hands were suspended in the air. Several officers ran over to the car. They made us get out and get on the ground until they patted us down. It was a good thing I had put my clothes back on before dozing or else Debra would've 'caused me to have to run out of the house naked.

Ms. Mamie and I were the only ones to get out of the car. The police made us stay on the ground until they were satisfied we were the victims. Two policemen were seeing after Storm. I overheard them say he had been shot in the face and in the neck. Storm's mother was going ballistic. I, on the other hand, knew it was over for him. I just didn't want to look.

One of Storm's neighbors invited me to sit on her porch until an ambulance came. An EMT went over to

Storm, and another one stepped over to me. "There's one in the house you need to check on," I said, pointing.

"We have someone going in there now, ma'am. I just need to look at you for a minute."

I don't know what came over me. "No! Leave me alone. Go in the house." I began to cry. "There's a lady in there who needs you."

"Yes, ma'am," he said, backing off me.

Ms. Mamie's screams were so loud, I wondered if the residents across the bridge in West Memphis heard her. A policeman walked over to me and began asking questions. I was dry, but I answered him as much as I could.

"How long were you friends with the deceased?" he asked.

I looked at him. I knew all along in my heart that Storm was dead, but hearing him say it was something different. I became nervous when I saw a stretcher come out of Storm's house, but I relaxed once I noticed oxygen over Candy's mouth and an IV bag held over her head. The officer repeated his question. "Ma'am, how long have you known the deceased?" I waved my hand at the officer then dropped my head. "I can see right now is a difficult time to answer any questions. Why don't I have one of the officers take you someplace where you're comfortable? I have your contact information. We can talk later."

He called an officer over to take me home. As I walked past Ms. Mamie's car, I didn't bother to look in. I knew although Storm's body was there, he was someplace beyond my reach. I got into the patrol car. As we were pulling off, I looked up into the dark sky. Just above Storm's house were two large stars. Of all the stars in the sky, these two stood out, and they were the brightest. I began to speak out loud. "Kerry and Storm," I said. I had ruled Jaabir out as one of the stars because I didn't think he'd hang out over Storm's home. I called Kerry and Storm's name again. Both stars grew larger and blinked one at a time as I called them out.

"Did you say something, ma'am?" the officer asked.

"No, sir. I was just thinking out loud," I responded.

He nodded and kept driving. *I know I was left here for a reason,* I thought, still staring into the sky. *I won't let either of you down.*

Epilogue

The kids and I had been having a ball since their summer vacation began a week before. I couldn't get enough of spending time with them. I was allowed to set my work schedule like I wanted, so I began to work from home as much as possible. My second Saturday with the kids, we went down to the river walk for a picnic. We found the perfect spot in the grass near a tree. As I sat on the blanket, I looked up and spotted my condo on the hill.

My phone rang, breaking my train of thought. "Hello," I answered.

"How's everything going?" Momma asked.

"Fine, Momma. We just finished eating our sandwiches. How are things going with you and my niece?"

"Well, I'll tell you one thing: I can't wait until her momma comes to pick her up. This is one nosy little baby. I wonder where she gets that from."

I laughed. "Okay, Momma, go ahead and pretend you're not nosy at times."

"I'm not nosy," she said, laughing. "Anyway, I'm getting pretty tired today."

"Momma, I told you to let her come out here with me."

"No . . . no, it's much too hot outside for this baby, but ask me again when she gets a bit older. I'm sure I'll take you up on your offer then." We both laughed. "Have you heard from your friend Candy? How's she doing since the shooting?"

"I saw her yesterday. She seems to be doing fine. She doesn't look like she ever had a scratch on her. That goes to show you what God can do."

"You said a mouthful, baby girl. Amen to that."

"I had been holding some money for her in my bank account because her bank credit was bad, but she's gotten everything all straightened out now. As a matter of fact, she's going on vacation with her boyfriend this weekend."

"She's been hanging with this guy for a while now. This is the same fella from the spa, right?"

"Yes, ma'am. I think they make a great couple. I'm happy for her."

"Well, a good man will come along for you, too, honey. Don't you worry, okay?"

"I'm not worried."

The children ran up to me. "Momma, can we go over closer to the water?" Robin asked, interrupting my conversation.

"Yeah, Momma. Can we? Please?" Zachary asked.

"Momma, your grandkids are ready to play, so I'm going to have to call you back," I said.

"Okay. Make sure you watch them, and don't let them go too close to the water."

"Yes, ma'am. Chat with you later. Love you."

"Love you, too," she said just before hanging up.

I walked down toward the river with the children. "Wait, li'l man," I said to Dillon. "Let your sister hold your hand."

He reached for Robin's hand then headed down the small hill covered with rocks. Once the children were as close as I thought they should be, I called for them to stop. They began to pick up rocks and toss them into the water. I watched from about six feet away.

A couple walked past me, holding hands. The woman reminded me of Candy, which sent my mind into reminiscing mode. I could hear Candy's laughter clearly in my head. Then I began to think of Kerry and what he might be thinking as he watched over me. I imagined he was proud to see me with my children.

Storm, I thought, *you made a lot of your wrongs right before you died. Because of you, my children and I are happy.* Then Jaabir came to mind. I wished I could take back the day he entered my office, but only because not meeting me would have spared his life. "I'm so sorry, Jaabir," I said aloud, looking into the sky. "And just so you know, I'd do anything to hear you call me Zahrah again."

"Anything, Zahrah?" a voice from behind me said.

I turned around and was startled by the sight of Jaabir. I almost screamed, but my breath was gone. I stood gasping until I could say something. "Jaabir?"

"It's me," he said, walking toward me. I felt like I was dreaming.

"How . . . what . . . where did you—" I attempted to speak again, but I was at a loss for words.

"Stormy spared me. He shot above my head then told me to run and to never contact you again. I heard about what happened to him, but I wanted to wait until you'd had time to heal before trying to get in touch with you."

"Do you know I feel like I'm dreaming right now? I wanted to die the day I thought Storm killed you."

He smiled as he walked closer. He grabbed my hands. "You're not dreaming. I'm really here. And you don't have to die. I'm here to give you one more reason to live."

I was confused. "What're you saying?"

He pointed to my kids as they continued to throw rocks into the river. "Those the little ones?" he asked.

"Yes," I answered, turning to look at them.

"You know I've always wanted kids. I'd love to adopt them and make you my wife. "

I began to feel faint. Not only was Jaabir standing before me, alive and well, but he was asking me to marry him. "I—"

"Before you answer . . . I just want you to know that I never stopped loving you during our separation. I just got promoted to head chef on my job, and I have a new home. I want to share it all with you and the children—if you let me."

Tears came to my eyes. "Jaabir, I don't know what to say."

"Just say you will."

I hugged him with all my might. "I will."

The children came running up. "Mommy, who is this?" Robin asked, looking up at Jaabir.

I smiled then happily reported, "My knight in shining armor."

Discussion Questions

1. In what ways do you feel Ivy and Candy were naughty?

2. Why do you feel Ivy gave in to Stormy so soon after discovering he had been watching her?

3. Was tough love the issue between Ivy and Bessie Mae or was it something else causing the distance?

4. Was Bessie Mae just for keeping the children away from Ivy? Why or why not?

5. At what point do you feel Ivy should've done something to remove herself from an unsafe environment?

6. Was Candy a friend? Why or why not?

7. What did you think of Jaabir? Was he the man for Ivy?

8. What was your favorite scene? Least favorite scene? Why?

9. Who was your favorite character? Least favorite character? Why?

10. Did you predict any of the story's events? If so, what was the giveaway?

11. Was the ending including the epilogue satisfying or just? Why or why not?

12. What do you think about the author's overall delivery of the story?

About the Author

Alisha Yvonne is a native Memphian and a rising voice in the world of African American fiction. She is the author of the *Essence* Bestselling titles, *Lovin' You Is Wrong* and *I Don't Wanna Be Right,* the dynamic March 2007 release, *Naughty Girls,* and *My Girl Friday,* November 2007.

Alisha is a bookstore owner, president of the R.A.W.SISTAZ Memphis Chapter Book Club, and a member of several online literary groups, including R.A.W.4ALL, Readers-andFriends, and FictionFolks. She's currently working on her 2008 releases.

Visit Alisha Yvonne online at *www.alishayvonne.com* or e-mail to *author@ebonyliterarygrace.com.*